WAR

Books by J. M. G. Le Clézio

WAR 1973
THE BOOK OF FLIGHTS 1972
TERRA AMATA 1969
THE FLOOD 1968
FEVER 1966
THE INTERROGATION 1964

J. M. G. LE CLÉZIO

WAR

TRANSLATED FROM THE FRENCH BY
SIMON WATSON TAYLOR

ATHENEUM NEW YORK 1973

Originally published in France under the title *La Guerre*,
copyright © 1970 by Editions Gallimard
English translation copyright © 1973 by Jonathan Cape Ltd.
All rights reserved
Library of Congress catalog card number 72-94243
ISBN 0-689-10547-9
Manufactured in Great Britain by
Richard Clay (The Chaucer Press) Ltd., Bungay, Suffolk
First American Edition

WAR

War has broken out. Where or how, nobody knows any longer. But the fact remains. By now it is behind each person's head, its mouth agape and panting. War of crimes and insults, of hate-filled eyes, of thoughts exploding from skulls. It is there, reared up over the world, casting its network of electric wires over the earth's surface. Each second, as it rolls on, it uproots all things in its path, reduces them to dust. It strikes indiscriminately with its bristling array of hooks, claws, beaks. Nobody will survive unscathed. Nobody will be spared. That is what war is: the eye of truth.

During daytime it strikes with the light. And when night falls it exerts the tidal force of its darkness, its coldness, its silence.

The war is all set to last ten thousand years, to last longer than the history of mankind. There can be no escape, no compromise. In the face of war, our eyes are downcast, our bodies offered as targets for its bullets. The sharp sword seeks out breasts and hearts, even bellies, to pry and gouge. The sand is thirsty for blood. The harsh mountains are longing to open up chasms beneath the feet of voyagers. The highways desire the ceaseless mutilation and death of those who travel them. The sea feels the need to throttle and choke. And in space there is the terrible determination to tighten the vice of emptiness around the stars, to smother the shimmerings of matter.

The war has whipped up its all-destructive wind. Burning gas pumps out of silencers, carbon monoxide spreads through the lungs and arteries. Mouths open wide, exhaling grey-blue smoke rings that drift up to the ceiling. Lips part, releasing

7

strings of words, mortal words that inspire fear. That is what it is: the wind of war.

Flashes of neon burst out around the girl's face, threatening to pierce her skin, to scorch her gentle features, to frizzle her long mane of hair.

The harsh rays of light stream endlessly from the electric lamp. Inside the glass bulb the incandescent filament shines brightly. That is war's game, the pitiless eye illuminating dazzlingly the surfaces of the room, fixing the image on the opaque film-strip.

Like the short flame that spurts briefly from a revolver's barrel, like the explosion of a bomb, like a stream of napalm flowing through a city's streets. Crumble and fall, white buildings, churches, towers! You no longer have the right to remain upright. Woman wearing that well-known mask, drop down, drop! You no longer have the right to face the unknown. The war's aim is that people should lower their heads and crawl through the mud and the tangled wires that cover the ground. Woman, your naked body is no longer an object of exultation. From now on it is destined for blows, for humiliating glances, for wounds that will bare life's innermost recesses.

Like a star's flame burning in the night simply to register the unspannable millions of miles: the gaze sparkling between the upper and lower lids. Like a drop of water, or of blood: the consciousness of this girl whose name means nothing and comprises nothing. There is no more solitude, no more haughty refusal: the pulsing war has annihilated them, effortlessly, with a single stroke of its light. How could one be alone while surrounded by this chaos? How could one say no, or even write down the letters

N O

when everything around one and within one is constantly saying yes?

8

So all this happened off-stage, in the third person. There was no longer any place for the I. With all witnesses in flight, there remained only the actors themselves. Eyes, legs, nipples no longer went by twos. Skulls were no longer filled with tender images, with tales, with reasonings. Great masses of numerals turned the sky dark, rained down, ploughed into the ground. Words no longer meant the same thing twice running, they no longer remembered each other. Perhaps people went on writing letters, perhaps ... Hunched over their sheets of paper, poets went on spinning their simple odysseys. Perhaps ... The stuffy air of cafés still vibrated to a few songs, the sound of a guitar, a woman's voice pronouncing words of love. Yes, yes, perhaps, perhaps ... But it was of no importance, meant nothing. These were merely sounds among a host of others, sounds emitted by the great vibration-creating machine. No, what needed to be told now, on that very day, was the truth of the crowd. There were no longer souls, no longer feelings shaped like islands. Thought no longer applied itself to its minuscule linear pattern. There was no longer any single entity.

So it all happens together. It all advances like an army of rats, with a single face, and breaches the ramparts. Like a floodtide with countless fulcrums, rising, rolling, pounding to bits. All the names. All the muscles. All life's fingers pressing, groping, forming their path. Who shall speak about the masses? Who is the man who will finally understand the route taken by the crowd? He is himself that path.

That is how the war started, probably, though by now it is too late to know precisely. It is spreading across the grey plain. It fills space. Sickness that ruptures membranes and sets the lymph flowing. It has chosen places inhabited by man. It has burst the dykes. It has touched the earth with the tip of its cone of pain, a single nerve among millions of nerves. It has sought out the body of one girl from among the millions of other girls. But of course war has always been war and exists outside thought. It is everywhere. In the night's dreams, in the sun's gradual setting, in love, in hatred, in vengeance. It has only just started.

It is not an accident. It is not an event. It is war.

It is inscribed on papered walls, within flowers, across rose-windows. It is engraved on the surface of glass and water, in the match's flame, in each grain of sand.

War that does not want to win, that has no need to win. It is no longer a question of man's squabbles or incursions, his Danzig corridors or 17th parallels. Those things happened very quickly, and those who died did not die fighting but by chance, because a bullet had traced a trajectory that passed through their chest or lung. There had been no connection between the eye that had conceived death and the steel tip that had inflicted it.

But the war I am telling you about ignores nothing, it is dead from one end to the other.

The heavy machine-gun, the Mauser, the crossbow, the blowpipe, the axe were basically tender because they were blind. They were only weapons. But the destruction I am telling you about has eyes. Its weapon is total, its crime unending.

War that is capable of beauty. Radiating the glow of flames or a marine sunset. Moving like a cat. Its hair seaweed. War that is alive, truth, future! Why has the world suddenly been obliged to reveal its secrets?

It is beyond the imagination of a girl. Were it within the imagination of a girl, there would be no problem. Her imagination would be prised up, wrenched out like a bad tooth, and everything would be normal again. Were it to happen within the eyes of a girl, her fate would be, of course, to have her eyes plucked out and replaced by two grapes. No, no-one's eyes are involved. It is beyond eyes, beyond imagination. It is not an aching nerve. It is beyond nerves. Be what you like, say what you like: but do not think that anything will change. Close your eyes, write little one-word poems,

10

take photos of women's breasts, caress smiling lips. But do not start thinking that anything is going to be at peace.

How to express that? To express it absolutely, there would have to be explosions and lacerations, there would have to be words come from outer space at the speed of light, words which would obliterate everything in their path, words like streams of molten lava, words which would whistle through the air and gouge great seething craters in the earth's surface.

One must, one absolutely must get out of oneself. And one must plunge so deep into oneself that one no longer recognizes anything, that everything becomes freshly invented.

It has arrived slowly, then, and settled over the earth. A flight of circles, for example, and the rings have floated down to the ground, one after the other. Somewhere in space there is a great snake winding itself around its prey, its silent body ceaselessly casting its coils. Each time a fresh piece of flesh appears, the great snake makes a knot around it and squeezes.

No, no, it is not that. A snake does not have that much strength. The battles that are waged for life are simple affairs. This is more clandestine, there are no faces or bodies. It is within things that the circles come into being. Everything generates circles. They swim around specks of dust, move apart, make matter tremble. Never-ending agitation that destroys every quality of permanence, of ecstatic immobility. Will-power is not external. Danger is not strange or foreign. It is fear that sets the world vibrating, that blurs images. Nothing is safe here any longer. Quickly, then, amass great blocks of stone and raise your granite monuments. Or it will be too late. Fear has no need of rocks and mountains. That is why men have erected so many pyramids and cathedrals, in their centuries-old struggle to prevent the liquefaction of the universe.

Dying is nothing. But to become water ... Then, as the water divides and retracts its membranes, to become gas. That explains the fear. The deserts of sand and bitumen are the last islands of consciousness among so many rivers.

11

Above the city, the clouds are about to burst. Nobody wants to disappear. After being born, one day, and seeing the sun, and conceiving the idea of dryness, nobody can ever have enough deserts and caverns in which to hide.

In the mouth, tongue wrestles with saliva. Words are a matter of teeth and hard palate and taut lips. Glands release the flow of saliva, through which words proceed to bubble. Sometimes one of these soldiers falls to his knees, lungs pierced. Then the flow of saliva that mounts in the throat and trickles from the mouth turns red. Instead of the expected shout of 'Help! Rescue me! Come, come quickly!' all that can be heard is a drowning gurgle, something like 'Arrl arroull! Oooooorrl! Ohoooooorrl!'

The sun's civilizations are doomed. They could not last. All the blocks of stone, the temples and the stairways, together, could not dam the encroaching waters. Stone is fragile, the harbinger of dust. Mountains are not higher than the clouds. Eyes are not stars, they are lamps flickering out. Thought does not move straight ahead, like light. Thought is a stream of saliva.

The solitude that used to reign, the kind that hurled you into the depths of space, that walled you up in its silence — the rapture of a body floating in muteness — no longer compels belief. When everything has become language, it is because all hope of understanding is dead. To be alone was to try to understand. But to be there with all the others, in the great whirlpool, swept along by the torrent that eats away the shores as it gathers speed, is not to understand. It is, fatally, to be the object of the great panic.

All the:

'I am'

'I want'

'I ... I love'

'I, I, myself, to me, my, mine, me, I, I, I!'

and all the old memories, the photographs full of shadows

12

and mystery, the sketches on scraps of paper, the poems about the I confronting the pageant of the sea, about the I confronting the beauty of birds, about the I sitting beside the woman busy listening to the beat of her heart, and about the I confronting Death: lies, blinkered lies! All a ruse to avoid seeing the war arrive, to forget the swelling thunder of the mob's boots, to pretend to be no longer there when THEY arrive!

The world has forgotten nothing. It takes its revenge, hastening up, for the massacre, from the depths of time. With a single stroke it will put an end to all the old dreams, all the anthems. It will cut short the refrain as it cuts the throat, it will spill thought and blood together.

It blows out its smoke rings, and the darkness increases.

What is the point of crying out? Bawl your lungs out, sob away: the world simply transforms your laments into noises, noises that will all clatter, groan, crackle, rattle, rumble, warble, scream, gurgle, whistle, sing and drum together. Listen, listen to the great music! You will never get away. To be alone. To be the only one. To be he who *is*, indefinitely. That was true peace. But today the soul has escaped through the gaping skull, diffusing itself across the heavens, vanishing over the ocean. Through habit, or through sheer cowardice, these odds and ends, these stammerings, these kinds of signature still survive. This is mine. That is yours, hers. Sometimes, those who have already been sucked into the common pit still imagine that they own things: mouths desiring to possess, eyes all set to conquer, footprints with which to measure the world. How to forget all that? Is there not a single crumb that bears your name? Is there not a dream, a breath of air, a gleam of light that belongs to you?

All belongs to everyone. Nothing to anyone. All is no-one. O human gaze, rediscover power! Conquer once again! The world is eternally the same. Each time a drop of water forms under the spout of a tap, it means that one can wrench something away from the nameless mass. Each time a life is born,

13

it means that a house has been built and that the rats will oust the occupants.

An army on the march, trampling the fields, destroying bridges, pillaging, raping, smashing. Invisible army, devoid of thought, devoid of actions!

Where does this enemy come from? Can it be possible that it springs from the mind, solely from the mind, to wreak its havoc? Can it be possible that man harbours such hatred for men, that the tree harbours such hatred for trees? Everything is designed for destruction and execration. Tenderness, security are wholly absent: there is only this ferocious army with eyes that blur the sight and make the body teeter in space. No interplay, no contest: just the need to win, day after day.

Evil is born at last. It had been talked about for so long that people were beginning to have doubts about it. Until this moment evil had been unimportant, it had its heroes and its judges. It had its frontiers. Its first appearance on the earth had been almost fortuitous, a storm-like explosion accompanied by condensation, concentration, thunder and lightning. Peace came close behind it. Today, at last, man knows evil. It is no longer the result of a conjunction of circumstances, it is no longer a mood. It is IMMENSELY EXTERNAL.

The evil — the war — is to have imagined the external. Then, having imagined it, to have opened the doors of the internal. The delicate substance has leaked out, to be absorbed by the dense ocean. Fear began its reign on the day that this girl blurted out, jokingly perhaps, or simply because it had suddenly become the truth:

'I am nothing'

followed by some declarations of freedom:

'I want nothing'

'I won't have children'

'I no longer believe'

'You don't exist'

The world had failed to crumble, as she had expected it to do.

14

Everything had remained intact. Vehicles had continued to move along the tarred roads, people had stayed on their feet, aeroplanes had gone on flying. The terrible thing was that something had disappeared, had withdrawn from the core of all beings. It was invisible, no-one knew what exactly: just something. There was a hollow, now, at the core of each object, a cavity with a very narrow orifice but an interior vaster than a grotto, rather like a woman's belly.

It is within these cavities that the war takes shape. Each object is a huge uterus, within the still vaster uterus of the world.

All these bellies give birth. War, this war, is precisely that: the act of procreation.

The world is born and man has no part in its birth. Surrounding man, surrounding the girl, the world is engaged in its great effort at parturition. The girl sees the spasms pass through the air and the earth. Some of them pass through her body like tremors. The world longs to materialize, drags itself painfully towards the exit, towards the light. A terrifying experience, surely, for the earthworm multitudes.

To have spoken, one day. To have said many words, to have put one's freedom into writing. And then, another day sees the arrival of the greater freedom, the freedom that had paid no attention to words, that had simply carried on its struggle for liberation: the child, as he is being born, will gulp down the whole sea of the placenta with a single lick of the tongue.

The girl does not want this son. She wants to poison him before he is born. How could one want a son who is going to kill his mother?

Consciousness no longer exists. The gaze has ceased journeying to and fro. Now it is no more than a desperate plunge towards the bottom of the well, towards the horizon's limits. The world is curved, its boundary wall can never be located. To start off afresh, it would be necessary to encounter the wall's final rampart, the one signifying that the mind had reached full circle. It is clear, now, that voyages are purposeless. What would be the point of recognizing the limit of intoxication, of discovering it, knowing it? Nothingness trickles away, flees. Emptiness does not even want to be known. Suddenly the chasm flattens out, the better to become unfathomable.

Knowledge requires that things shall first have been encountered, yet has anyone encountered them? And self-knowledge requires that one should first have touched oneself like an object. Worlds — and this is what I wanted to say, above all — are beyond discovery.

People are faceless from now on.

Yet the girl I am telling you about had a face. This is more or less how it was: a mask of soft white skin, with a rosy flush on the cheeks, on the chin and on the wings of the nose. With a few dark blue veins at the level of the temples, with a few wrinkles at the corners of the eyes and on the forehead, with two or three pimples, and a hundred or so freckles.

Profound face with slight elevations, face of stone polished by water, face that affronted time. She carried it before her, and the wind glanced off her prow, parted at each side of her nose, swirled past her cheeks.

Her face was not a random affair. It was she who had fashioned it, with her hands, perhaps, or else with her thought. She had modelled it to summon light, to pass through rain, to soar among the air's layers. In the centre of her face she had created this pyramid-shaped appendage pierced by two holes, so that the cold air might penetrate right inside her body, sucked along these hair-sprouting canals to be purified, warmed and humidified.

Beneath the nose there was this hollow, this shallow little gutter along which mucus was able to run.

Then the lips, the two purplish-blue bulges scored by little wrinkles, tiny cracks. Through this entrance the outer world flowed down the throat, bathed the cells, invaded,

16

cleansed, spread its thousands of fingers. When the lips parted, revealing the buccal cavity with its secret odours, the world did not hesitate—it entered. It was for that purpose that the girl had opened up the doorway at the bottom of her face. This had been the first onslaught upon silence. The head had ceased to be a stone tumbling through the sea's night. The current had entered, bringing with it voices and non-stop music.

I wanted to speak about the eyes, too. The girl had imagined the world's light, had dreamed of landscapes flaming in the sun, of deep nights, of beauty. Then she had traced flowers of two kinds on her face, two blue grottoes that were soon glowing and through which the shimmering light entered. Around these sparkling grottoes she had outlined the petals of the black, tarry eyelashes that blinked lightly to open and close the pupils' holes. It was from these objects, alive in the face, that perception had emerged. It was they that had suddenly made the world immense.

The eyes looked. The universe lay before the eyes. After the girl had finished tracing these two fabulous designs on her face she had realized that nothing would ever be the same again. That is why, each morning of her life, she had sat in front of a mirror and had re-enacted the ritual of creation of the eyes, with her little paint-brushes and her tubes of black paste.

After that, the face had been given the finishing touches: just two other holes for hearing sounds, and millions of hairs planted in the skin of the skull to prevent the face from opening up and spilling its contents into the sky.

And then the face dissolved. It lost its features one by one, quite simply. The nose ceased cleaving the wind, ceased resembling the jet plane's muzzle of rounded metal off which reflections glance. The eyes melted, smearing the cheeks with mascara, and the eyebrows' arches faded away. The mouth closed, first of all, and the lips knit together; scar-tissue

17

covered the wound, and finally nothing remained but a scarcely visible mark, a sort of violet weal covered by transparent skin.

Then, all the small signs of life vanished. The moles, the hairs of the body and the head, the dimples, the wrinkles, the flaps of the ears, the tendons and the veins.

What has been demolished in this way, with sledgehammer blows and charges of dynamite, is a building. The lofty, beautiful façade has crumbled, freeing clouds of dust and swarms of cockroaches. The windows remained, for a brief moment, blind, hovering in the sky, so open that they had become invisible. Then, in one last effort, they in turn fell, floating down to the ground like dead leaves, and this was the sign that there would never again be any place to dwell.

Without warning, the immense explosion erupts in the deserted city where all the men and women are in hiding. A volcano opens its jaws in the centre of the port, spewing its column of colourless flames into the air. Paving stones soar upwards, then hurtle down again, smashing through the roofs of houses. Windows shatter. Floors ripple underfoot, eardrums are burst by the suddenly liberated weight. And the noise arrives, flattening everything against the surface of the earth, the cyclone of noise that sweeps over the city like a giant shadow, making straight for the girl, threatening to engulf her, to grind her to dust.

Where to hide? Where? Is there one place left, in the whole world, that the noise has not invaded? Is there a lake with transparent glacial waters, a lake as pure as a mirror, on a mountain top, a lake of silence into which one might plunge and wash oneself clean?

A long deserted beach, burning hot under the sun, with waves breaking endlessly along the whole stretch of sand, and swarms of flies buzzing around the heaped seaweed?

Is there an asphalt road, unconcerned with happenings on either side of it, that stretches straight ahead until it perforates the horizon with a single clean stroke, opening up in space a great gash through which perspective's receding lines might at last escape?

Is there — and this is the question, the real question — is there one girl, just one, whether she be called Bea or Eva or Djemia, who has not experienced the war? Just one who has not made war with her body, with her gentle face and moist eyes, with her mouth and teeth, with her hair? Just one who has been neither prey for the hunter, nor hunter herself? On all sides are watchful gazes, darts bristling from loop-holes. On all sides, breastplates, shields, scabbards, arrows, machine-gun barrels.

With the din of massacre in her ears, she flees, running barefoot across the ruin-covered desert. Along the dusty ground, pitfalls open up frantically, making weird sucking noises. The girl avoids them by jumping, sliding, zigzagging, hopping on one foot. She runs towards a dome, a knoll of stony dirt that dominates the plain. She runs towards it because she knows it is her last chance. Just before reaching it she trips and falls. The pain is so terrible that she cannot even cry out. She thrashes around in the dust like a fear-crazed, panic-stricken bitch. Falling spreadeagled, she has scraped one forearm against a flint. Blood starts flowing from the wound and, with the blood, her life. Quickly, very quickly, the process of disintegration sets in. Her flesh, her bones, her thoughts melt on the desert's flat slab. Death, delicious and horrible, comes to alleviate her pain, little by little. She becomes almost weightless. She floats. She is intoxicated.

Or else, some other night — January 10th, for instance — she dreams that she is lying on her left side, on a bare mattress. In the room, the faceless form has arisen and moves slowly forward. She has not seen it, but she knows: the flashing knife-blade advances in the gloom, a streak of horizontal light amid all these shadowy shapes. After an eternity of time, the blade enters her back, exactly between the shoulder-blades, and makes straight for her heart. The knife point

19

touches the heart, punctures it, rips it, splits it open like a tomato. And she feels the fiery liquid spread and seethe inside her body. The pleasure is so strong that she faints.

Or again, May 12th. The girl dreams that she is hanging from a gibbet.

August 19th. She falls.

August 20th. She drowns herself in a water-tank.

December 4th. Two great spotted dogs devour her.

Come now! Do you really not understand? You never did encounter these monsters, these shrieks, these voices! This war of yours is a product of your imagination! The dreams are self-explanatory. These abominations surrounding you are phantoms, mere phantoms! The apparitions emerging from the sea are wisps of fog! Just relax, now. It will all fade away. Face up to these chimeras. Slay them with your unblinking stare. Nothing can withstand the sun. Dread, uproar: this whole frenzy comes solely from within. See how peaceful the world is. Nothing is wrong! The earth has never been more placid. Sunsets have never been tamer. As for your chasms and abysses: puddles, mole-tunnels!

Where do you hear cries? There is nothing but silence, as usual, flat cold impenetrable silence. Where do you see eyes? Rest assured that there is nothing to be seen but a few glaucous orbs sunk between baggy lids. It is all within you, within you!

Nothing to make a fuss about, that's for sure. Cascades of sparks, fireworks! Mere mechanical displays, lasting a few minutes at most. Cars speeding along their tracks? But they are stopping, they are on the point of stopping! The sounds of words: a little buzzing for your ears! There is no cause for alarm. Never has the world been etched in clearer relief, never have the whites been more white, the blacks more black.

There is nothing to run away from. Hiding-places? What for?

You are losing consciousness? But you are no longer alone.

20

You are slipping into the whirlwind that embraces everyone else in time and space. Madness leads to nothing. Men have never been more real, do you hear? Never.

You would do better to study this girl, as you call her. Look: she is walking along the street, window shopping. She stops. She bites her forefinger. She sets off again. Her heels tip-tap. One, two, one, two! She skips over a step. She enters a big store. She is radiant among the neon lights. Her hair, sparkling like spun glass, frames her plaster-white face with its blackened features. Her eyes move. She has seen something on the display counter. She reaches forward, her hand opens, then closes again. Her fingers with the painted nails are holding a little notebook bound in blue imitation leather, on which is printed in gilt letters:

'EZEJOT' DIARY

The girl opens her red mouth and speaks. She says:
'Ah yes ...'
'Good ...'
'And that?'
'What?'
'How much?'
'Yes yes.'
'Euh thanks.'
It's not true. It's not true. You are lying on purpose, so that people will believe your fabrications. You are alone, quite alone, conjuring up fantasies from deep within yourself, and hoping to spread them through the world. To justify yourself, you want to annihilate the difference between the internal and the external. You want to live as one dreams, and vice versa. But the world is not listening to you. It continues its regular motion, and with its powerful arm driven by a concealed piston it traces long geometric lines which efface all your scribblings.

Within this girl, as you call her. It is there. Not only in the

21

depths of her warm lithe body, not only on this transparent skin, these breasts, this belly, these legs, this face. But also in these sheaths of nylon and wool, these brassières, these suspender-belts, these court shoes, this white oilcloth raincoat. She is neither free nor under restraint, this human silhouette. No-one is making war, no-one is killing. There is only this strange yet intimate force at work.

The girl you are talking about wants a child. It is inscribed in her body that she will have several: little men and little women who in their turn will want children. Bellies and children go together.

All is within her. The girl I am telling you about does not possess just a single body and a single soul. She possesses thousands.

Where it has been possible to establish the position of a mass of one milligram of silver to within 0.1 millimetres, the uncertainty concerning the speed of that mass necessarily exceeds a thousand millionth of a thousand millionth of a micron per hour.

Werner Heisenberg.

The girl called Bea B. had seen the city take shape around her head. That had not happened all at once, far from it. It had needed years, years with the kind of months and days that one counts on the fingers while studying the leaves of a calendar, or by marking a little cross every twenty-eight days.

The first day, there had been this hotel room with yellow wallpaper and a blue curtain drawn across the window. That day, everything had emerged from the bed, from the sagging mattress and the white sheets. Emptiness had made off, half flying, half swimming; it had spread out through the cold air, it had run through the street, it had lifted the room up to the top of a kind of tower that soared above the sea of sounds and movements.

By the eighth day, all sorts of roads had taken shape like the rays of a star, or like the spokes of a wheel. In the centre, at the hub, Bea B. was seated in a chair, listening to the sounds of water draining and flushing away along the walls.

On the thirtieth day she had seen faces. At the side of the clusters of houses, a man with shining eyes and a vertical crease between the eyebrows.

By the seventy-third day the frontiers had receded farther. Beyond the vista of roofs and terraces, following with her eyes the channels of one-way streets, she could see the looming shapes of great tree-shaded gardens, lawns, fountains, gravel paths. Tiny children ran, shouting, up and down the paths. Pigeons scratched and pecked. In a shady spot a steady stream of men filed in and out of a brick-walled urinal.

The one hundred and second day brought a vast ring of outer boulevards; the following day an airfield, a grey desert over which aeroplanes crawled slowly.

Etcetera. Using her head, the girl, Bea B., tunnelled a hole from the fifth-floor hotel room down into the ground, forcing coils of rubbish and assorted objects along it towards the open. Each day, the area expanded. Miles of roadway unfurled, sheets of asphalt, hoardings, walls. Each day, there were more windows, more pavement kerbs. The unknown crowd assumed habits, names: they called themselves Monsieur Cordier, Monsieur Gioffret, Madame Duez, Madame Lemploy, Monsieur José Martin, Madame et Monsieur André Vignaux, Elizabeth, Antoinette, Dick Flanders, Jo, Evelyne, Nicole Nolon.

It was difficult, under the circumstances, to retain one's identity. So at night-time the girl, Bea B., sat down on her chair, beside the bed, and looked at herself in the mirror set into the wardrobe door. She studied her hands resting on her knees, and the tin ring that little Johnnie had once presented to her, on the beach. She studied her knees with their two white kneecaps, then she studied her two naked feet with their splayed toes. She studied her face, with its two green-grey-blue eyes and the dark shadows beneath them. She studied her hair, strand by strand, distinguishing the hairs that were raven, brown, light chestnut, auburn, white.

She made the following grimaces:

1. Mouth turned up at the corners, incisors showing, one eyebrow raised, the other lowered.

24

2. Eyes narrowed, directed downwards.

3. Both eyebrows raised, with three wrinkles running across the forehead, and two more above the eyes.

4. Cheeks puffed out, nose turned up.

5. Mouth wide open, and right at the back the uvula trembling.

Then she got up and walked around the room, in front of the mirror. She went up to it, then backed away from it. She performed a striptease. She danced. She sang, out of key. She pretended to be Ava Gardner in *The Barefoot Contessa*. And then Theda Bara in *Cleopatra*.

Sometimes, too, she talked to herself in a gruff whisper. She said:

'It's true. Honestly, it's absolutely true. When you said that to me, yesterday, I just didn't know what to reply. You know, I always have the feeling of being out of things. I mean, everything that happens seems to be at a great distance from me, and I don't really understand what people want from me. So I don't know what to say. And then there's this sort of feeling inside me that I can see something alive in people and yet I don't trust that feeling. Well, that sort of thing. You know, when I left home three or four years ago I wasn't like that. When I first came to live here I used to go out every evening, hanging around night-clubs till four in the morning, and so on, wanting to do the same as all the others. I used to see so many people. And I imagined that being a journalist was a serious business. So I really made an effort. There was this little gang of fellows and girls I went around with: we used to meet at some special café every evening. There was Jérôme, Louis, Antoine, and then that fellow with the shaved skull—Pedro, I think his name was. And the others, Sophie, Roseline, Thérèse Balducci, Françoise. I got really involved in their scene. I thought it was all so important. I had no time to think. And then, little by little, everything changed. It happened gradually, without my realizing. I simply noticed that I was no longer listening to what the

25

others were saying. When they got into discussions I lit a cigarette or just went away. And then I started writing my articles at the café, with a dictionary. Whenever I ran out of ideas I opened the dictionary and chose a word at random. *Liver*, for example. The first definition was *viscus*. So I wrote a piece about visceral behaviour. How people felt when they had a liver complaint. And the universality of the viscera. The hidden organs that govern life. The skin being the surface of the liver. Or else, *python*, for example. The obsession with pythons. People see pythons everywhere. Pythons wriggling everywhere, into beds, inside people's clothing, into baths. Or again, Hiiumaa. The island of Hiiumaa. There are 15,000 inhabitants on the island of Hiiumaa. Which means that one has about one chance and a half in three hundred thousand of coming across a Hiiumaaian one day.'

She stopped talking long enough to light a cigarette in front of the mirror.

'Anyhow, you see the kind of thing. But at the paper they were all delighted. That was the last straw. They illustrated these things with absolutely beautiful, rather pretentious photos that Henri took. It was the same with Henri. He was delighted, too. He thought we were going to get married, he wanted us to have a child, a son. He wanted all sorts of things. But I couldn't keep up with him, though I pretended to go along. The point is, everyone seemed to be positively radiating intelligence, whereas I'd have preferred the whole world to be silent. Their minds were so full of important ideas that they didn't want to bother themselves with day-to-day problems. That's why I came to live here, to have time to look at what was really happening. They tried to make me understand. They arrived one after the other, my parents, Henri, Jérôme, Pedro, and all the others, plumped themselves down in my room, and said their bit. Then eventually they lost interest, and even stopped ringing up. They found someone to replace me. Funny, huh? I would never have believed that one could disappear so easily.'

26

While this was going on, the rest of the city was busy digging its crater round the girl's head. The streets spun around the mirror-wardrobe, thrusting their perspectives very far into the depths of the glass and the silvering.

Somewhere in her head there was a fixed point. A white spot on a convolution of the cerebrum, perhaps, or else the memory of a pain. The day when she had been walking barefoot along the beach and had trod on the rusty nail protruding from an old plank.

The day, the terrible day, when she had realized that she would never be really alone.

So then she began mapping out the city, to stop the whirling motion. But it was not easy. She started off from the centre of her head, and tried to count: first whirlpool, second whirlpool, third whirlpool. Current. Reef. A cape. String of islets. Sand-bar. Thudding of rollers. Fourth, fifth whirlpool. Vast esplanade, oil-slick, smooth sea. Calm, calm. Off-shore breeze. Flight of seagulls. Shallows. Short beach, dotted with stranded jelly-fish. Air corridor. Break in the clouds.

The map disintegrated continually. Everything was still hazy, in constant flux.

She started again: first peak. Second peak. Cliffs. Ravines. Glacial valley, long and curving, blocked by névé. Puy. Third peak. Fourth peak. Sea of ice. Sea of dazzling snow. Black peaks thrusting above the snow. Shadows creeping along the fissures. Wind of silence.

Or again: first nebula. Second nebula. Third nebula. Pocket of emptiness. Constellation. Galaxy gliding through the black desert. Nova. Dead silence. Pain of sharp stars in the centre of the immense anaesthesia. Falling. Fourth nebula.

And this is how things really happened: in a room with yellow walls, at night, around 0 o'clock, a girl was seated in a chair in front of a mirror-wardrobe. She spoke aloud, puffing at a cigarette, and thinking of some fellow named Henri, or Stephen. Then she took up a little book covered

27

with blue plastic material, on which was printed in gilt letters:

'EZEJOT' DIARY

and with a ballpoint pen started writing rapidly:

Saturday 9 January

Been here a year already. How time flies! Yet I still don't know a soul. I divide my time up between lectures, the library, cafés and my own room. It's cold. Raining. Men are a bunch of creeps. One-track minds. Girls, too. Me too! What a load of rubbish. All this business about sex. Why on earth should some people have one sex and others have a different one? It's completely ridiculous. I've been going to the cinema. The last thing I saw was Skolimowski's *Walkover*. In the street, I intercepted Monsieur X's blue gaze. He is ugly but personally I find him beautiful.

Then she put the blue notebook away in a drawer, and smoked another American cigarette. She went across to the window and watched the street through the slits of the closed shutters. She brushed her teeth, standing over the washbasin, rinsed her mouth and spat.

That night she dreamed that a great train with wheels as sharp as those in ham-slicing machines was journeying to and fro across her body, transforming it into a series of neat round slices.

The war is not on the point of ending, far from it! It still erupts savagely: eruptions of light more murderous than bullets, eruptions of eyes from their sockets, eruptions of metal. All things are rampant, bent on annihilation. Death to everything that is self-contained, everything that is inherently singular! No more thought! No more action! From now on, surrender ... The war bursts from mouths of flame. The screens are rolled back and the gun barrels unmasked. A black car drives down the sloping street: suddenly a machine-gun protrudes above its roof and starts mowing down the passers-by. The word kill is hidden everywhere, echoing in every other word. But it is not a question of killing. When the blood finally gushes from the wounds, what peace! When the bus leaves the roadway's invisible grooves and crushes two or three children or a couple of women against a wall, something becomes freed. A sort of joy or truth manifests itself.

When violence becomes crime, it invents freedom.

But everything that is contained! Everything that is squeezed tight into the volcano's subterranean gallery, and that nothing can save! The spasms that rack the bowels of machines, all the jolts and quiverings: savagery! blind hatred! ignorance! dumbness!

What exists in the depths of the colour black, in the heart of the flame. The will to obliterate the world's outlines, to cancel utterly. Unending miscarriage, dilation of muscles, grimace, yet nothing comes!

The world watches with its millions of eyes, and its stare is more fascinating than the pupils of tigers. It thrusts its syringe deep into the soul, and sucks. The stare wills one to drain oneself of one's substance, to contribute to the fearful haemorrhage. The universe is a vast empty space that needs endlessly to be filled to the brim. Such things should never have been allowed to come to pass. The dragon with gaping jaws has peopled the sky and the earth. He has endless need of fresh flesh to gorge upon, and he is never satiated. Soldiers, deliver us from the world! He is too substantial. We shall not be capable of resisting, we shall glide gently towards his great mouth in which the digestive glands are already visible.

In the city, the eager whirlwind is born and has fashioned its funnel. How to resist so much intelligence, so much beauty? Must one make oneself ugly, like some black object curled up into a ball in the dust? I want to be transformed, this very day, into a dog's stale turd coiled like a snake on the pavement. Perhaps I will not be noticed. Perhaps I will not be noticed by *him*?

Monsieur X, you who are a soldier, come to my aid. Fight him. Slay him. Crush him under the wheels of your motorbike. But first gouge out his eyes, all his eyes. He has so many. In the evening, when the sun sets, these little glass globes streaked with threads of colours can be seen shining behind the windows of cafés. In the morning, when the sun rises, they are all bloodshot.

Smash all electric light bulbs, demolish all illuminated signs. They, too, are eyes, that do more than stare: that devour. On the façades of buildings and all along the streets they glitter together in the night as they trace their symbols. I have no time left to think. I dash myself against them like a foolish moth.

An end to being! Existence is a never-ending rout, a stampede towards all these luminous dots. The messages draw nearer together, encircle us. All men and all women are victims. They are already in the dragon's mouth, and they do not even realize it. They are fornicating between the dragon's very jaws!

No way of remaining alone. I have lived in hiding for so

30

long now. I was buried under old rags, I was a black dot among countless black dots. But the war is a lighthouse that, in a single flash, can send its beam out into the night to worm out nooks and crannies. A column of light tunnelling the darkness to force the terrified beasts from their lairs.

Fear: the eyes dilate, the heart beats furiously in its narrow cage. Everything grows hard. Impossible to escape. The doors are closed, all the doors that control the entry of things. Before that, one could enter into a tree or a telegraph pole. One fitted oneself inside, standing very straight, and became as cold as cement. Or else on the great stony beach, a few inches away from the sea. The sun blazed down. The waves burst over the pebbles, one after the other, with a raking sound. The sky was blue. Then one could close one's eyes and, by lying on one's back, enter into the beach. One became as flat, as stretched out as the beach, with millions of round pebbles piled deep.

One was like this ▬ and then also like this ●

Who opened the flood-gates? Who demolished the dyke that held back the sea? And who switched on these sun-guns everywhere? Now there is no more sea, no more beach. There is mind everywhere. Nothing but mind.

The earth is a patch of tar, the water is made of cellophane, the air is nylon. The sun in the centre of the fibre-board ceiling burns with its great 1,600-watt bulb. Somewhere, there must be a vast factory, its fiery machines throbbing as they churn out ceaselessly all the products of falsehood: false skies painted blue, fake mountains of duralumin, tinsel stars. Trees of indiarubber sway in the breeze from ventilators. Their green leaves never die. In fruit-baskets, the violet grapes, the bananas, oranges and apples never rot away. The machines have shaped them and stamped them out. Artificial geraniums sprout, without hope of growth, in flower-pots. Nylon fur-coats sparkle in the light. Space no longer exists, and everything is flat. Burglar-proof windows have barred the way to the infinite, sheets of tin and layers of cement have obtruded

31

themselves everywhere. Rain falls occasionally, but it is no longer rain. The drops are pellets of translucent plastic that roll harmlessly off the roofs. The cracks in the surface of the macadamized ground will remain unchanged for all eternity. The world is polished and new, smelling of chlorophyll and benzene. Crystalline powder, phosphorescent snow, rigid structures whose components are immutable. Everything is simply horny matter and mother-of-pearl. Rivers of steel glitter everywhere, and the sky revolves very slowly, pivoting on its immense hinges.

In a setting filled with circles and cross-strokes and occasional triangles, men and women glide past each other. They come from the end of the world, from where the rumbling machine moulds bodies and faces, and they calmly cross the impenetrable street. The air's fringes play upon their shining bald pates. Their piercing eyes glitter behind the lenses of spectacles. Their metallic lounge-suits are buttoned down the front. Their varnished shoes creak. Their hands are closed over hard bone-like objects: umbrellas, bags, satchels, white cigarettes. Over the ground pass bakelite Negresses, nylon Chinese, pink celluloid Whites and leatherette Red Indians. Their thoughts emerge from their mouths like the thin squeaks of bats, or else form clouds of steam in the sky, like polystyrene foam.

Monsieur X, come, together we will track down the spot where the great factory turns out all these things.

But now there is no longer a girl. The one called Bea B. has disappeared. She has vanished. All that remains, where she was sitting in front of the mirror-wardrobe, or walking quickly down the multicoloured streets, is a sort of mechanism with protruding cog-wheels.

The moulded body, with its two linked symmetrical segments, is topped by a doll's face. Plastic sphere with vague protuberances, on which the eternal features are painted. The short nose with its two apertures, the twin arches of the brown eyebrows, the eyes of green bottle-glass, the eyelashes

32

of black-tinted nylon, the eyelids that blink, the unwrinkled brow, the strands of chestnut hair stitched together on the skull's cap, the ears made of gristle, and the lips lacquered blood-red, lips that smile gently without saying anything.

Perhaps the war has already overwhelmed her, petrified her, just like that, with strokes of light, noise and movement. Perhaps nothing more is needed to conquer her. Perhaps, indeed, she exists as an automaton, a carnivorous doll that will never grow old, never die. Perhaps all her gestures and all her desires are wheels that rotate and light bulbs that flash on, deep within the shell of her body. And her thoughts, her words: the marks of stiletto heels in the asphalt, cigarette stubs, reflections on the surfaces of cars, magazine pages showing nothing but photographs of unknown people.

> *But it was not a novel, it was a letter, and it is also what I would think if I were not a little girl, that is to say if I had the courage to be ugly all the time. There are so many powders for the face, so many shades of lipstick, so many false eyelashes, so many coloured lining pencils, so many dyes for the hair, that being a coward no longer means anything.*
>
> Claude Grenier.

'You know what we're going to do?' said Bea B. to Monsieur X.

'We're going to go over to the attack.'

She got up and started walking around the room in her bare feet. She lit a cigarette with a match.

'We're going to become soldiers and demolish everything, that's what we're going to do.'

She sat on the edge of the bed and looked at herself in the mirror.

'Do you agree?'

She decided her eyes were still too gentle, and put on her dark glasses.

'We're still talking too much.'

She got up, put on her shoes, opened the door and went out.

'FORWARDS!'

First, though, a uniform. All genuine soldiers wear uniforms. It would be possible to dress as a café waitress (Monsieur X as a bartender). Or else as a nurse (Monsieur X as a doctor). Or else as a Sister of Charity (Monsieur X as a clergyman). Or else as a prostitute (Monsieur X as a pimp). Or else as a widow (Monsieur X as an undertaker). Or else as a student of molecular physics (Monsieur X as a professor of political economy). The great thing was to disappear, to be very far away, in unsuspected spots.

Bea B. bought a housemaid's costume. Monsieur X, a plumber's outfit. In his right hand he carried a little iron tool-box, like those that plumbers usually carry.

First, they went into this café at the end of a street full of people and vehicles. The café was called the Rond-Point, or the Pergola, or Sanborn's, or something similar.

They went and sat down at a table, and drank bottled beer while they chatted. Bea B. told Monsieur X that they must never again talk about important things. They must say very simple things, without attempting explanations. For instance:

'I'm going to tell you how I took the plane. Well then, I was in the seat next to this character wearing spectacles. He was reading a newspaper. On the other side of him there was this little porthole and these little nylon curtains that were blue with a pattern of little yellow flowers. And so I sat in my seat, waiting. From time to time I leaned across the character with his nose in his newspaper and I saw clouds that looked like kapok. And then, do you know what, an air hostess suddenly came up and handed me a plastic tray. So I put it on the little table that unfolded in front of me. It was really very odd: on the tray there was this kind of plate shaped like a figure eight, containing a wedge of meat, some string beans and some mashed potatoes. And there was a little plastic bowl, too, containing some fish and some salad. And then there was another little plastic bowl containing slices of pine-apple. And do you know what, right in the centre of these round slices there was a candied cherry!'

'No!'

'Honestly! And that's not all. There was also a glass of

35

mineral water, and a little cellophane bag that held a fork, a blunt knife and a small spoon, and three tiny packets, one of pepper, one of salt and one of sugar.'

'And then?'

'And then there was an empty cup, and a paper napkin.'

'So what did you do?'

'So I started by eating the fish and salad in the bowl. It wasn't too bad.'

'And then, after that?'

'After that, I ate what was on the figure-eight-shaped plate. The meat and string beans. But not the mashed potato.'

'Why not?'

'I don't know. I think it was a bit dried up.'

'Did you take a drink?'

'At the end. After I'd eaten the pineapple slices and the cherry. Oh yes, I forgot to tell you that there was also a bread-roll, and a little pat of butter wrapped in gold-coloured foil that had the brand-name Viralux or Luxor or something like that on it.'

'You ate it?'

'No, because the bread was stale. After that, I drank the mineral water, and wiped my mouth with the paper napkin, and rolled the napkin into a ball. And then, after that, I lit a cigarette and scattered the ash around a bit, over the mashed potato in the plate, and into the pineapple juice in the bowl, and the character sitting next to me watched with a rather disgusted air. When I had finished smoking the cigarette I stubbed it out in the fish bowl, among the leftover bits of lettuce, and that produced a weird crackling sound.'

They began sipping their beer in silence. Then Bea B. asked:

'And you? What have you been up to?'

A little later, Monsieur X started up his motorbike and they drove off to watch the cars and lorries going by on the motorway. They stopped near a bridge, and watched the string of vehicles moving along the road. The weather was chilly, because it was winter time. Drizzle fell sporadically from a grey sky.

The vehicles whizzed along the highway, engines screeching harshly. Bea B. saw them arrive from very far away, balanced squatly on their four tyres. The sky's reflections glistened on their rounded bonnets, on their metal bodies. The windscreens were like fragments of mirror. As the cars came up to the bridge they could see the wet asphalt racing away between the front wheels. Along the embankments, the telegraph poles jumped backwards, one after the other. The cars arrived, then in a split second they had passed, sundering the bridge's shadow and vanishing uphill.

There were thousands of vehicles, all similar and yet different. They were moving along in three lanes, the fastest on the left, the slowest on the right. They followed each other in a line. They overtook each other, and then there was a sort of yellow star that blinked on and off just above the front wheel. Before reaching the bridge they followed a long curve, without swerving an inch. The roadway was marked out with a series of lines in white paint, and the vehicles drove between them.

From time to time, heavy tankers rumbled by, skirting the kerb, and the ground trembled under their wheels. There was no end to it all. There was no end to the machines. They flowed on endlessly, disappeared, flowed, disappeared. The wet road surface made a continual swishing sound beneath the tyres, while clouds of exhaust gas clung to the embankments. The grey sky was blank. But at ground level there was this rapid movement that raced through the air, this wind that whistled in the ventilators, these chromium-plated radiators in which reflections glowed. Talking was no longer necessary. Bea B. and Monsieur X smoked their cigarettes, sitting on a gravel pile near the bridge. They watched the traffic go by. Sometimes they just watched a small strip of the road, and then it was as though they had been looking at a door continually opening and shutting. Or as though it were

37

a sky in which the sun has slipped behind the clouds, and dark patches and clear spots follow each other, accompanied by flashes of lightning. At other times they looked up the road, tracing it back with their eyes to its point of origin somewhere in infinity, and then the roofs of the cars were piled on top of each other.

No-one could see Bea B. The car windows were opaque. The motorway was a hard desert on which the rain fell in winter, off which the sun's heat bounced in summer. Perhaps the world was made of metal, and that is all there was to it: sheet metal, chrome, bolts and rods. Perhaps mankind had vanished, all the men and all the women.

The motorway had plunged into a great gully of cement. It had the appearance of a frozen river, a motionless glacier, a dried-up watercourse, something like that. Even the noises were no longer distinct. They arrived like the roaring of an aeroplane engine, each blade of the propeller, prisoner of the central boss, emitting its long screech. Each wave thundered against the ancient beach's wall of pebbles, making its own particular din, but it was always the same wave in the process of falling.

Of course there were a number of things that remained incomprehensible. But that was the result of being at the edge of the road. To understand properly, it would have been necessary to lie down on the wet asphalt, by the side of Monsieur X, and feel all the tremors run along the earth's surface, all the round rubber-sheathed wheels, all the burning sparks of engines turning at 4,000 rpm.

Rectangular coaches passed by, with their human cargo imprisoned behind the windows. These people saw nothing. The tinted windows had made night fall, and the little drops of rain that streamed backwards made them think that they were travelling deep beneath the sea.

Up front, the twin windscreen wipers folded in two, then forced themselves up again, squealing against the glass of the great wide-viewed window. But nobody saw anything. They

38

did not see the vast roadway stretching from one end of the earth to the other, they did not see the gentle curves, or the telegraph poles, or the grey sky. They did not see that the world had become metal. Nor did they see the concrete bridge, nor, at the foot of the bridge, this heap of sand with this motorbike lying on its side nearby, nor, on the heap of sand, this strange sight: two bodies lying pressed against each other, clothes dishevelled, struggling together, breathing heavily, mingling their gasps, their limbs, their bellies. With the whole world in the grip of war, who still cares about a pair of bellies?

Forwards, Monsieur X! Let me ride behind you on your mighty 500 cc BMW, and we shall speed through the streets of the city. We shall circle the block fifty times, then maybe take a few one-way streets in the wrong direction. Your bike has a headlamp and at night you will switch it on and the beam of yellow light will sweep the darkest shadows. The sound of your engine's exhaust will shatter the night's silence, sending echoes bouncing to and fro in the buildings' entrance-ways. With your powerful bike you will overtake all the cars, almost brushing against them as you pass. Each time a new street appears, to the left or to the right, you will tilt the bike over to one side, without slowing down, and we will watch the sloping ground as we take the turning. It will be like being in a plane. The wind will blow very hard, there will be blinding swirls of dust. Our mouths and nostrils will be filled with cold air, and our eyes with tears. We shall never go to the cinema. In those sealed halls the people slumped in overstuffed armchairs will be enduring suffocating heat and humidity. But we shall not join them. The bike will whizz past the waiting queue, giving us just time to read the posters, THE TRAPEZE, WAY OUT WEST, CASTLE OF THE SPIDER. We shall drive right to the outskirts of town, into districts containing nothing but gas-works and marshalling yards. Doing ninety miles an hour, we shall roar along the outer boulevards that cut a swathe through waste ground. When we are tired and freezing cold we shall stop at a café. But not the kind of café to be found in the centre of town, where people sip coffee and discuss psychosis and metempsychosis and things like that. No, some café for heavy-transport drivers, for

40

plumbers and electricians, for small punters. You will pull up in front of the door, and we will walk into the café and tell the fellow behind the counter: 'Two beers.' We will drink the glasses of beer, and smoke cigarettes, and never say anything brainy, just: 'Cold, huh! Really not too warm outside. Beastly rain. Well, so long as it's fine tomorrow for the match.' Sometimes we will go as far as the airport and watch the planes take off. We will try to understand why they taxi gently along the concrete runway, their coloured lights winking on and off. Then, how they manage to soar away from the end of the airfield, leaping high into the sky with their four jets screaming.

After that, we went into two or three bars, drank more beer and listened to the music. This very beautiful music came out of a metal machine. The same sort of machine as cars and aeroplanes, with a lot of shiny chrome and winking lights. The barmaid's hair was dyed white. She leaned over the machine, dropped a coin in a slot and pressed some buttons with her forefinger. The machine had a motor whose wheels turned secretly inside its belly. It was so full of electricity that there was a halo of sparks around it, and the girl's fingers crackled as they touched the buttons. The electricity ran through her veins and forked out into the room, giving off a peculiar blueish gleam like fluorine. And each time that the music started coming out of the machine, everything else was forgotten. They were war songs, that's why, their rhythms were all made for killing, for savagery. First, a few heavy, very deep thuds which reverberated in the ground and penetrated you from the feet upwards, spreading, continually spreading out. Sounds of death, no doubt, and it was possible to feel the cold making its divisions within the spinal cord and the loins. The sounds fell slowly, slowly, lingering on for hours. Then came other sounds, sharp hesitant notes blending in with the great deep thuds. At that stage it became quite clear what all this meant: it meant that there would be no more future, that the past had ceased to exist, and that all time's holes had been probed, had been scraped to the bone.

The electric machine hurled sounds as far as the end of time, obliterated all the years' numerals: 637, 1212, 1969, 2003, 40360, Aa 222, Year VI. Nothing remained. It hurled its notes as far as the end of language, too, it crushed words underfoot. One became dumb: there was no more to be said. The machine thought for you, I swear it did, it had a monopoly on thought. Nothing but circuits of wires, fog-lights, small symbols stamped into the cellulose plastic, and dizzy movements in the condensers. Everyone in the bar was like that: sitting in a chair, in front of a table, eyes engaged in seeing the window's white rectangle, while the machine grimly aimed its waves at these minds, slowly setting the rotors turning, making the fan blades whirl faster and faster under the alternate blows of the electric current, and IT WAS THAT THAT CONSTITUTED THOUGHT.

Then, words could be heard boring into the café's silence; they emerged from the scintillating machine and vibrated in the hermetically sealed air, and the people there heard these words with blank minds. The voice murmuring against the microphone was very gentle, very faint, the voice of a young woman or maybe a child, but its words devoured space. They rippled through the network of electric wires, became amplified, reverberated, spurted from the mouths of loudspeakers, ran quickly along the ground, or just flew slowly through the heavy air. They said nothing. They were beyond intelligibility, simple vibrations drowned by the vibrations of the guitar and the double-bass, and the young woman doing the singing was visible everywhere, opening and closing her thick lips. The words danced in the café's cube of air, accompanied by cigarette smoke, slurred whispers, the clearing of throats, the sounds of water and breathing. They said nothing. Or rather, what they said was:

Ba de bi dooo   doo da ti da dooo
Wha di toodoo daaa ni na beuh deuh dooo

42

Chitti dan wi   wachamidamoo doo doo
Ra la mi   ma ma mi   ooh oh eh eh
Ta long whon di   nimamoo   wa ta
Ti da doo bi da   Wa   wa

And this was truly the most beautiful language imaginable, gentle incantations full of moist noises, murmuring, spelling out their simple sounds, agglutinating their powerful vowels. It was a language that hurled one backwards, that made one forget the war, perhaps. Or maybe it was their own war-chant that was coming from their electric mouths in long-drawn-out stresses, and for the first time the question of defeat no longer seemed important.

In any case, this language was not that of woman, or of man, or of any living thing that kills for food, or of dogs, or the offspring of cows, or ants. It was more like a language of trees and plants, a tremor concealed within the fibres, a vibration in the sun's light or the rain's downpour, an out-crop of roots.

Monsieur X, this is what poetry has become, today. No longer little phrases jotted down in notebooks, no longer little lines carefully arranged on sheets of paper by beslippered poets in stale-smelling rooms with closed shutters.

This was it, true poetry. Emanating from the mouth of a bulky thinking-machine at the back of a plastic-coated café. The poetry that should be the same for everybody.

Would you care for a short list of some of the great poems of our time?

Shaking all over (Johnny Kidd and the Pirates)
Heloise (Barry Ryan)
Satisfaction (Rolling Stones)
Obladi oblada (Arthur Conley)
End of the world (Aphrodite's Child)
Shake it, baby (John Lee Hooker)

43

I'm sick y'all (Otis Redding)
Sous aucun prétexte (Françoise Hardy)
Kansas City (James Brown)
Sir Geoffrey saved the world (The Bee Gees)
A whiter shade of pale (Procol Harum)

When there is no living word left upon the earth, that will mean that the war is over. It will be peace, then. It will be possible to open one's eyes again, and look around. It will be possible to hope for happiness in both love and business affairs. There will be nothing left to invent. It will be possible to sprawl on a beach, in the sun, without seeing the great bleeding hole in the sky, and it will be possible to walk in a city of fifty million inhabitants without scanning walls for crannies that have no eyes pressed against them, without deliberately seeking out the company of the blind. No-one will feel obliged, any longer, to possess genius, and to live alone on the top of a pile of garbage, cursing. No-one will write any more of those intimate little poems inscribed laboriously on a sheet of paper with a ballpoint pen, the words set down one beside the other, taking great care that they are poetical words, and not banalities of one kind or another, such as

'I enjoy living'

or:

'The sky is blue'.

When the war is over, Monsieur X, we will spend a lot of time in these plastic cafés. We will listen to the language that stirs in the silence, and the electric music with its different accents. We will go to the cinema to watch the very white images of a man and a woman, naked, caressing each other for hours on end. We will go to the theatre to see a very beautiful play in which everything will be obvious from the beginning: the stage will be covered by a network of electric wires, and rails, which will constitute a sort of map of human thought revealed at last in its totality, and that will mean that one will have emerged from the labyrinth at last, for good. No more departure or arrival! No more dream or reality! No more why or how! Everything will be clear. Everything will be true. Everything will be beautiful. Maybe we will both be dead before all this happens, but that's another story …

> *In case it should help in making my intentions clear, I may say that it was after having constructed a pair of spectacles, the lenses of which bristle with needles threatening to* pierce the eyes, *that I felt the urge to recreate objects in terms of the memory, instead of actually showing them.*
>
> Daniel Spoerri.

Each succeeding day, evil makes visible progress. It does not really advance. It stays put. Only, things become more clear-cut, develop angles, solidify. Hooks and claws appear, peculiar hands with outstretched fingers that emerge from the ground or from walls. Everywhere, mouths gape open, giving a glimpse of yawning red throats. There are wheels spinning very fast, with wisps of smoke and streams of sparks escaping from their smouldering hubs. There are eyes that open in the light, eyes whose hard glances seek to vanquish. In the tarred streets the air is a motionless block; but the bodies of tiny specks of dust vibrate across it. Each of these is a planet, inhabited by a man endowed with vision and judgment. Drops of rain fall from 16,000 feet or more, each one tracing a long glowing ray in space.

Solid buildings straddle the earth, bearing down with all their massive weight. Everywhere, it is possible to feel the pain inflicted by their foundations, to feel the zones of congestion on the skin. Thirst, too, an unquenchable thirst that parches language in the mouth and turns the blood into paste. Ribbons of bituminous crust wind like tightly-squeezed lodes

46

across the earth; these are the long asphalt roads that cars pound ceaselessly. And the grey, blue or black sky is contracted between the walls of houses as aeroplanes pass painfully through it.

Everywhere, at random: telegraph poles carrying endless wires, the white towers of skyscrapers, tunnels through which blind trains burrow, streams, rivers, drains, building sites, factory chimneys, antenna-festooned metal turrets, waste land, reservoirs, motorway intersections, railway junctions, traffic lights, the snarling of engines, clouds of fumes, windows. All that: all these aches and pains, all these teeth, all this skin.

One calls them by their name. One looks them in the face. And they stare back with steady, hate-filled eyes. One talks to them occasionally, telling them things in a worried tone of voice because fear is stirring within. One stops in front of a traffic light and says:

> 'Oh how beautiful you are, I love you, you know, metal pole, I really do. I love you because you have a beautiful cast-iron base for dogs to piss against, and because your roots are invisible beneath the pavement. I love you because you are not a tree. And yet you bear beautiful fruit at the top of your body, three beautiful fruits, a green one, a yellow one and a red one. If you were a tree you would not be so beautiful. Trees die. Sometimes they are struck by lightning and split in two and turn black. Sometimes a man comes along with a power-saw and cuts the trees up into matchsticks. If you were a man you would not be so beautiful. Because instead of having three lights that wink on and off you would have eyes, and it would become obvious right away that the whole set-up serves merely to churn out thoughts, to think ME ME ME and then again ME ME ME and then

47

ME GOD GOD, so what's the point? You are an iron pole, a beautiful iron pole with three lights. Down below, you have a beautiful electric motor that hums, and you never stop flashing your three lights on and off, GREEN LIGHT and the cars dart forward with roaring engines, YELLOW LIGHT and they all go crazy, some braking, while others accelerate and rattle on, RED LIGHT and their over-heated engines come to a halt. Inside the cars' shells, people get impatient and start picking their noses, but you don't give a damn, you just wait, then you put on your GREEN LIGHT and the people hurriedly feel for the little stumps protruding from their gear-change boxes.'

A little farther on, stopping in front of a manhole cover, one says:

'Beautiful beautiful manhole cover.'

There are so many things to greet, everywhere in the city. One recognizes them, in passing by, because they never move. They are there one day, and also the following day, and also the day after that.

The girl called Bea B. looked at the temple-like edifice that had been built in the centre of town. It was a pyramid, a pagoda, a cathedral and an acropolis all at the same time: a vast white building with glass panels from top to bottom, colonnades, a pointed roof. The entrance-way was quite extraordinary. Standing on the opposite pavement, Bea B. studied this giant portico with its four glass swing-doors through which the crowd was squeezing.

People went in and came out in a never-ending stream, shuffling their feet as they pushed at the golden, S-shaped handles that glittered in the four glass doors. Like grotesque black insects, the people were continually swallowed, then

48

regurgitated, by the great building. The light from the neon strips at the back of the display windows and above the doors made big white haloes in the daylight. The entire population was heading for the temple. It had been built there, in the very heart of the city, and people were heeding its summons.

Surrounding it, along the pavements and in the air itself, were all the signs that provoke fear and forebode a hidden God. People had come thronging to the temple from the other end of town, from dark dismal suburbs. They joined the mainstream of the crowd, following in the footsteps of those who had preceded them, rubbing elbows. Descending from their cars and buses, they walked submissively towards the immense façade.

The girl did as they did. She crossed the street, plunged into the flood of men and women, swept onwards with them towards the four doors of polished glass with their S-shaped handles of glittering metal. In front of her, a man in a raincoat pushed the glass swing-door and held it for a grey-haired woman who held it for a woman in a check coat who held it for a woman in a fur coat who held it for a thin man who held it for a woman with a child who held it for Bea B.

She took it by the golden, S-shaped handle and pushed it open a little. She went through. Then she held the door for the outstretched hand of a woman wearing glasses who took it without saying thank you.

The girl advanced into the hall. She noticed that the ceiling was resting on cemented pillars. All around, display counters made of plastic shone whitely. The crowd meandered around these, wandered off, split up, and solidified again, their legs working busily. Bea B. walked straight ahead, between two rows of counters. Her mind was blank as her body manoeuvred itself between the bodies of hovering women. Others were moving in the opposite direction, and she just had time to glimpse their black eyes opening onto their white faces.

Bea B. passed an area reeking with perfume. Women in pink blouses, standing behind illuminated show-cases,

49

watched her. Their painted faces were identical. Their red nylon hair was arranged in complicated coils, their lips smiled impassively.

Bea B. arrived in front of a large cardboard placard featuring two huge eyes that followed you as you walked past. Eyes like a pair of insects, rainbow-hued caterpillars of some kind, magical, great greenish-blue circles bordered by a fringe of black hairs, floating in the centre of the white cardboard.

Underneath the eyes, Bea B. read:

> Bar the way to
> Those tell-tale
> Little wrinkles!
> Wage war on them with
> HELENA RUBINSTEIN'S
> Skin Dew

No sooner had Bea B. escaped from the eyes' dominion than something else happened: in the middle of the crowd, far behind the rows of counters, a woman was standing under a neon strip light. Bea B. saw her pallid, uncontoured face and hands, rather like a corpse's, and her tight-fitting dress that was a violent, unreal purple-blue, and she had the feeling that it would be easy to vanish altogether. She gazed for several seconds at this petrified woman. Then the shifting crowd suddenly swallowed up the chalk-white woman in the violet dress, and the vision entered deep into her own being, an unforgettable absorption of something incomprehensible, a sharp anguish against which she was powerless.

Bea B. went on wandering through the department store. Everything she saw was both very ancient and utterly new. There were wavelets skimming over the surface of the sea, and fissures in the chasm's wall. There were signs to be discovered, and scar tissue, and bone fragments. Or else she was inside the belly at last, in the centre of the living pyramid. And the things she saw there were all tokens of what would some day appear outside, when one had finally emerged into real life.

She saw the following things. Severed legs standing on a pedestal. Bottles full of amber-coloured liquids. Photos of smiling women showing their white incisors. Tubes of red, blue and pearly light that were more beautiful than flowing lava. Glass portholes set in the ground. Great stretches of plastics bare of grass or dust. Figures swaying in the sky. Ventilators. Radiators. And all the time, everywhere, hordes of blank, irresolute faces gliding along at the tops of bodies. All this happened here, inside the white hall of the great temple, far from time and death, in the frail bubble welded to the earth's surface; while infinity pressed in from all sides.

Shoved along by other arms and hips, the girl eventually reached the centre of the hall. There, the staircases of twin escalators climbed upwards, unaided, and a large glass panel displayed columns of small words:

> Adjustments, Claims
> Baby Garments
> Bathing and Beach Apparel
> Bathroom Fittings
> Beauty Salon
> Bedroom Furnishings
> Bedspreads
> Bicycles
> Blouses
> Bookshop
> Carpet Centre
> Children's Departments
> Chinaware, Pottery
> Clocks and Watches
> Coats, Men's
>   Women's
> Corsets and Brassières
> Cosmetics and Compacts

51

Curtains and Draperies
Dresses
Dressing Gowns and Housecoats
Dressmaking Patterns
Drugs, Prescriptions
Electrical Appliances and Accessories
Foodstuffs
Furnishing Fabrics
Furniture, Suites
Fur Salon
Games and Toys
Garden Furniture and Supplies
Glassware, Crystal
Haberdashery
Handbags
Hardware
Hat Fashion Boutique
Heating Units
Hosiery
Housewares and Gadgets
Jewellery
Kitchen Centre
Kitchenware
Knitting-Wool
Knitwear
Lamps
Leather Goods
Linens
Lingerie
Men's Clothing
Men's Furnishings
Perfumes
Photography Equipment
Radios and Television Sets
Rainwear
Records and Record Players

Refrigerators and Washing Machines
Restaurant and Snack Bar
Rest Rooms
Shoes, Men's and Children's
        Ladies'
Silks, Synthetic Fabrics
Silverware
Skirts
Souvenirs of Paris
Sporting Goods
Stationery
Teenage Fashions
Toiletries
Tools, Power and Hand
Trunks and Travelling Cases
Typewriters
Umbrellas
Wallpapers
Whitewood Furniture
Woollens

That was the programme. Now one could start wandering around. One would follow the movements of the throng, and explore the world. One would let oneself be swept along between rows of clothes-racks, one would steady one's feet on the steps of the escalator, one would clasp the rubber handrail with one's right hand, sometimes one would stand in front of an iron door waiting for the queer box-shaped machine, crammed with buttons and lights, to hoist you from floor to floor.

Bea B. decided that she would stay in the shop for a long time. She could pass whole days there, months even, years perhaps, without ever leaving. She visited the first floor, which was filled with clothing: pink woollen dresses, check overcoats, black raincoats. Here and there, giant mannequins reared up from their plinths, arms outstretched.

Men sprawled on leather couches, reading newspapers. The women's heels trampled the pile carpeting, raising little clouds of dust. From the ceiling, clusters of electric lamps ceaselessly manufactured dazzling light. Concealed in the angles of walls, loudspeakers broadcast a continuous, remote music.

Bea B. felt a strange tiredness sweep over her. She sank into a leather armchair near a pillar. She lit a cigarette and flicked the ash into a vast ashtray, a sort of column supporting a copper bowl that was furnished with a spring mechanism. The girl pressed down on the button with the forefinger of her left hand, and watched the metal disc spin its way down towards the bottom of the bowl.

She might have thought that it was exactly like the circles of the infinite which comprise the intellect's only real movement. But she was not thinking about that, or about anything of the sort.

From her red travel bag, upon which was written TWA, she produced the little blue rexine notebook, upon which was written in letters of gold

'EZEJOT' DIARY

and she wrote on a fresh page:

'I feel so depressed today! I've been wandering the streets. I went to the café. I didn't have a sou, and it was cold, so since I couldn't go to the cinema I came into this big store. I am very tired. There are so many things here, such beautiful things, and so much money and so on that it makes me feel quite ill. It's a long time since I caught sight of Monsieur X. What a life! The very idea of existing for eighty years seems incredible!'

She paused for a long moment, trembling slightly, while the

tip of her ballpoint pen hovered above the paper. Then she added very rapidly:

'Shit. Shit. Shit. Shit. Shit.'

After that, she put on her dark glasses, rested her head on her right hand, and went to sleep.

No-one took any notice of her. Assistants scurried silently by, on either side, carrying costumes hanging from long rods. Women with varicose veins lurched about in front of revolving hangers laden with costumes. Long-haired girls turned the sleeves of the raincoats inside out, to see the price hidden inside.

In plywood cubicles, women got undressed and then got dressed again in front of mirrors. They inspected themselves in red, in blue, in yellow, in green. They combed their hair.

The uproar inside the store was deafening. Uninterrupted music flowed from loudspeakers, mingled with the snatches of words, always the same ones, that came from mouths.

'Organdie, but bigger, but more'

'Which? Which did you say?'

'There, there, the, lower down, the less tight-waisted one, I'

'Red and blue, red and blue'

Inside the temple, everything was powerful and gentle; movements glided along smoothly between rubber handrails. Lifts hummed as they went up and down, escalators hoisted their loads with tireless motors. There was nothing to fear, here. It was at the heart of the war, the mysterious ark that floated above the terrible waves. At last the girl could get some sleep, shielded by her dark glasses and her hair. No-one would come to kill her. She could dream about translucent landscapes, in colour, about the faces of lovers, about caresses in the warm hollows of her flesh. This tower, this refuge, had been set here for her, and for all men and women. Thought had been made concrete, here, a block of cement with broad

55

white bays and beautiful lighting. All that is hard and mortal — sun, rain, wind, sea, forests and deserts — had been hidden away. What had been created was step-by-step thought, leading from first floor to second floor to third floor to fourth floor to fifth floor to sixth floor. Basement.

The soft-drink stands gushed forth fountains of soda and orange juice. Ripe fruit from every corner of the globe filled the display counters. Cellophane-wrapped meats waited in open-topped freezers. The yielding carpets, the rich colours of the wools. The snow-white stationery. The heady perfumes. All the flasks of alcohol, all the cigarettes.

The girl slept there, in her first-floor leather armchair. She was not expecting anything. She was like the others, with them at last. She breathed slowly, her drooping head resting on the palm of her right hand. Behind her dark glasses the eyelids were closed. Behind the eyelids the eyes shifted upwards a fraction.

The non-stop music wrapped a warm cocoon around her body. People's thoughts, rapid words flowed around her, without doing her any harm. She was part and parcel of the shop, a commodity like any other, an article in the first-floor department. That was perhaps the resting place, found at last in the midst of the chaos of centuries and territories. A stage marked in the immense labour, a dot, a cipher, a number.

One day, catastrophe is bound to strike. Everybody knows. Everybody expects it. It is brewing in the very depths of the universe. Finally its blood-flecked slaver will cover the whole earth. Things will vanish as easily as they had hitherto existed, a complete and evident annihilation. Things: mankind's tender creations, the jewels, clothes, paper flowers, hubcaps and photographs.

Catastrophe rumbles around the great white temple. Strange premonitory tremors come from outer space. Sometimes something appears on the wing of a Pontiac or perhaps on the smoked lenses of a pair of green-framed sunglasses, something terrible, an evil sign, a dazzling reflection, and that means that the day is a little nearer. There is a girl who, from time to time, starts thinking about this fissure, this empty space; the two edges of the soul try vainly to knit together. If one only knew how to see, one would see something terrible through the gaping cleft: the end of the world, the end of cities.

So the temple is also the temple of oblivion. Those who enter, pushing one of the four glass doors in which S-shaped handles of golden metal gleam, do not really know it but they have come to seek refuge. They are fleeing a war that is more terrible than man's wars. Their aim is to seek, in the depths of triple mirrors, for example, infinite objects that resemble them.

No-one will be spared. Those who are fighting, and those who are lying down; the gorged, the drunken, the sclerotic, the crazed, the doped, the somnolent. The war is coming closer, is already here. The enemy is already in the citadel. In the great temple, greedy hands grasp objects. But who can say whence the evil comes? Is it not already gushing from the loudspeakers' little holes? Is it not descending with the light from the neon tubes? Each time a woman hides herself away in the trying-on cubicle, and slips a violet dress over her skin-clad body, is she not unwittingly putting on THE ACCURSED DRESS that is fated to cling to her in the same way that nylon burns and encrusts itself, boiling, in the flesh?

Meanwhile, the girl, Bea B., was asleep, with her hair and her dark glasses, and with her chin resting in the palm of her hand.

When the inevitable catastrophe does strike, I shall not be caught napping. My eyes will be wide open and I shall look. You know, Monsieur X, I have learned quite a lot since I was born. I won't recite it all to you because it would take too long, and anyhow you wouldn't believe me. Sometimes, when I have learned something during the day, I have an urge to ring someone up, it doesn't matter whom, and say:

'Hello? You know what I've just learned?'

'No, what?'

'That a cigarette left resting on the edge of a glass ashtray will become mottled with damp patches.'

'Oh yes? Why is that?'

'I don't know.'

'And what else did you learn?'

'Yesterday I learned that one shouldn't walk under a ladder because that would mean passing through the triangle formed by the ground, the ladder and the wall, and it is unlucky to pass through a triangle. And also, that the secret of staring steadily at people without falling into the abyss is to fix one's gaze on something just above the eyes, the eyebrows, for instance, or just below, like the bags. And then I learned that cyclones don't revolve in the same direction in the southern hemisphere as in the northern hemisphere. And that messianic civilizations arise during troubled periods. And that in Arabic there are solar consonants and lunar consonants.'

It is good to learn things, even if one forgets them later on. When one learns things, one tames them. Otherwise, one grows afraid. I shouldn't think that you are ever afraid. I have seen you walking in the street. You walk very straight,

58

and never look at anybody. You always look as though you had just stepped out of a bandbox. That must be because you are a soldier.

I'm afraid all the time. When I'm in my room I'm afraid that someone will come in. When I'm washing my face, and my eyes are full of soap, I'm afraid that someone might creep up behind me and stab me to death while I can't see anything. I'm afraid of the mirror on the wardrobe door, and of the one above the washbasin. I'm afraid of rats. I'm afraid of clothes hanging from racks. I'm afraid of the dark. I sleep with the shutters open, so that I can watch the street's lights pass across the ceiling.

And when I go outside I get so scared that I can't even walk. My knees knock together, and I stumble all the time.

The ground I walk on is a slimy mud. My feet sink into the pavement, and it needs a terrible effort to pull them out again. Behind me, gaping holes slowly close up again, and as I walk the sound my shoes make is not 'tap! tap!' but 'plop! plop!'

I'm afraid and yet I frequent all the spots where things are humming. I go into the glittering cafés that are filled with ogling eyes. I go into the cinemas where this great white light bursts upon the wall at the far end. I walk up the broad avenues where everyone is scurrying to and fro. At midday I am out of doors, and at seven in the evening, too, when the armies start marching, jostling me with their faces, their elbows and their feet. I do all that because it is impossible to get away. I want to see the war. I'm not one of those people who hide away in the depths of their burrows, convinced that the world no longer exists.

I do all that, too, because I want to know where thought is to be found, and who fashions it. Thought sucks me in, draws me towards it from the depths of my hiding-place, and I go down into the street. I want to see the signs of madness, the colours, the dangerous movements. I want to understand why everyone is dancing. Perhaps that is another thing that I might learn, one day. Perhaps I might understand, then, how the war will end, and who will win it. Each time I am in the street and come across one of these extraordinary faces approaching me, on top of its body, through the crowd, I try to enter the eyes so that I can see what there is on the other side. I know that there is an unknown world, a labyrinthine path.

I no longer want to be myself, nothing but myself. There are so many things drawn upside down, so many things written with dots and dashes. There are so many blueprints. All the people who have been shut into their shells are moving along the street, just like black cars with raised windows.

Perhaps if I were a thunderbolt I could smash all that to pieces. If I were a motorbike, perhaps I could zoom straight through the mass of cars, levering open a whole lot of shells as I went.

Or alternatively, there must be a word, a real word, capable of shattering all these matrices unaided. Not a clever word, or a word of love, but some commonplace word that would explode in the flesh like shrapnel in the skull of a rhinoceros. One word, one single word. But however hard I search for it I never find it. Some word like JAGUAR or OM or ZINC or TRUTH. There must surely be a word to stop the war. But what can it be?

And in the center of a cluster of ten thousand stars, whose light tore to shreds the feebly encircling darkness, there circled the huge Imperial planet, Trantor.

But it was more than a planet; it was the living pulse beat of an Empire of twenty million stellar systems. It had only one function, administration; one purpose, government; and one manufactured product, law.

The entire world was one functional distortion. There was no living object on its surface but man, his pets, and his parasites. No blade of grass or fragment of uncovered soil could be found outside the hundred square miles of the Imperial Palace. No water outside the Palace grounds existed but in the vast underground cisterns that held the water supply of a world.

The lustrous, indestructible, incorruptible metal that was the unbroken surface of the planet was the foundation of the huge metal structures that mazed the planet. They were structures connected by causeways; laced by corridors; cubbyholed by offices; basemented by the huge retail centers that covered square miles; penthoused by the glittering amusement world that sparkled into life each night.

One could walk around the world of Trantor and never leave that one conglomerate building, nor see the city.

Isaac Asimov.

How eagerly people wait for the earth to disappear beneath the cities, so that it will never again be possible to talk about trees or plants or bushes! May it come soon, the layer of tar or cement that will cover every surface! No more mountains and lakes, no more beaches, no more water, no more rivers, nothing any more! Just cement and tar everywhere, plus prestressed concrete. Since the war which is shattering the ancient dreams is advancing rapidly, would it not be better to have done with them all without delay?

Forests, rivers, grasslands, grottoes, valleys: all are towns, now! Vertical posts, covered drains, esplanades, cellars, streets. Each day, something is torn away. On the surface of the earth, deep in man's heart. Enough suffering! Let nature change its name: let it now carry a street name, a number, the symbol of a brand-new block. As for those who baulk, those who close their eyes, and those who photograph a blade of grass trembling in the breeze: may they all be crushed by the steamrollers, may they vanish pulverized into the snout of the pounding machine!

One day, around noon, somewhere in the vast city, the girl, Bea B., takes up a position near the crossroads and gazes at the intersection as though it were a sunset at sea, or an ice-floe, or a field of wheat with crows wheeling overhead, or something like that.

Her heart beating very fast, she leans against the wall, in the sunshine, and tries to understand what a crossroads really is. She tries to see it, beyond fear, with a look that is neither piercing nor evasive. She follows the swirling lines with her eyes, she studies the flat surfaces, she enumerates all the signs, she wants to conquer doubt. Deep inside her, a word waits to be spoken. She says, gruffly and throatily:

'Crossroads ... Crossroads ...'

It is incomparably more beautiful than the sea, incomparably vaster, with delirious depths, and flashes of light that dazzle the vision. There is so much movement, so much detail that the girl plunges down an abyss, falling for a long while before suddenly surfacing again. She is drowning. Now she is hovering in mid-air, suspended from a grey cloud. The sea is nothing. Nobody has ever seen it. The infinite in all its blackness, forests, deserts: none of these exist any longer. Everything is contained in this crossroads, the magic meeting-place of these four valleys that came from unknown parts and ended here, at this spot, in this cross-shaped forum.

The struggle must surely have begun in this very place. All the disputes of this and other worlds have chosen this landscape, out of so many others, as their field of battle.

There are so many things here that it is difficult to know where to begin. First of all, there is this roadway of black macadam, with its millions of tiny granules of stone embedded in the tar's magma. A congealed mass, slightly convex towards the centre, stretching out endlessly along the four roads. It is a flow of lava, but a tranquil one that never seethes or bursts apart, a frozen river with countless branches, pressing its crust hard against the earth's surface.

The tyres of vehicles pass with a liquid sound over the black roadway. Sometimes the crust has given way beneath the weight of a lorry, or has melted in the heat of the summer sun, and then small blue-clad men have arrived with machines and filled in the hole. Here and there, patches are visible, greyish blotches on the tar, and the wheels of passing cars bump over them.

The black roadway is new. It can never come to an end. The light from the sky cannot penetrate its dull sheen. The rain, when it rains, flows over it and runs down its slopes towards the gutters. The wind, when it blows, does not raise waves, but skims over the hard surface, grabbing dust-heaps and greasy papers, then rushes along the roadway, to be engulfed in the corridors of side-streets. In the centre of the crossroads there is an invisible point from which whirlwinds spring.

Bea B. is studying the crossroads, trying to understand how the four rivers of macadam come together and in which direction they are rolling. But they are headed neither this way nor that way. They are headed in all directions at the same time, reaching the edge of the universe in a single second. The black solid mass, without speed, without passion, that provides the city's primary element; the throbbing ground beyond which there is nothing. All comes to a halt here: imagination, hope, violence, all the war's secrets.

Bea B. retreats, leaning her back against the wall of the pharmacy. She gazes at the roadway with utter concentration, willing herself to enter it, to become a crossroads. She stretches her body out on the hard black surface, arms crossed on her chest, and cars and people's feet pass over her.

There are pavements, too. Imagine strips of grey cement, about one foot high, bordering the roadway: shorelines, as calm and flat as the river itself, following the contours of the houses. At the edge of the pavement the cement strip is kept in check by a sort of step of white stone. On the left-hand side of street number one, the pavement makes an angle, then sets off again in a straight line. But on the right-hand side, at the angle of street number one and street number two, the strip of pavement becomes rounded, and the stone step has been carved into an arc. Why should that be so? Has the current from the river of tar worn away the point of the angle, or is there some mysterious factor, in the wall of the house, or in the nature of things in general, that has required the equilibrium of asymmetry?

Bea B. looks down at the area of pavement beneath her feet. Like the rest, it remains motionless, a grey and white surface protruding above the black roadway. This is the haven of pedestrians and dogs. This is where children arrive, panting, after having run, hopping all the way, across the street's dark ocean. The pavement is inscribed with a series of geometrical designs: squares traced in the cement with a ruler. Squares for skipping from one to the other, while walking along. Squares to drive one crazy in trying to count them. Squares to prevent crêpe soles from skidding on rainy days.

Squares to let people know that this is human territory, adorned with tattoos. Because of the squares drawn on the pavement, the roadway's black stream is a place of ill omen where death and the unknown and the inhuman prowl.

Everything is so simple, at this crossroads, that one must never think: how might this be otherwise?

Bea B. studies all the signs installed along the pavement. These objects in the landscape, motionless as trees or rocks, are no-parking signs. They stand upright at each side of the crossroads, their grey metal tubes topped by discs painted blue and red. And here and there, along the ground, are the grilles of drains, rectangles of black cast iron where for years waste matter has accumulated. In their centres, a rosette of moulded metal spells out the letters S.E.V.

Bea B. notices a curious kind of island in the middle of the crossroads, a long rectangle of cement floating upon the black roadway. At each end, the island is terminated by a stone-bordered circle that serves as base for a luminous winking turret. Above the turret on the left a signpost says: THE HARBOUR.

Bea B. is not engaged in thought. She has no time to think. All her time is occupied in seeing everything connected with the crossroads, all these lines, all these volumes, all these colours. She looks at them as though for the last time. As though, after her, after them, nothing could ever exist there any more. A rapturous joy has taken shape under the eyes of the crossroads, a joy that animates it now. Everything – the black roadway, the walls of the houses, the movements of the vehicles, the vertical posts, the winking lights – is extremely pure and violent and simple. So, no need any longer to think, to question empty space. The gaze encounters things, hard stratifications.

How to put it? It was something like the explosion that occurs when a fireball suddenly splits open and spurts rays of calcined debris. An immobilized explosion, one without beginning or end. It was not destructive. It had no origin. It was there, in the city, with its four barbed arms and its restless nucleus: a star, a star.

If the world really has a centre, a navel, then this must be it. If the universe is really in the process of being perpetually born, then this must be the egg. Here is the aerolite's point of impact as it plunges into the field of dust. Here is the sort of festering boil that the lava throws up in the plain and that is named Paricutin.

Bea B. watches the explosion, her back resting against the white wall of the pharmacy. She is not afraid any longer. The armies may come, but she will not be crushed beneath their murderous boots. The crossroads stretches out, huge and peaceful, just like a river that has ceased to flow. No waves break. One does not see walls crack and crumble under the mud's pressure. One does not see the sky speed away, ploughing its terrible wake of empty space.

One sees only things that are transfixed by sunlight, their shadows marked in black upon the ground: iron posts, women's legs, car wheels. One day, perhaps, the girl called Bea B. will have penetrated the war so deeply that it will be like the eye of a cyclone: a deep silent calm that bears down upon the earth, setting barometer needles fluttering.

Up and down the pavements that line the crossroads, things are happening: a man enters a bar, brushing past the machine that dispenses soft ice-cream just outside. He vanishes into the blue shadows. A woman and her child follow the lines of the pavement as far as the angle, then turn into the other street.

There are broad yellow stripes stretching across the road. Little flocks of pedestrians cross over, while the cars come to a halt on either side of the yellow stripes. An old man steps down from the pavement, in front of the pharmacy. He looks to the left and to the right, then walks in the centre of the yellow stripes. When he reaches the refuge with its two winking bollards, he raises his right foot and steps onto the little island. Then he again looks to the left and to the right, and steps down onto the road once more. First he moves hurriedly, then slows down. He raises his right leg, as before, and steps onto the opposite pavement. He stops there, a moment, peering vaguely to the right, then disappears behind the angle of the house.

All sorts of things are happening. Bea B. watches it all go on, from her vantage point in front of the pharmacy. Men in boiler-suits clambering down from a big lorry. Children shrieking as they chase each other. A fat woman, carrying a bag, who looks up at the house-tops, tilting her head right back, and calls out in a piercing voice:

'Yoo-hoo!'

Next to the bar, the wall displays a series of wordings: BUTCHER / BANK / MACCARI & FRANCO. Between the butcher's shop and the bar there is a door. A young woman suddenly appears. She looks straight ahead. Her face is pale, framed by long brown hair. She is wearing a coat of black plastic material. Standing on the doorstep, she looks straight ahead. After a while, a white car arrives, driven by a young man. The young woman crosses the pavement and climbs into the car. The white car moves off, disappears from sight.

A man dressed in black lights a cigarette with a match.

A red-haired dog starts barking.

Bea B. looks at the crossroads with her eyes wide open. The light is so harsh and so white that the girl is obliged to put on her dark glasses. Minutes do not count, neither do hours. Names, words are of no consequence. There is no sense of place. It is like facing a glacier, or a high mountain with sheer ridges.

And then, slowly, menace descends. It is fatigue, no doubt, or else mysterious fear that has taken hold like a sickness.

Imperceptible ripples appear on the convex black roadway. Above the buildings, the sky clouds over. The broad yellow stripes painted on the tar begin to sparkle. The iron posts planted in the ground send out stars of bewilderment and grief. The manhole covers, the squares on the pavement, all the scars, the excrements, the old dried-up gobs, the fag-ends have multiplied. For centuries, now, people have been scattering these leavings over the ground; for centuries, now, the dust has been falling. The four roads' summons is a wind that stabs the midriff, a gasping wind.

Bea B. looks at the crossroads with eyes hidden behind dark glasses. But she does not see the crossroads. She sees the future, displayed there, in a flash, on the tar surface, painted on the plastered walls, moulded into the slabs of cast iron. The future has arrived in one stroke, swallowing up all the other landscapes on earth. It has swallowed up vast beaches facing the sea, deserts, grey cliffs, plains of wheat and corn. All these have vanished. The four rivers of tar have flowed from one end of the world to the other, and have then become petrified. The iron poles' roots reach down to the centre of the earth, to the nucleus of molten metal which nothing can abate. Engines race crazily, hidden under the bonnets of cars. Trams plunge ahead, sending out showers of fat sparks.

Who has won the war? But it is something other than war. It is more long-drawn-out and more terrible, it is an uninterrupted movement that no-one has been able to understand. The fact that the girl is facing the explosion, on one particular day, at noon, her eyes concealed behind dark glasses, means that she is in the process of understanding. Something has swept through the universe. But there are no real cities, merely tiny cell-like compartments for these insects. Who is concerning himself with the towns and cities? That is another matter. It is in the mind of Bea B., and at the same time it is beyond time and space. It is a story of life and death, a love story; and, too, it is a stupid story, a fable for caterpillars and goldfish.

Bea B. is looking at the crossroads, so near to her, yet so alien, because it is also her own face. She knows that it is here, in the abstract design of these walls and pavements, that the secret of her consciousness is dissembled. If, some day, she should come to understand the reason for the existence of these no-parking signs, these squares traced in the cemented ground, these angles, these yellow stripes painted on the macadam's black river, then perhaps she would finally understand who she is, down to the last of her cells.

When she had had a good look at the crossroads, Bea B. went away. But she told herself that she ought to go back there often, to do a little sightseeing whenever, wherever four roads converge.

Each day, the girl fought against fear. It was an invisible
battle: waged within her own being, against outside forces.
She had allies fighting alongside her. There was one who
lived in the sky and who looked so like the sun that they
called him Mr Sun. And there was one who had the form of
a cloud, a white and grey ball floating very high in the air.
That one was Mr Cumulus, or Mr Cumulo-Nimbus. They
were not people to whom it was easy to talk, in fact there was
a certain air of haughtiness about them. But when she raised
her eyes she could see them there, in their familiar positions,
and she knew that she was not alone. It was odd, having all
these friends in the air, on the water and under the ground.
When the girl went out she found them almost everywhere,
and that made her less afraid.

There were other, more secret friends that she alone was
acquainted with. The figure four, for example. She had never
mentioned it to anyone. Nobody suspected that Four was her
friend. It was a peaceful numeral that surely had no purpose.
Bea B. had been thinking about this numeral for a long time
now. As soon as she had found out that it existed she had
realized that it was her own numeral, and that it would remain
engraved in her memory. She had no desire to divide it or

70

multiply it, like people do. She accepted it for what it was. When she came across it by chance she felt almost joyful. She turned the pages of a book and gazed at the number written on the white page

4

or else she wrote it in the pages of the blue notebook: Four.

It performed no services for her. It was content to be there, in sums such as 4034, 44, 74104. In addresses such as 4 rue des Oliviers, in telephone numbers such as 88 12 24, in packs of cards, in the names of kings, on the leaves of calendars, 4 April 1944, for instance. It lived inside words, too, formed fours, on all fours, foursquare, quatrain, crossroads. In its honour people wrote four-line poems, such as:

> El dia 23 de julio
> Hablo con los mas presentes
> Fue tomado Zacatecas
> Por las tropas de Insurgentes

But there were many other letters that traced their outlines upon the plaque of silence. Letters which sprang from the ground like clouds of insects. Bea B. saw them flying around her, in the evenings, in the night's black air, or else at noon, in a haze of dust. Great care was needed to avoid the risk of suffocation. Bea B. took a big sheet of white paper and on it she wrote what she saw:

F K Four   &   *Four*   Four   FOUR

           2   Four   G G H

                         f   M M

   For Four   f f

              C

  S F O D D   N P

            Z

71

```
ZyZ     W W
                    uu
aAa     HI!              Tt          Hhuh
                V
    Z                       (N)
        th'W
                f
        K
```

All the swarms of flies, may-bugs, vultures, pterodactyls and vampires: they fly back and forth above the seemingly ruined city, seeking blood, seeking sap. Where do they come from? So many furiously waving legs, so many wing-sheaths, membranes, talons! Might they be the war's real messengers? The girl looks out of the window of her room on the fifth floor and sees the air tremble with these winged cloud-formations.

Lower down, in the street, whole packs were on the move. Hordes of wolves, peccaries, baboons. Caravans of ants in search of a body. Oozing streams of snakes, scorpions, black spiders. They were all words. But equally they were unknown threats, desires, glandular secretions. One was never left in peace. Fondly imagining one was secure at the top of one's tower, here on the fifth floor of the building. Getting into bed and burrowing inside the sheets and blankets. Until the fluttering, quivering army discovers you there, in your nest, and gnaws you to the bone.

The girl could do nothing about it. For this is fear, which enters the body and then breaks out in tiny drops of cold sweat.

The girl, Bea B., wanted to break down all barriers. The barrier of silence, and then also that of noise. That of sleep, that of death. She was alone, yet gripped by thousands of hands, arms, legs. She possessed an eye, a single eye swimming in the centre of her black consciousness, as well as dust-specks of eyes that sparkled in the night from one end of the world to the other.

It is so that they will no longer be afraid that men read pornographic publications in squalid little shops. They stand around in the ill-lit back rooms, fingering the magazines. The glossy pages are filled with black-and-white or coloured photos of naked women, women with heavy breasts, white bellies pierced by a navel, buttocks, legs, feet with corn-encrusted toes. One of them is spread over a double page. She is smiling gently with her great red mouth, and her tow-like mane is draped over her right shoulder. Her left arm is positioned across her belly so as to conceal the pubis. All the rest of the body is visible, in salmon-pink hues, with odd reflections at the points where the spotlights are aimed. To start with, there are the two plump, round breasts, the left one slightly larger than the right. Each of these sleek balloons displays a big reddish-brown blotch with a protuberance in the middle. These are the areolas, where the skin is marked by a series of small swellings rather like goose-pimples. There are grey shadows in the form of half-moons on the two breasts. Beneath them, the heavy belly traversed by folds and punc-tured by a puckered navel. Then the fat round hips, and the long rosy thighs, and the wrinkled knees, and the shin-bones, and the ankles where the veins are just visible, and the two long feet each ending in five toes: one big toe with a split white nail, and four small toes of diminishing size, the last one curled inwards.

Bea B. was genuinely fond of pornographic publications. These magazines that she bought at the news-kiosks and took back to her room were also personal friends of hers. She gazed for a long time at the photos of naked women, and it was one way of fighting silence.

Each one had her own name, her own life, her own thoughts. It was only necessary to take a magnifying-glass and scrutinize the folds of the flesh, the swollen mounds, the breasts, the hair. Their story soon swam into focus.

They had names. It was all written down in large letters beneath the colour photos, for example:

Rita Rose
the summer's belle
is a woman without secrets

When the hot sunny days arrive, Rita escapes from town and runs across the fields. She likes woods and birds and fields of wheat, and also stock-car racing. She comes from Holland, and feels nostalgia for the broad plains and the wind.
Which doesn't stop her having her feet planted firmly on the ground.
'Happiness', Rita tells us, 'is to be beautiful and free.'
For our happiness too …

Nadja Séguilah
Daughter of the Aurès
the Savage
the Berber
the Amazon

Sabine Sun

Her preferences:
Czech films
American short stories
mineral water
sad men
Russian music
and riding in the sidecar of a motorbike

These days
Amphitrite is simply
a big girl.
She no longer heeds Neptune's call,
she disdains chariots
even if they are
drawn by dolphins.

Tritons and sea-horses have remained
in the ocean's stable
because Annabel
has no need
of anyone's help to get ahead.
It is quite enough for her to rise
from the waves;

ANNA BELLE

when this child appears
the circle of her friends expands
continuously.
But don't start thinking
that Annabel will allow herself to be caught
in your net.
No mesh is tough enough to withstand
her fierce strength.

Bea B. had many such friends. They were true friends, who
never changed or grew old. They lived peacefully in the pages
of magazines, without worrying themselves about hunger or
cold. They knew nothing of the war. They had nothing to
fear in their Technicolor world. No-one wanted to destroy
them. They were pure and beautiful, their triumphs came
easily, just like that, lying on beds or astride black motorcycles. Their look was unclouded by fear. Between the heavy
lashes, the star shone steadily, shedding light like a diamond,
but never any tears. They bore magical, gentle names, Sophie,
Handa, Molly; names like whiplashes, Vick, Dolores, Patri-
cia, Estelle, May; names like the names of cars. Perhaps they
were already on the other side, soldier-women from Venus or
α Centauris, who had decided to conquer the earth. Perhaps
it would be easy to go away with them. The girl would strip
off all her clothes and, naked but for a bronze pendant and a
leather headband, would hurl her tall bronzed body into an

assault upon the planets. She too would have her own name, and her disturbing story would figure on the pages of pornographic albums:

> Bea of the war
> the very real queen
> of a future Ys
> she
> who wishes to save
> the world
> from boredom.
> Wreaking vengeance
> on all contempts all nullities
> she gives her body
> and takes it back again
> her body made of bronze
> which, with a single sweep of the arm,
> will send crumbling into dust all the old decaying walls
> of Jericho!

It was truly difficult not to be engulfed. It was difficult to swim above the muddy waves when they wanted her to founder. She would need to be prouder than a ship, harder than a torpedo, more mysterious than an iron submarine. All around her, endlessly, people were sinking, disappearing into the terrible depths. The light gnawed away, the noises and odours nibbled at the flesh, everything everywhere ate ravenously.

Or else it was a gigantic fire, an endless blaze ravaging the earth. Flames higher than buildings danced over the ground, and the heat transformed everything into water, then gas, then nothing.

From her high room, Bea B. watched the inferno. She saw the street's corridor stretching away to infinity, and it was a throat, a long gullet whose burning acids dissolved its victims ceaselessly.

Down below, on the pavement, people were moving forward, never suspecting what fate had in store for them. She knew them all well. She watched them vanishing in death's direction, her heart heavy, her eyes brimming with tears. She murmured to them, from behind the window-pane, and each word created a halo of steam before her lips:

'Farewell, Monsieur Geoffroy ... And Madame ... Farewell, Dick ... Farewell, Jules ... Farewell, Simon. Farewell, Monsieur Soulier. Farewell Sébastien. Farewell Héloïse. Farewell Lucie. Farewell Germaine. Farewell, farewell ...'

She wanted to lean out of the window, to cry out to them with all her strength:

'Stop! Stop! Don't go in that direction! Come back! Danger! Danger! Come back quickly!'

But no-one would have heard.

It is not too late yet, Monsieur X. We shall fight. We must take the initiative, we must fight back. We shall make use of any weapons that come to hand. We shall fight against the motorways with your mighty 500 cc BMW. We shall speed like the wind among all the black cars, and each time you pass one it will be like inventing a new word, *Schlemp, for example, or *Grunge.

We shall use music as a weapon, howling like coyotes for hours on end, and then croaking like frogs for hours on end.

We shall fight the shop windows by breaking them with iron bars, and by listening to the alarm bells clanging in the night. Is it not a fact, Monsieur X, that there are not enough bellies for all the waiting kicks, not enough mouths for all the waiting punches? The crushing sky is made of concrete: we shall set up iron spikes which will pierce it through and through, we shall construct towers of Babel which will transform it into a great landing in a building.

At night, the city shuts its doors and assumes its dead mask, its mask that wishes to see nothing. So we shall race the engine of your bike in the silence, and wake up everyone who is asleep while I cannot get to sleep.

We shall fight the clocks by tearing their hands off, we shall fight the lamp-posts by smashing their bulbs with shots from a catapult. There are so many things to do. We must start right away. When we have demolished everything, just like that, house after house, street after street, town after town, then perhaps it will be time to think of other things, agreeable things such as daybreak or forests of poplars. But for the moment the poplars are inside matchboxes, and each tiny stick is tipped with a red head that explodes and flares up. Meanwhile, the world is strewn with cigarettes, waste paper and Pepsi-Cola crown-caps.

I want to wage war against everything that moves, against everything that eats. I want to wage war against everything that passes by too rapidly for the eye to see, streaks of lightning, flashlights, cars, reflections, winking lights, drops of water, men's words, women's glances, the flights of flies and aeroplanes. I no longer want people to change their names and their ideas all the time, I no longer want to see films unreeling at twenty-four frames a second, or to hear the vibrating rhythms of electric guitars. I want, I would like to make something stop, anything at all, an electric light bulb or an oil-drum would be fine: I would get inside, and at last I should have peace.

Let us try with an electric light bulb. I don't know whether you have ever looked at an electric light bulb, Monsieur X. Maybe not. It is something really extraordinary. First of all, there is its base, a sort of disc of black bakelite with two small blobs of lead rising from it, gripped by one end of a brass tube that spreads out, near the other end, to a wider circumference. Near the end of the brass tube that is gripping the bakelite disc, two short prongs are sticking out opposite each other. All this is extraordinary enough, as it is. But there is more. Rising from the brass and bakelite and lead base is a huge bubble of transparent glass that is pear-shaped rather than spherical. It is the most beautiful, most perfect thing imaginable. A bubble of very thin colourless glass that catches fleetingly an endless range of grey, blue, mauve and reddish reflections. Inside the bubble there is a kind of little crystal tower like a lighthouse, resting on the bakelite foundation. The tower's base is rounded, but a little higher up it flattens out, and an air-bubble can be seen trapped within its mass. Two wires ascend, from the left and the right sides of the tower's base, passing through the lighthouse's plinth. Inside the glass, these two conducting wires are red, but on emerging

79

from the tower they become black. They splay out as they rise, leaning slightly backwards at the same time.

Right at the top of the tower the glass bulges out, and it is from here that the seven wire filament-holders radiate, like the rays of a star or the legs of a spider. Of these seven little lengths of wire, four point upwards and three downwards, and they are all fused into the top of the glass tower. Each of these metal arms ends in a loop, and the fine, trembling filament zigzags its way through these loops, circling the lighthouse and so surrounding it with a sort of heptagonal crown. The filament begins its voyage from the tip of the left-hand conducting wire and ends it at the tip of the right-hand conducting wire.

I have never seen anything as beautiful as this electric light bulb. Something is written on the very summit of the glass bubble. This is what it says:

Electric light bulb, electric light bulb, save me! Come to my aid. Permit me to enter your sphere of silence within your fragile glass bubble. Let me glide along your wiring, let me pass through the bakelite and lead entrance-way and rise inside the brass tube, all so very quickly, and then gush out into your universe where emptiness reigns.

I shall no longer be called Bea B., nor you Monsieur X, and Pedro will no longer be called Pedro, nor Rita Rose Rita Rose. We shall no longer be saddled with all these stupid names, all these names of people who think. We shall all call ourselves by one identical name, something tender and genuine, a name that will launch our bodies in unison, in

80

swift particles, in an assault upon the glass bubble. We shall call ourselves ELECTRICITY, for example.

Somewhere in the room's darkness, the girl's hand feels along the wall, fingers outstretched. Suddenly her hand encounters an object protruding from the dividing wall. The forefinger rises towards the china hemisphere and discovers a little switch. With a rapid movement the forefinger presses the switch downwards, and a click can be heard.

What happened then was quite extraordinary. Within a hundredth of a second I had sped along the cord hidden in the wall and inundated the miles of wiring with my fluid body. After spurting as high as the ceiling, I flowed down again along the plaited cord that dangles in the centre of the room. I passed as quick as lightning through the brass tube, then scaled the little glass tower in the centre of the bubble. The tenuous tungsten filament lay there before me, a fragile slender crown. Then in a flash I set my body ablaze, since otherwise it would have overwhelmed the element, and began bombarding the room with photons. In the middle of the floating globe I lit my arc of light and heat, and it was as vast and as beautiful as the sun, a thought gleaming by itself in the night, a living thought that I fabricated ceaselessly with my speedy body.

Electric light bulb, which I have inhabited. Come and join me here, Monsieur X, inside the crystal globe, in the vacuum-filled space-ship that explores the world. There is no more I, no more you, no more they, in the middle of the electric light bulb. There is nothing but this action, this W of white-hot wire which comes to life as our strength pours through. I lead a clear-cut, useful existence. I am not afraid of anything. Hanging from the ceiling, all the time, with my eye which scans the shadows and repulses darkness and dust. Come, let us scale the tiny glass tower together, and you too shall utter your commands. It is an ideal place from which to wage war. It is a place for being big and fierce, for being ablaze. When night comes, we shall wander around all the rooms and

81

caverns of all the buildings, spying things out. We shall see the people moving around, eating, coupling together on mattresses, or else writing, as they lean upon the plateau of a table. We shall make journeys. During the day, flies will come and settle upon the glass globe. At night-time, we shall madden the moths and mosquitoes. And when we die, it will not be with a few last gasps and rattles, but with a terrifying explosion while a round spark rolls around in the glass bubble. Come!

And when we grow tired of living inside electric light bulbs we shall drop them from the window onto the roofs of passing cars, and we shall listen to the noise that they make as they burst.

There are so many things to learn to see. Nobody marvels at anything. People are living in the midst of miracles, without even noticing them. There are so many extraordinary and beautiful objects, things with chrome plating, with wires, with engines and lights! There are scissors, ballpoint pens, watches, inkpots, driving mirrors, bottles of soda water, forks, cigarettes, window-panes, hair dryers, scales for weighing things, pullovers, automatic lifts, bicycles, coins, typewriters, transistors.

Transistors. The other day I opened up my transistor radio for the first time. When I saw what was inside I almost closed it up again right away. It was terrible and secret, like the entrails of a living being. Wires, coils, tubes, little balls of plastic, soldered joints, tin plates, screws, little bits of metal. At the top left-hand side, there was a sort of tube around which was wound an endlessly twisting length of very fine red thread. Nearby, I saw a half-moon made of superimposed metal plates, which revolved upon itself and dovetailed into a sort of comb. In the centre, there was what is called a loudspeaker, a disc of black cardboard in an iron armature, with a wire leading up to it from either side.

It was a labyrinth, and anyone who entered through one

of the orifices in the white plastic shell would have to walk for hours and hours before he could get out again. Although the radio set was scarcely larger than a book, everything was written inside it. Perhaps, indeed, it was the pattern of destiny that had been outlined there, within the white shell. The complex pattern of everything that had happened on earth for the past ten thousand years, of everything yet to come. Who can tell? Perhaps the world is simply a network of wires and coils, with, here and there, the little cylinders of transistors and condensers. If one fails to see that, it is because one is inside, advancing there between rows of soldered joints. To see all that, one would need to be suddenly thousands of miles distant, thousands of centuries distant. You know, Monsieur X, I think that at last I understand what is troubling me, and what makes us all blind: it is that things are separated from one another. So we become telltales; so, too, we tell tales that pass for history. We want there to be a voyage, a way through. Thus we continue, from one coil to the next, and each time we say: this is the centre, yes, this must be where the navel is.

That is why I do what I do: I study lots of things in that way, trying to make out the paths the wires take. Crossroads, department stores, beaches, highways, towns. Fields seen from the air, continents displayed on maps. They all have their wires, their connecting threads. Somewhere, a plan of the war exists in outline. If I find it, we shall all be saved. You see how simple it is, once one has thought about it. There must surely be a diagram. Perhaps we shall come across it in some book or other: the Bible, the Koran, or Bartholomew's Atlas. Or else in cinemas, when the house lights are dimmed and at the same moment the screen blazes up in ten different towns, with *Ivan the Terrible, Nosferatu the Vampire, Ngu, Viridiana, Il Crito, Caballo Prieto Azabache, High Sierra, The Mother, Pickpocket, Fires in the Plain.*

I am convinced that in the end I will find the plan. It must have the form of a gigantic town, with streets and boulevards,

83

bridges, tall buildings and railway lines; the map of Berlin, of London, of Tokyo. The map of Helsinki or Bogota. Avenues ten miles long, as in Mexico City. Open drains full of muck and rubbish, as in Tegucigalpa. Alleys scarred by shell-holes, as in Vientiane. Deserted concrete esplanades, as in the Los Angeles area. Underground passages, as in Paris. Jetties, as in Dakar. Brick walls, as in Khabarovsk. And then it will also have the form of deserts of rose-red sand, the form of mountain faces. The plan is inscribed in the sky, with the clouds and northern lights. The plan is in blue lakes and reservoirs on the tops of mountains. The wind blows over the ears of corn, opening up paths among them. The wind sweeps clouds off the dunes, at El Paso. And in Holland the wind skims the snow off the surface of the ground. There are fresh clues that must be followed up. If one knows the plan one cannot get lost. It creates the stars and galaxies that stretch to the outermost limits of space. It floats in the very centre of the void, surrounded by its ring of iridescent particles: Saturn's beauty. It breaks and ripples along jagged bodies: the sea's curved mass. Impossible to take one's eyes off the plan. Come with me, Monsieur X, help me to find the labyrinth's exit. Come and grope along the mirrors until we have found the one that opens like a door.

Instead of making films and writing poems, Monsieur X, I will tell you what would be a good idea: we should construct, on a theatre stage, a great network of wires and rails, with a whole lot of lamps and machines. Then, people would come and look at it, and for once they would see something that resembled them, without beginning or end, all solutions deliberately exposed to view. They would no longer need to wait for time to elapse: they would be able to see everything that is bound to happen. And that would be like being God, or destiny, or something of the sort.

Perhaps the plan is in the language that emerges ceaselessly from the radio. I really like listening to the radio. I sit on the edge of my bed, in my room, and place the little white plastic box on my knees. I open up the aerial. I really like to see the metal aerial pointing in the direction of the ceiling. And then I turn the knobs and listen. I listen to all the noises that pass through the radio set.

There are very clear voices that seem to be speaking into your ear, and which say:

'This is Radio Monte Carlo. We have just presented your programme, Jazz in the Night'

Or perhaps:

'The Masters of Mystery'

Or again:

'Your Station of the Stars!'

There are raucous voices that say lispingly:

'The Voice of America, Radio Tan*geeee*rs'

Occasionally one hears distant voices which come from the other end of the earth, appear, disappear, drown each other:

'... the working-class forces ... communiqué from the central committee of the party ... the clique of Soviet renegade revisionists ...'

And:

'Nuo Mikalojaus Konstantino Čiurlionio (1875–1911) mirties praslinko daugian kaip penkias de šimt metų ...'

And also:

> почему ж вы не плачете? прячете
> свои слезы, как прячут березы
> горький сок под корою в морозы?

I allow myself to be transported far, very far away, by these voices. I make my home upon the waves that surge back and forth across the earth, that dash themselves against the clouds' dome, that hunt eagerly for all the wire aerials.

I like the parasites, too, that live in radio static. Some of them are very deep-toned and go woooouwoooouwoooou without stopping, while others are piercingly shrill and go iiiiiiiiiiii. There are all kinds of them, mysterious animal voices that speak to me, that call to me:

    tik tik gloup tik tik gloup tik tik glouip
    crrrouiiiccrrroouwooiiik
    jjjjjjjjjjjmmmmmmmmmmmmmm
    phiouphiouphiouphiouphiou
    dddongdddongdddongdddongdddong

    tchtchtchtchtchtchtchtchtch
    hom! hom! hom! hom! hom!
    uuuuuuuuoooooooouuuuuuooooo

I listen to them for hours on end, twiddling the knobs and gazing at the metal aerial pointed towards the ceiling. How I would love to learn the language of these parasites of radio static. I am convinced that there are secret messages meaning: 'We shall attack at dawn tomorrow,' or: 'We are about to dynamite point 123. Evacuate vicinity.' While people are sleeping, and when the radio falls silent, I listen to the parasites in the static and I stay awake.

Upon the ocean full of signs
full of letters
Lost in the midst of the constellations of signs.
Where to go?
Where to go?
Upwards? But there are signs.
To the left? But there are signs.
Forwards? But there are signs.
To leave, and then forget, but dreams are signs.

The dumb man grunts and splutters
over his glass of beer
and his hand rises towards his mouth and makes signs.
The water obscures
the wind
the stones
the trees, the trees!
So much antiquated science is suffocating the world.
To emerge from silence
one single time
everything would have to become dumb all of a sudden.
Then one might hear perhaps
perhaps one might hear
the immemorial humming of the woman's voice that goes

  huuuuuuuuuuuuuuuuuuuuuuuuuuuuuuuuuuuu

near, nearer, right inside the ear.

> *The dog is placed in a dark room and at a given moment, an electric light is suddenly switched on; after half a minute, and during the ensuing half minute, food is given to the dog. This is repeated several times. Eventually, the light; which hitherto has had no importance for the animal and has not activated its salivary glands, now, through the repetition of its simultaneous appearance with the food, becomes a special stimulant of these glands. Each time that the electric light illuminates the room, salivation may be observed. Under these conditions, we say that the light has become a conditional stimulant of the salivary glands. In the present case, the salivary gland is nothing more than a simple indication of the animal's reaction to the outside world.*
>
> Ivan Pavlov.

The moment that a girl is let loose upon the world, all these flagella can be seen flinging themselves at her, all these tresses, all these strands of seaweed can be seen reaching out to her to cover her. She escapes, fleeing with all her strength. She runs down a vast avenue, almost brushing against the walls of the buildings. On the roadway, the caravan of black cars with rubber tyres moves faster than she can do. Each time the girl passes a door or window, a shadow springs out and starts pursuing her. She runs. She goes as fast as she can. She hears her heart thumping in her chest, feels it swelling and subsiding crazily. She runs so fast that she loses her shoes. But she has no time to stop and put them on again, so she abandons them on the pavement and continues running barefoot. Her face is thrown back, her mouth agape, gasping for air. Her hair floats in the wind, sometimes flapping over her face and getting into her mouth so that she cannot breathe.

She does not look where she is going. She closes her eyes so that she can run faster. She trips over things, bumps into lamp-posts and passers-by. The soles of her feet slap the ground, she scrapes her toes against sharp pebbles. But she has no time to look back at the traces of blood she is leaving behind her. She has no time to cry out or to think. She has no time to know what she is doing. She runs, she escapes frenziedly from the shadows that are tormenting her. She knows, without needing to think about it, that if she stumbles they will all fall upon her, glaring at her with their goggle eyes. She no longer even has time to be afraid. Quite simply, her body has become a crazed machine with feet that pound over the cement surface of the avenue.

If she could think, if only thought existed, she would be free: then it would be easy. She would stop immediately, in the middle of the avenue, and confront the pack. The warm sun would bathe her face, would make a golden halo round her hair. And she would look at them all, these black cars, these buses, these men with tightly stretched masks, these white buildings, these windows. Suddenly, her breathing would become calm once more, and she would look at everyone with untroubled eyes. She would cross her arms, smiling, and say, almost without moving her lips:

'Who are you?'

And immediately, all this would disappear, would retreat underground. The vast city would start to boil and blister, and would gradually sink out of sight. The cars' bodies would melt onto the cement, the houses' windows would close their black scars, the lamp-posts and passers-by would come into leaf. And people's silhouettes would become transparent, golden-hued blobs through which the light would easily pass, as though through flower petals.

Give a word to the world, just a single word, and lo and behold the whole language immediately breaks loose. A word meaning *silence*, or perhaps *peace*, *love*, *enjoyment*. And language rushes headlong in pursuit, surrounding the word with its pale ravenous Cytophagas. They who say *hatred*, *hatred*, *torture*, *doubt*, *contempt*, *hunger*, *destroy*. One wants to be alone. One wants to forget. But these gouts of memories gush forth, these hordes of rodents, these flocks and swarms. In her high room, the girl would like to be unique. She would like the dance of falsehood to end. So she puts her hands over her eyes, and plugs her ears with cotton-wool. She sits at her table and writes down in the little blue plastic-covered notebook entitled

'EZEJOT' DIARY:

It must be late. There are no more sounds inside the building, and outside, the lights are nearly all switched off. I am in a room with slightly yellowish walls. It apparently measures fifty feet in each direction. There is a bed, there are two wall-cupboards with a big mirror on each of their doors, but there are no windows, well yes, there is what is practically a French window (which I like), and then by the bed there is a night table that has on it a white telephone, a blue alarm-clock and a white lamp (with white lampshade). There is also a fairly comfortable armchair, a wardrobe with four drawers and a table at which I am in the process of ??? the fact is I'm not too sure what I am doing let's say I'm writing, smoking, and eating chocolate.

I am tired, my eyes ache, I've got a splitting

90

headache (too much smoking, I expect) and what's more I haven't eaten lunch or dinner. I ought to sleep, but I shan't be able to. I feel very uncomfortable, my eyes feel peculiar, so do my ears and legs. Of course, all that is not very serious, still it is just possible that it is an expression of the fear I am feeling. Yes, it is the fear which is making me neurotic, but why am I so anxious, I don't know, I feel that I absolutely must answer a question, that's very important, right, I'm ready, I can answer all the questions in the world, but I can't find them, any more than I can find THE question.

I have a tremendous desire to walk, walk, talk, hear, see, listen. I can't. If I start walking I will wake everybody up, I couldn't even speak, they would not give me time, and as for them, I do not want either to see or hear them, so what then? I scratch my legs, my eyebrows and my head.

I feel as though I were trussed up and unable to free myself. I can picture my grandmother assuring me that there is not a single bond to prevent me making use of my arms and legs and hands, and calling me a lunatic. Perhaps she is right, it is mad not to be 'happy' and 'do as all the others do'. That's true. So suppose I am mad, suppose I really am off my head? What to do, in that case? CURE MYSELF!!!

The 4th

It is 8.30. I have slept well and the weather promises to turn out as fine as during the past few days. So much the better!!!

P.S. for Monsieur X's special attention

The same day, fifteen minutes later. I send you these few lucubrations, though I really don't know why. Yes, I know: find the question that I am asking myself.

Bea B.

A few words, like that, in all the din. A tiny lamp trying to burn in the middle of the enormous night. The girl would like to batter walls down with her body. She would like to get out. Will she succeed?

The girl tries to pass through to the other side of the mirror fixed to the cupboard door. She sits down, facing it, and strives, with her eyes, to see what lies within it.

The girl is seated at the café terrace, and she tries to understand where people are going. Or else, at night, she lights a cigarette and watches the glowing tip. The essential thing is never to get lost. There are holes everywhere. The sun is a hole. The earth is a hole. Glasses of water on tables are holes. Wash-basins, sheets of paper, walls painted yellow, shop windows, even eyes, are holes. If one does not watch out, one is bound to fall.

And meanwhile, a few inches away, a few years away, far from her, the city climbs and descends. It extends its sheet of bitumen and its blocks of cement, its esplanades and its squares. It undulates. It vibrates. It contains the gentle heat, 21°C or so, and the noises. One does not approach it. One does not enter it. Men and women move along the straight streets.

Here is the reign of quantity. No individual thoughts, no more desires. No attention is paid any longer to anyone at all. The reign of multiplicity of things destroys solitude ceaselessly. One should speak of infinities peopled with planets, or of all the hairs planted on a woman's skull. One should use a hundred thousand ballpoint pens, perhaps, to say that, and a hundred thousand blue notebooks containing two hundred pages each. One should bring together the world's photographs, newspapers, cigarette butts.

So, too, when fear appears, in front of the sun's hole, or at night-time in the depths of rooms, it is not a single fear but millions of fears that grip the heart. When cries emerge, harsh and strangled, from throats, it is a flight of bats suddenly darkening the sky, passing across the sun like a cloud of smoke.

One should speak of that as one speaks of the sea:

The sea is invention.

Blue, pale, swollen, stretched out, movement that rises and falls, that reaches deep into the conscious mind, that reaches into death itself, but where is death?

A girl is sitting on a bench, one day, around noon, facing the sea. She looks at the sea. Here is what there is:

First, the coast with its sharp, bristling, fissured crags, and its white rocks bereft of grass.

The blue sky. The sun on the left, shining.

Finally, stretching out before the young woman, the sea's bulging mass. Blue, too, but shimmering with metallic and glassy reflections, criss-crossed by waves, in constant motion. That is what she wants most of all. The girl has arrived from the planet Jupiter, or from even farther away, and she does not know what this sea may be. Is it an animal? Is it an idea? Is it a toxic gas? Is it a klaxgoriam? She does not know. She does not enter it. Nor does she taste it. It is made for the eyes, only for the eyes.

She looks at the sea. The sea looks at her. Alternatively: no-one looks at anyone.

One should speak of that as one speaks of the sea. But how to say it? The war has entered the soul through the pores of the skin, through the lungs as they inhale. The war has blended into the landscape of life. Where there should be a field of corn swaying in the wind, with the blue sky overhead, there is a sort of green and yellow hell, with shivers running through it, and a great mouth with azure gums that sucks everything in. How to remain oneself, high up there on the headland, how to be bold enough to look around calmly? A storm sweeps in, the kind of storm that sends tidal waves and ground-swells to suck at one's feet. How to be oneself, there, confronting the others, confronting the worlds, with a scornful smile and a lion-tamer's bragging eyes? When the ocean of munching insects, with their thousands of feet and antennae, is rising higher and higher?

There is no refuge left for anyone! The grottoes are gullets. The pyramids are teeth-lined wombs. The lighthouses that shine in the night are the single eyes of gluttonous Cyclopes. Love's sleek bodies suddenly bristle with scales. The warm rooms snap their jaws shut with a noise of shutters. The books are boxes in which the breath is confined. The image, the one and only image vanishes in the mirrors! The poems, listen to them, listen to them attentively, say:

> Grrrr grrrraooh!
> Hargn!
> Hargn!
> Rahoo crrraa
> Ra-a-ah ra-a-ah
> Nyok!

> *His reason tottered, for he was remembering what the Follower had written on the 'card'.* You are now caught ... in the most intricate trap ... ever devised.
>
> A. E. Van Vogt.

The war continues. It seems endless. Whichever way one turns, there is nothing to be seen but knives, spears, flashes of light, gun muzzles.

One night, the girl called Bea B. visited a district where violence reigned. It was a sort of city within the city, a district where thick neon tubes glowed night and day. Once there, one forgot everything. There was no longer any way to know the time, or what the weather was like, or even where one was exactly. One entered as though penetrating the crater of a volcano, and one lost one's last name, one's age, one's vigour.

Bea B. saw that the people were no longer the same as before. They went on foot along the narrow streets, having abandoned their cars. Their normally pale faces turned the colour of blood. Their eyes had altered, too; they shone, deep in their sockets, casting odd metallic gleams. Some of them were harsh and leaden, like drops of ink.

Bea B. walked in the centre of the crowd. Among the frontages of bars and night-clubs, many hieroglyphs were written with neon tubing. These all flashed on and off again so quickly that there was no time to read them. But all the lights shone so fiercely that they created rays and eddies. In the night, all these thousands of suns shaped like Os and Ms and Zs

95

radiated their waves. Under the electric lighting, it was about as hot as on the shores of the Dead Sea at two in the afternoon.

Long cars with gleaming coachwork crawled along the roadway. Behind the closed windows, faces stared outwards. They, too, shone like light bulbs, or like cat's-eye reflectors.

The ground rumbled beneath the girl's feet. A dull continuous vibration that entered the body and penetrated the organs. The noise of an engine, perhaps, in action beneath the tarry crust, or else the distant, fearful murmur of a stampede. That was one thing that could not be forgotten. There was no doubting that each second produced movement, car wheels, human feet, earthquake tremors.

Bea B. walked along the pavement, brushing past the arms and legs of the crowd. Light struck her face, hollowing blue shadows under her eyes. Electric light. Sometimes, she passed so close to a lamp that she was instantly covered from head to foot with a mass of tiny drops of sweat, and her clothes and hair became dry and frizzy. Sometimes, she was swallowed up in such holes of darkness that her pupils dilated and she glided between the obstacles with blind gestures.

The lines of cars swept onwards, headlamps blazing and engines roaring. The smell of petrol and oil floated along the walls. Suddenly there was a clamour of hooters. One of them started off, for no reason, and the others all joined in, bellowing, croaking, trumpeting in unison. Then the din stopped, just as abruptly, again for no reason.

Once, a car slowed down near the kerb, and a man leaned his head out and said loudly:

'Hop in!'

But Bea B. stared at him uncomprehendingly, and he drove away again in his shimmering car.

A little later, the girl noticed this place on the other side of the street, with a crowd outside jostling to get in. It was a

96

wide door set in a red wall, and above the door two magic words winked on and off:

VOOM   VOOM

There was nothing else but this red wall, and these two words lighting up and going out again. People were queueing up to go inside, by way of this wide dark door. They disappeared. Most of them were young folk, teenagers wearing canvas trousers and lumber-jackets. The girls' hair was golden, the boys' jet-black. Their silhouettes floated briefly against the red wall, then they passed through the door and were lost to sight.

Bea B. crossed over, dodging the traffic, and went up to the red wall. She tried to overhear what the people were saying. She heard a few snatches of conversation, such as:

'Paulo, did you see, Paulo?'

'Hey! Jacques!'

'Evelyne?'

'I didn't go, you know, I'

'What?'

She walked towards the door. Above her head the two magic words appeared, disappeared, and each time a little more of her energy seeped out. The blood-red door seemed to rear up as high as the sky, a rock-face, the hull of a giant steamboat, the façade of a forty-four-storey skyscraper. In place of the sun, or the moon, there were these two words written in neon, words which blazed forth and melted away unceasingly. No doubt they had replaced all the thoughts in the world. It was this, no doubt, that the world was thinking now:

VOOM   VOOM

For a long, long time the girl sidled along the red wall. She already knew what awaited her on the other side of the door, she already knew what the two brutal words were saying. But she wanted to go in. They wanted her to go in. The door was bigger and then bigger still, an opening towards the inside of the secret tomb. On the other side, it was a new world; one had only to enter it to see that one had never ceased being there.

The girl slipped into this kind of grotto with a group of young people. Her eyes absorbed the room with one glance, a deep hall-shaped room, carpeted in red, filled with hundreds of moving, insect-like bodies. Here, too, there were lights; great coloured beacons attached to the ceilings and walls, and revolving slowly. In the centre of the room, an eye outlined in neon tubing continually raised and lowered its eyelid, fringed with lashes, over its blue iris.

All this was very strange and very mysterious, and at the same time very close and very comprehensible. It was something like a temple, when the high priest turns towards the faithful and says something in a sing-song voice in a language that no-one understands. When the god with the grinning face starts speaking behind the emerald-encrusted gold statues, and the great hall is suffused with a red glow.

The girl did not seek to understand. No-one sought to understand. Something terribly urgent was taking place in the world outside. These people had come to take shelter in this red bastion, and they wanted to forget, to pray, and to shout out loud.

In the centre of the room was a sort of arena. The neon eye opened and closed its lid, the red and green lanterns swept the ground with their rays. On the plastic floor, the legs of men and women moved rhythmically. Between the thudding feet, rainbow-hued reflections advanced, elongated themselves.

Bea B. wove her way around chairs and tables, hugging the walls. She watched the big blob of light where the dancers were stamping up and down. She watched the fluid body stretched out on the ground, there in the centre of the room,

98

with black shadows dancing over it. The heat was stifling; she swayed with the clouds of cigarette smoke and the noise. The long, snake's body set its scales glinting as it writhed in agony. In the four corners of the room, the mouths of loudspeakers vomited the noise of endless music. But it was as though nothing could be heard. Bea B. continued to advance between the tables, skirting the various groups. In the corners, couples were glued together in a single body with four arms, and two heads joined at the mouth. As she passed by, people got up and spoke softly into her ear, but she did not hear what they were asking her. She made her way slowly around the arena, tripping over feet, bumping against tables. Under the blue eye with the flapping eyelid, men and women were jumping up and down. Their expressions were serious under their dark glasses, and smoke came from their open mouths. Under their feet, the great luminous body undulated and shimmered. It was an animal, half woman half fish, a manatee, perhaps, slowly displacing its tons of oily flesh. At moments its white belly became visible as it thrust up out of the water, tense with effort. The women's stiletto heels pierced its skin, making little stars of blood spurt out. Then it plunged, and the sheets of greenish water closed over it. At the other end of the arena, it stuck out its black snout, a formless mask containing two holes for the eyes and two more for the nostrils. Its groin split open beneath the lacerating feet, and a shrill cry could be heard, a cry that stabbed the air in the room: waaaahoo! Or else its blue back floated between two waters that lapped it like an island. It was the source of all the music: the dull thuds that shook the walls were its heart-beats, hoarse snarls were torn from its lungs each time it breathed. Everyone wanted to kill it, but it had no wish to die and resisted fiercely. Sometimes it was even possible to see its heavy breasts heaving among the dancers' legs.

Bea B.'s mind grew dizzy, and she felt the need to sit down. She went on skirting the walls until she reached the far end of the room. There, in an angle of purple shadow, she came

99

across an empty chair. She dropped into it heavily, and closed her eyes.

From the spot where she was sitting, Bea B. could no longer make out the shape of the manatee. All she could see was the globe of the neon eye and, just below it, the heads of the men and women who were busily marking time.

How far away one was. How much one had forgotten. There was no more free space outside, there were no more plains or mountains. There was no more blue sky with clouds floating in it, no more sun, no more wind or rain. All that was lost. There was no more beach stretching its white-pebbled length, sloping gently down into the sea, with lines of waves breaking diagonally across. Since early childhood the girl had been in flight, without knowing it. They were all pursuing her. They had set their packs of savage dogs upon her, they had forced her to run on and on ... But there is no escaping the war. It snuffles you out, in the darkest recess of your hiding-place, and drives you from your hole. Then there is no choice but to be off again, to go a little farther still.

The war closes its traps upon the girl, once more. In one of the town's districts it has raised a red wall with two crazy words that flash on and off. No question of going anywhere else. The door is wide open, the corridor slopes ineluctably downwards. Then she finds herself sitting in a chair, in this kind of grotto where men and women are dancing. She is drinking beer, watching heads bobbing in the red shadow. She can hear all the cries emitted by the manatee as people dig their heels into its body. She has stopped thinking. She no longer wants anything. She is almost no longer there, the eyes and mouths have drained her. Soon she will be of no further importance. Under the light-cluster, Bea B. watches Monsieur X dance. He is very tall and very strong, and pumps his arms forwards, then backwards. From time to time, he turns his head in her direction and smiles a grim smile. She can see his eyes moving in their sockets, and the drops of

100

sweat that plaster his hair to his forehead. He says nothing. It is a long time since anyone has said anything.

A little later, Bea B. closed her eyes again. She leaned back in her chair. Cigarette smoke swam behind her eyelids, rose and fell in her throat. She listened to all the sounds the music made. It was the sea, no doubt, hurling wave after wave against a huge rock. Dull reports echoed from the base of the rock, then the water withdrew with a sucking noise. An avalanche of pebbles thundered down, pools cascaded, millions of bubbles streaked the liquid mass, hissing shrilly.

Perhaps that was why the people were dancing: to do as the sea does. But it was impossible to tell, because it was all happening there at once, very quickly, without any time being wasted. Bea B. watched all the heads moving in the semi-darkness, and the air was moving too, and the blood-red lights, and the eye with the flapping lid. Her will-power was gone. The great sealed room with red walls was like a compression chamber, and the invisible piston was thrusting hard. There was also this emptiness hollowing itself out like a syringe in which the bubbling liquid is rising. Because it was here, it was nowhere else. But it was difficult to say where one was. It was difficult to say who one was. One's name was Bea B., perhaps, and a little farther away there was Laure and Agnès and Dorothy. How to tell? There were so many things. Everything was so squeezed and mangled by the light, everything was exploding so quickly with roars, with rumbles of thunder. So many heads and arms, so much sweat and breath, so much vocal resonance. The great machine for extracting souls was in operation. It moved its driving-rods, it detonated, it threw out sparks. Finally, there was a common enemy that they had invented. They had given it the body of a manatee, and now all they had to do was kill it with their feet.

On the pebble beach, in the scorching sun the two little boys whose names were David and Curti had sent the body of the octopus flying aloft. Remember how it happened? It happened on a big pebble beach, in the autumn. They had yelled something. The little girl had come nearer to see, and she had seen the two little boys dragging something out of the water with their sticks. They were pulling with all their might, yelling:

'Easy does it!'

'It's clinging hard, the bastard!'

'Brain it!'

'Hold on, it's coming!'

'Arrh! Arrh!'

Then they had lifted it up on the ends of their sticks and had hurled it as far as they could, towards the back of the beach. The octopus had flapped through the air and had come down again at the feet of the little girl who had hastily jumped back. Now it was thrashing around on the scorching pebbles. It was black, gleaming with water and frothy slime, and its tentacles were curled round the little stones. Then it had raised itself and started walking. It slid over its own substance, so rapidly that it seemed to be still there when it was already a long way away; it was running towards the sea. The two little boys were running alongside it, hitting at it with their sticks. The blows resounded dully on its soft body, as when one hits a pillow.

'Stop it!'

'Impossible, there's no way to stop it!'

'Bash it in, otherwise it will get back to the sea!'

'Smash it with a stone!'

But the stone rebounded from the black body, and it continued gliding down the slope that led to the sea. The little girl walked behind, her heart thumping.

'Hold it with your stick while I turn it over.'

Then the little boy called David had knelt down on the pebbles and had turned the octopus over with his hands. It had gashed the skin of its belly, and had pushed its gluey body through the wound. It was that that proved the octopus's undoing. All this slime that it had put on its skin to make it

102

slippery now sealed its fate. Its body glanced off itself very easily, turning inside out like a glove. First the internal organs passed through the gaping wound, then the head, and then the tentacles. When the whole process was over, the little boy tore his hands away from the suckers. The little girl saw that both his forearms were smeared with black liquid. On the scorching beach, the octopus died slowly, trapped in the sac of its own body. Its pearly organs palpitated in the air.

'It's suffocating,' said Curti.

'Yes, that's the only way to fix them,' said David.

Then, when it was completely dead, the two little boys had stuffed it into a bag and gone off with it.

Now there were a whole lot of people on the pebble beach, under the light of the lamps. Or perhaps one was inside the octopus's black and red body, and one was writhing in agony. However hard one looked, one could see nothing but one's own lungs, intestines, heart, liver and kidneys. Death was going to come, yes, come right here, to this bloodstained room!

Bea B. drank from her glass and let her head fall back. The music hammered its blows interminably. Sometimes it seemed as though one had been asleep for hours and had woken up just as things were starting up again. Sometimes one had a half-formed thought, such as:

'Suffocation'

'Loathing'

'Monsieur X Dance Drink Smoke'

But perhaps it was simply that these words were written up in luminous letters at the back of the room. Nobody was speaking to anybody. The men were dancing up and down in front of the women, were lying on top of them, were feeling at them with their hands and mouths. Bellies were quivering less than an inch from each other, uniting invisible sexes. The beacon lights flickered as they changed colour. From time to time, the centre of the room emptied, and all that remained was the red and blue and green pool rippling on the floor. Bea

B. listened. She was listening for the moment when the record ended, the single second of terrible silence that reigned over the world before the next record started off. She tried to enter into the empty second, like a cat leaping between two cars, at night, on the road. At that moment, everything was white.

But occasionally the new record began before the other had finished, and there was a still more terrible second when the two musics were intermingled, and then everything turned black.

A moment came when the girl heard a record that she liked. It was Nina Simone's *I've got the life*. She got up at once, walked over to the centre of the room and began to dance by herself. There was no-one else on the dance floor. The men and women had been pushed back against the walls, forming a closed circle of red darkness in which their eyes shone. The girl watched them as she gyrated. Then she forgot them immediately. Her legs moved fast, now, impelled by the music's rhythm. Far away, beyond the heads, beyond the red walls, the voice of the unknown woman sang, uttered its series of little cries. Bea B. did not understand what she was saying. The sounds were deep harsh outbursts that filled the whole room. They were addressed only to her, though, to no-one else. Every part of the girl's body was penetrated by the music, by the voice's tremors, by the beat of the drum and the slurrings of the organ.

She was frightened. She looked at the floor beneath her feet, the swift slippery floor that returned her jabs like a rubber membrane. The light beams frightened her. She felt the red and blue and green reflections flow over her skin, slowly or very quickly, like water. She danced. Time went slowly, the air was hushed, there was no wind, no earth, no sun. She swayed her hips and her shoulders, hugged her elbows against her sides. Her mind was a complete blank. It was all happening much lower down, somewhere in the region of the solar plexus, as though there were a new organ,

104

a heavy heart, a living animal in her guts that dilated and contracted. She danced around her spine, and the invisible axis went from the ceiling to the earth's centre. She span round very fast, her legs whirling on the fluorescent floor. It was a motion comparable to that of the stars and planets, a simple spiralling motion which descended the well of the music. There were other satellites around her now; she saw them pass, yellow-haired heads, black bodies, torsos, shoulders, legs, red hands. They advanced, swaying, in empty space, approached each other, drew away. Faces hovered close to the young woman, turning towards her to show white masks with eyes that were gems. Then, still in empty space, they retreated at full speed.

The girl went on dancing on the same spot. She bent her knees and flung her arms forward, snapping her fingers. The heat was dense. Drops of sweat trickled down her cheeks, her back, her arms.

With her two feet she struck the elastic floor. A moment ago, the manatee shape had disappeared. It was she, perhaps, who had become a manatee. So she dived in; she leaped and plunged in the water, again and again. Her hair floated around her, like the tentacles of the octopus, and her body gleamed with frothy slime.

There was nothing left to kill. The pack had surrounded her and was prancing up and down in one spot, making enormous efforts. But it was a futile activity, a need to be in motion in the midst of general immobility, a need to speak with gestures.

As she danced, the girl spoke with Monsieur X. She threw out her chest, turning her head slightly to the left, and that meant:

'Am I alone? Am I quite alone?'

And at the other end of the room she saw the man who was flexing his long legs, and that meant:

'If you move like that, you will never be alone, if you move like that.'

She twisted her hips and crossed her hands in front of her belly, while the light turned from red to blue. And that meant:

'I want to be she who moves, not she who sees.'

There was a man who made a leap forwards, and a young woman with golden hair who made a leap backwards, and the blue light trembled, and the neon eye opened its lid, and the music let out a shrill cry mingled with a deep snarl, and that meant:

'You are beautiful.'

She closed her eyes for a moment, and when she opened them again the light had turned orange, and the walls of the room were covered with vertical shadows:

'I am with you, yes I am with you.'

On the moist ground the knot tightened, then unravelled again. Legs glided and walked. Shoulders shook, heads floated like buoys, breaths exhaled in unison. The cigarette smoke formed strange tiers and clouds, a bearded man was kissing a red-haired girl, the wrist-watches and dark glasses glinted. The roofs of the houses were covered with dust, the cars were screeching around curves, and the sea's grey waves were breaking along the sunny beach. That all meant:

'Go on! Go on!'

And she replied to Monsieur X, leaning her body slightly forwards, with the sweat plastering her hair to her neck:

'I'm coming!'

This was how she spoke, wordlessly. She made a drawing with her body, then erased it immediately. She knew that there was nothing here, nothing there, but empty space, so she stretched out an arm, and put forward a leg. No-one could see her, any longer, in the middle of the throng. No-one tried, any longer, to trip her over, or to talk to her.

When the music stopped, Bea B. went to sit down again. She threaded her way through the tables without noticing anyone. She sat down in her chair and drank what was left in her glass. She felt very tired, and slept for a few moments.

106

When she woke up, she saw that there was someone sitting next to her. It was a young woman aged about thirty, with a very pale face. She was dressed in black. The young woman leaned over towards Bea B. and, speaking right against her ear because of the noise, said:

'Are you by any chance ...?'

Bea B. could not hear the name that was mentioned. She yelled in reply:

'No!'

'You look like her.'

For an instant, Bea B. thought of leaving. But she was too tired.

'Do you come here often?' said the young woman in black.

'No,' said Bea B.

'I saw you dancing, just now,' said the young woman in black; 'at the beginning you were all by yourself on the dance floor, it was great, it was really great.'

'Thanks,' said Bea B.

'You dance far better than the other girls here.'

Bea B. noticed that the young woman in black was wearing a ring on her left hand. It was a cheap tin ring with a stone of blue glass. She wondered why this woman wore such an ugly ring. The other leaned over again and spoke in a deep voice that murmured strangely amid the bursts of music:

'What is your name?'

And since Bea B. said nothing:

'Why were you dancing by yourself, like that, just now?'

'Because I felt like it,' said Bea B.

The young woman in black had two creases around her mouth, and heavily made-up eyes.

'Weren't you afraid, doing that?' she asked.

'What?'

'That, dancing by yourself, like that?'

'No, why?' said Bea B.

The young woman in black smiled, and leaned over

107

towards Bea B. She studied her with black eyes that shone in her pale face.

'You looked as though you were afraid,' she murmured.

'Everybody is afraid,' said Bea B.

She was wrong to have said that. Because immediately the room became black, and red, and stifling, with walls so thick that it grew impossible to breathe. At the same time, the music began to growl from deep in its throat, and the sounds that came out were like sneering laughs, and mewings, and sighs. Silence and immobility rushed back, glided up people's legs, and emerged from the little cylinders of cigarettes like a deadly gas. The lamps revolved, the neon eye opened and closed.

'You look so like this girl I used to know,' said the young woman in black. She was – she was like you, she had eyes like yours, she was afraid all the time, she wanted me to protect her, she was afraid of everything, just like you.'

The woman drew a silver cigarette-case from her bag, and lit a long white cigarette. Bea B. noticed that her hand was trembling a little as she lit the cigarette with a lighter.

Then the young woman leaned over towards Bea B. once more. She whispered in her deep voice:

'Look at them. Look at them.'

The lights suspended from the ceiling were like propellers, they turned so fast that it was impossible to see them clearly.

'They – they are so active. They are not afraid of anything. Look at that girl over there, the one in the black dress. She's not afraid. And that one over there, with the peroxided hair. She's not afraid. No-one's afraid. They move in the way they've been told to, they are all alike. No-one could ever recognize them. They are stuck together. And look at *her*, the one with the freckles on her arms, she's not afraid of anything. She would never dance all by herself. Her eyes are not panic-stricken. One doesn't feel her heart beating madly in her chest. Look at them and tell me if you can see anyone who's afraid, any girl who's afraid like you are.'

Bea B. did not reply. She stared at the dark little room with the bodies swarming over each other. She saw the taut masks, the glowing brutish faces with their white teeth. The eyes shining like steel screws, the blonde hair suffused with light, the naked shoulders glistening with sweat. She saw the gyrating hips, the stamping feet. It was too late. The pack had closed its circle, she could no longer get inside. The music had become incomprehensible, a succession of gurgles and hiccups, a peculiar din that sucked its sounds down towards the centre of the room, leaving pockets of empty space behind it. She could no longer understand anything. The young woman in black leaned right over her, murmured gently into her ear while holding her hand, and Bea B. no longer understood what the other was saying. Time, the future, were far ahead of her, they had fled as fast as they could, they had abandoned her. Over there, at the other end of the room, people were laughing, shouting, dancing. They were hot. They went on talking with their bodies, with their eyes, with their bellies. They were talking, and the whole room was answering, like bats do when they cross flights in a cave.

'Come on!'

'You're beautiful!'

'Agnès! Myriam! Elisa!'

'André!'

'It's marvellous to feel as happy as I do!'

'I'm roasting!'

'Come on! Snap your fingers! *Snap! Snap!*'

'I love you!'

'I love you!'

'I'm there! Here! There!'

She had to go, right away. Bea B. got up abruptly and walked towards the door. She heard the young woman in black call something out, behind her. Without once looking back, she passed through several layers of smoke and light, walls of men and women. Her heart pounding, she ran along the corridor and through the door. Already, the room was far behind, buried in the centre of the earth, gradually smouldering into nothing. Outside, Bea B. felt the cold air, and above her, between the roofs of the houses, she saw the black sky. Cars were still moving along on their rubber tyres. Groups of humans were still walking on the cement pavement. Everything was calm. No-one seemed to be preoccupied with any malediction, but who knew what they were hiding deep inside their skulls? Nothing had changed, as though the centuries had never passed. Perhaps, somewhere, there was still a great red wall with two words written across its top in letters of fire, two magic VOOM VOOM words blinking on and off. Perhaps there was some deserted avenue down which Monsieur X was, even now, hurtling at a breakneck speed on his 500 cc BMW.

Numerous fires are burning deep beneath the earth's crust.

Empedocles.

The terrible noises of war: in the street, in front of a sort of crossroads, the men have arrived with their machines. They have parked themselves at the bend of the pavement, in the sun, and they are digging. Under the iron points of the pneumatic drills the ground is splitting, bursting apart, scattering in dust. The machines with their scorching engines are working at full speed, chattering explosively. Compressed air is circulating in the rubber tubes, bursting out of the valves with shrill whistles. The men are hunched over the ground. They have brown faces, and broad, scarred hands. They say nothing. They lean on their pneumatic drills, and before their eyes, holes open in the ground. The noise is so powerful that it covers the face of the earth. There is no way of escaping it. Machines full of hot grease shudder on the roadway. They are beautiful yellow-painted machines with engines that growl at the air around them. The blows of the metal spears reverberate in the ground, then echo in the air. The sky is a blue-painted lid pressing down on the city's walls. Cars glide peacefully along the street's lanes, and the noise of their engines mingles with the noise of the machines. The men's shapes are almost lost to view, by now. The noise hovers in the air like a cloud of gnats, swaying from left to right, and up and down. Perhaps the planet is the skin of a drum, vibrating under the endless blows. Or again, perhaps the universe is

111

only an immense ear endlessly stripping away the linings of its auricle and devouring the noises with its ear-drum.

The ripples send their rings spreading very fast through the atmosphere. Deep beneath the surface of the water, the noise sweeps forward even more quickly, hurling its waves down to the very bottom, then flashing to the surface again.

Somewhere or other, a hidden loudspeaker is pouring forth a continual uproar. Everything issues from this mouth, the noises of engines, the roars of jet planes, bomb explosions, Italian hooters, fog-horns, the screeching of cranes, the rasping of cement-mixers, trains crossing iron bridges at sixty-five miles an hour, women's heel-taps, the cries of birds.

The work site is huge, hollowed out of the centre of the town, and surrounded by a wooden fence. At the bottom of a crater, motor-pumps suck in lakes of mud and spew them out again with enormous belches. The blows of a steam-piston send a block of metal, an anvil, rising slowly up an iron tower; then, when it has reached the top of the tower, the machine trips its cables, and the block of metal crashes back onto the ground. And a terrible thud makes the houses shudder on their foundations, a deep heavy blow that echoes through far-off valleys.

Lorries move off in procession. As they pass, windows rattle. The lorries have great snouts painted red or yellow, roaring engines, crushing tyres. They thunder down the highways in a cloud of dust, their four headlamps blazing. Their metal doors carry names written in white letters, *noms de guerre* like CADENA, INOX, MAGNE; and there are other aliases on their bonnets, FORD, CHEVROLET, CHAUSSON, DATSUN. They drive through the unknown town, on their high wheels, changing speed all the time. Sometimes they brake heavily, blowing out compressed air. Their sheet-metal shells sparkle in the sun. They transport long steel rods that dangle and sway at the rear, mountains of gravel, sometimes huge blocks of rock that weigh many tons.

The noise of war spreads out, surges forward. In a single

stroke it reaches the depths of the blue sky, reverberating against the cloud layer. The noise of the pneumatic drills fills the crossroads so loudly that the cars seem to be moving in silence. The noise yells with all its might, it rumbles inside the earth's caverns. The noise of the ocean's waves shattering against the sheer cliffs, the noise of the sea's breathing as it storms the dykes and estuaries with its millions of cubic feet.

The noise detonates with such violence that suddenly nothing is safe any longer. What has become of the beaches, rivers, forests, mountain peaks? The tarred road has opened up, and spread out like an airport runway. The outlines of the buildings have fled to the distant horizon, and now all that is left is this great grey desert sparkling in the sun. Great metal aeroplanes, their jet pods spouting flames, are gliding along this esplanade, then tearing themselves away from the ground and climbing skywards with piercing shrieks.

All the noises, all the noises: there was no end to the number of them that could be identified as they arose. The whirring of scooters, the rattling of mopeds, the grating of trams, the growling of cars. The blasts from hooters, shrill, *pip pip*, *tüüüüüüt*, or deep, *honk honk*, *beep*, *rrreuh*. The crash of sledge-hammers against the ground, the screeching of brakes, the tattoo beaten by goods-waggons at railway junctions. The air is knocked off balance. The ground skids away. There are harsh changes of colour: reds turn purple, then purplish-blue, then brown, then black. Shapes, too, are undergoing transformations, as they get carried away by whirlwinds, sucked in by waterspouts, their shattered fragments hurled for miles. Window-panes have become opaque, true mirrors of polished metal from which the light rebounds and melts away.

Sometimes, mysterious tremors sweep across the face of the earth. Or else, puzzling pains begin to grow along the pavements, tender spots that sprout their stars of nerves upon the walls. The landscape tries to breathe, but cannot. Seized by a sudden cramp, it chokes for whole minutes on end.

The noise blows harder than the wind. First it is cold, then it scorches like the mouth of a furnace. It twists iron poles, it uproots pylons. When the wind dies down, everything resumes its place, but there is something in the position of the doors and windows that is different from before. Something is grimacing. Nothing is safe, any longer; the noise has made everything fragile. It has cracked glass and stone. It has loosened the metal girders inside the reinforced-concrete blocks, and it would need a mere flick of the finger for the whole lot to come crumbling down.

It is a cone of annihilation that has settled over the town and made it so friable. The noise, the great sand-making machine. Everywhere, thundering engines gnaw away at partition-walls, demolish ramparts. They open breaches to the sea's invasion. One day the outer walls will give way and the terrible flood will leap in with one bound, to submerge the entire world in a fraction of a second.

Not many real actions still take place. Cars advance, men advance in the streets that are like gullies; but they move fitfully, with sudden lurches that betray sickness. It is true: everything is in motion, nothing remains stationary. But the movements enter into each other, cancel each other out. It is a drawing that is being simultaneously sketched in and erased. No-one ever changes. No-one is ever farther away, or else-where. The ponderous machines shake all over as they pound, smash, excavate. Wounds open up in the roadway. Tyres trace series of letters, rub them out, write them over again. The writing says

xxxxxxxxxxxxxxxxxxxxxxxxxxxxxxxxxxxxxxxx
iiiiiiiiiiiiiiiiiiiiiiiiiiiiiiiiiiiiiiiiiiiiiiiiiiiiiiiiiiiiiiiiiiiiii
zzzzzzzzzzzzzzzzzzzzzzzzzzzzzzzzzzzzzzzzzz

Waves of faces pass along the pavement, then vanish, and other waves appear. Eyes, mouths, nostrils swim through the fog. They come in their thousands, emerging from the un-known, moving towards the unknown funnel. Gleaming eyes, black and green globes in the centre of their gangue of eye-lids, surrounded by lashes and wrinkles, eyes that roll, close, wink, fill with tears. The eyes see. But the noise drives them off into the infinite, and they recede swiftly, taking with them their cargo of fleeting images. The mouths advance, too, some closed, some open. They breathe. They speak. What they are saying is hardly audible. Words that hover in space, and that are melted instantly by the surrounding uproar.

'What I say is'

'Ah how true that is, Monsieur Russo'

'Chock'   'At Baden-Baden'

Nostrils engaged in breathing, two by two. Sometimes they are blocked, and a peculiar valve-like wheeze comes out. They quiver. They draw avidly from the reservoir of the air, which penetrates noisily into the lungs.

The faces advance steadily through the thick air. One does not know them. Doubtless, one will never know them. One is imprisoned in the plexiglass shell, unable to touch anything. Thousands of such faces, transmitting speech and thought. All these things and all these people that one comes across and passes, that one forgets. Impossible to halt. Impossible to hold back. These are the armies of the war of movement and noise. They arrive and disappear again. For a tenth of a second, they shine out, with two clear innocent eyes. Or else the worn face of an old woman, sucking her gums as she advances. Another face, brown and hard, with lines of sorrow around the mouth and lines of anger between the brows. Another one, and another, and yet another. A girl with still unformed features: the lightning of her glance flashes once and is extinguished. Still another face, chalk-white, a woman's mask on which the eyelids are emphasized with a stroke of charcoal, the lips with a red line, and the hair curls back along the forehead in separate locks. There is so much hermetically sealed beauty passing in the street, while the noise erupts all around. The mechanisms are perfect, they have secret works: smoothly operating wires, coils, muscles. The bodies are metallic shells over which the uproar swirls. Everything is closed. To understand, tin-openers would be needed. The noise bursts against the polished skins and spreads in thousands of phosphorescent droplets. But perhaps it is the noise that drives all the men and women forward. The snarls of the engines push the silhouettes forward, on their waves, as though onto the crest of a roller, and these outlines will finally break into foam at the other end of the world.

Already, there is almost no-one left. There are only these ceaselessly intersecting movements, these machines equipped with two legs that straddle the ground, and two feet that slap the cement and tar. The noise has filled the world, leaving no room for anything else. The noise has driven all words and thoughts very far away, and replaced them by systems. Everything, today, is noise — even the silence. The roadway's black river is a permanent snarl over which the snarls of the cars and lorries glide. The outstretched branches of the trees vibrate. The white buildings hundreds of feet high are vertical howls, each window a loud noise opening up in the muttering air. The light explodes as it falls, the black shadows are blobs pressing against the ear-drums. Very far away, beyond the thunderous city, there are the dull thuds that echo from the bald mountains, there is the sea's rumination. Each man, as you can see, is a cry. They wander around the labyrinth, emitting strangled cries:

'Ho!'

'Hey there!'

'Psst!'

'Wow!'

'Hallo?'

'OK! OK!'

And across the face of the earth there is this great distant vibration, this membrane sending out its countless ultrasonics, and at its centre the sun's searing scream.

Perhaps one day there will be a face, a real face, that one could spend centuries decoding. It will not move. It will not

116

blink its eyelids. It will not make grimaces. It will not peer anxiously to the left and to the right, on the lookout for danger. A face one will be able to read, line by line, without its melting away among the other surging faces. Maybe it will be the face of Monsieur X, or of some unknown girl. Then, there will be no further need to prowl the streets. It will suffice to shut oneself in one's room, and to look at oneself, and it will be like a mirror.

That is the way the girl called Bea B. travelled around, in the centre of town. She traversed the noise's turbulence, made her own way through the light and movement. She offered her body to the terrible blows that rained down from all sides. But she had already lost consciousness, unless she had simply ceased to struggle. She walked with the others, in the sun, listening to all the noises. They entered her endlessly, intoxicatingly. Never before had there been so many forces at play in the world, so much power. Everything, every living thing, had its own weight, was buttressed. It was like a battle, when the shells crash to earth, opening up dusty craters. One could not fail to see the machines with sweating muscles working at full pitch. A bus passed down the street, its metal panels and its windows rattling away. The girl looked at the bus, and she knew that it was eternal, so to speak, a truth, a truth with broad tyres resting upon the earth, a truth that was a war-cry.

An aeroplane flew high in the sky, a cross of white metal against all the blue. She stared after it as though it had no right to disappear, as though it were the true sign, awaited since time immemorial, that was about to proclaim to mankind some astonishing piece of news.

As the girl crossed the street, she glowed in the light. Mirrors fixed to walls, and the plate-glass windows of a flower shop, allowed her to see herself arrive, walking slightly askew, with her white legs moving past each other, her body clad in a light-coloured dress, her face modelled by the shadows and

117

by her long hair swaying around her neck. And she too was a noise, the tick of a metronome, a deep murmur that wanted to say so many things to the world:

'I like noises, all the noises. There are people who say that some noises are hideous and others beautiful. But personally I like all the noises. There are people who listen only to particular noises. But personally I listen to all the noises. There are people who say that certain things are noises, while other things are not noises but music, for instance, or poetry, or moans of love. But *I* say that all noises are noises.'

She saw them arriving from far away. She gave them orders, made them circle around. Each time an engine rent the atmosphere with its shrill shriek, her face assumed a sort of smile, and her eyelids blinked rapidly. Each time there was a traffic jam behind a stationary lorry, she stood at the edge of the pavement and opened a mouth deep down in her guts: then the many hooters all began screeching in unison, and it was no longer possible to feel sad, or lonely, or forlorn.

The noises brought the great walls crashing down. The noises respected nothing. Standing on the road's shattered surface, a man with red, sweat-streaked skin pushed a small lever down and immediately his pneumatic drill went into action. The iron point quivered as it penetrated the bituminous crust. Black dust rose in the air, while fragments flew in all directions. Then, all of a sudden, there was no more emptiness, no more desperate hope, no more demons or gods, no more spirals of nebulae floating in the dark vertigo. The world was a slab of earth being ripped up, desires were shudders travelling up a steel machine, men ceased to be vague, their thoughts became precise, went stubbornly to work at one single point of the globe, and words filled the four corners of the room-like space with snarls of hatred and violence.

Now and then, I step out of myself and hurl my shape against a brick wall. After throwing it, I nail it to the wall. I do not do that with my thoughts or my desires. I do it simply as one would undress before going to bed. I tear off the image of my body and my face, and spit it onto a hard surface. I remove my eyes, and there they are: two glass spheres shining in the centre of my shadow. I strip myself quickly, quickly, with rage and exultation, with misfortune, with every possible misfortune. And naturally, when I hurl my body, thus, against the brick wall, I also hurl all that my body contains. I expectorate all knowledge. I have not read, I have not lived, I have not known, I have not experienced birth. All these years, all these days, all these words, there, there! Plastered in outline against the rampart's surface, exiled there. What! Is that all it was? This absurd silhouette, this smudge, this grimace! All the hopes, fears, systems! It was so small, after all! It stuck fast against the patch of wall, it could adhere so easily, with its hairs and its scales! It could so easily be hidden! Then, from the other side, at that point in empty space where I am no longer to be found, a strange wind starts blowing, a wind that prods and hurts, a throbbing of the air that is neither foreboding nor pain, but, of all things, laughter, LAUGHTER!

At dawn the next morning, the Carthaginians applied themselves to collecting the spoils and viewing the carnage, which even to an enemy's eyes was a shocking spectacle. All over the field Roman soldiers lay dead in their thousands, horse and foot mingled, as the shifting phases of the battle, or the attempt to escape, had brought them together. Here and there wounded men, covered with blood, who had been roused to consciousness by the morning cold, were dispatched by a quick blow as they struggled to rise from among the corpses; others were found still alive with the sinews in their thighs and behind their knees sliced through, baring their throats and necks and begging who would to spill what little blood they had left. Some had their heads buried in the ground, having apparently dug themselves holes and by smothering their faces with earth had choked themselves to death. Most strange of all was a Numidian soldier, still living, and lying, with nose and ears horribly lacerated, underneath the body of a Roman who, when his useless hands had no longer been able to grasp his sword, had died in the act of tearing his enemy, in bestial fury, with his teeth.

Livy.

Ten thousand years of history: ten thousand years of war. Above the mud-coloured earth, aeroplanes fly ponderously, carrying their cargo of bombs. Occasionally it is possible to make out the threads of roads, the filaments of railway tracks.

Or else a sort of greyish patch, made up of thousands of tiny cubes huddled together, stretching the length of a valley like some kind of mildew. The bare quadrilaterals of airfields slip slowly into the distance. Columns of pale smoke rise straight upwards from the heart of the forest. The bombs explode in silence, sending up series of smoke-wreaths that hover motionlessly above the ground. The world is a puddle of foul slime. The plane's nose thrusts forward, on and on, through the troubled, bubble-streaked air. It is searching to destroy. It is prowling at 25,000 feet above the muddy canopy, and its shadow flits across the tree-tops. The clouds divide, then re-mass. Occasionally a storm breaks out, below, and lightning flashes puncture the mist.

In the lush fields, men have been fighting for days, years, centuries. They crawl, they slither along ditches, sub-machine-guns clutched in their fists. They creep forwards on all fours, making no sound at all. Their eyes search for any-thing that moves or glints. There is some mysterious secret factor within them that commands them to advance, to crawl just a little farther still. Above their heads, the sky is empty. They listen to the blood pulsing through their arteries, in their necks, their chests, their groins. The sweat pours off them.

They have been fighting for so long, now. They no longer know why, having forgotten the reason. But did they ever really know? The earth, the whole earth is a reason for fight-ing. So are life's gestures, the birds that fly, the squeals of dogs and pigs.

Those who imagine that they command these legions are mistaken. They yell out their orders, they study their maps and yell:

'Advance!'

But the conflict is so old that their orders are no longer of the least importance. History is spread over the ground, here, and the hordes of tiny men are converging upon it. The groups seek each other out, cross paths, clash, slaughter. They

121

race across steppes on horseback, hurry down hills and mountain streams. They mass along opposite river banks, then abruptly at midday they utter piercing cries and fall on each other.

In the forest, they glide along like snakes. Their naked bodies are painted with red and black tattoos. Perhaps it is always the same man fighting. Suddenly he stands up in the centre of the clearing, brandishes his spear and runs off quickly into the bush. His painted mask remains rigid, stuck to the face's skin. If only one could stop him, if only one could rip off his countenance with its glinting eyes. 'Stop, Monsieur X! Stop a moment! Look around you! Stop a moment, and look!' But he does not listen. He heads into the wind, brandishing his spear above his head. And here his very image appears before him. A man looking just like him, painted red and black. The two savage forms leap at each other. When they meet, there is this fraction of time during which they are floating and dancing in space, while the two spears clash together. Then they separate, and now it can be seen that one of the men is sprawled in the grass, and that his flank is pierced by a large red hole.

Or else he has put on an iron mask with slits for eyes, and a heavy coat of mail. The clanking of old iron accompanies him as he walks. His feet shod with steel boots thud into the ground. He cleaves the air, a figure-head of silence. His breath hisses through the chinks in his helmet, and his spurs click. Above his head, the man's mailed gauntlet waves a sharp sword that flashes in the sun. 'Monsieur X, what are you doing? Look at the sun shining on your iron sword! Look! I beg you, stop and watch the sun's reflection on your sword!' But he does not look. Through the slits in his helmet, his eyes can be seen sparkling. The man follows his eyes, striking the ground with his steel feet as he walks straight ahead. And, always, there looms the image of the other, the one who seems to be emerging from a very limpid mirror, who is advancing to meet him, brandishing an identical

122

sword. The blades clash, draw sparks from the helmets as they glance off them. The points seek to penetrate the coats of mail, to prise off the helmets. Finally, one of the two crashes heavily backwards. And the sword's blade plunges between the helmet and the coat of mail, at the neck, and severs the carotid artery. Then the man goes away, and the other one, on the ground, dies imprisoned in his metal shell, his face still hidden.

The war never stops. It sweeps continuously through the world, with all its ships, its horses, its tanks, and its aeroplanes. Endless noise rises from the fields and valleys, deep growls, explosions, shattering cries, the whistling of bullets. At night, the forests suddenly glow in the light of flames, and during the day, columns of black smoke obscure the sun. Perhaps there has never been peace on earth, perhaps silence has never existed.

The armies march towards each other, they descend the flanks of the mountain. But there is never any sign of real hatred. All that can be seen is this mechanical movement, this calm movement which governs the troops' deployment. If there were hatred, or anger, everything would be very simple. But there is never any anger. The violence is mysterious, forging ahead according to a plan that nobody knows. All is precise, evident. The ground is like a desert, mile upon mile of naked stone. And the air: transparent, dry, hard. And the water, and the sun: they show no signs.

Sometimes Monsieur X lifts his head and looks up at the sky. But he sees nothing intelligible written there. So he goes on walking. His clothes are glued to his skin with sweat, his face cleaves the air without receiving blows. His feet strike the ground rhythmically, advance along the pathway bordered by tall grass. When one is a soldier, and making war, life is one unbroken march towards a meeting with empty space. Day after day, one passes villages, watering points, camps. But there is always farther to go. The reason always lies beyond, on the other side of the river, then on the other side of the hill, then on the other side of the ricefields.

The lorries rumble along the dust-track, crossing bridges, fording streams. From time to time there is an engagement. Sub-machine-guns crackle a few miles away. Shells dig craters. And when one arrives, it is already over. There is nothing.

In the evening, sitting on the ground, while mosquitoes swarm around, there is time to write by lamp-light:

Dear Bea B.

I have been here about a month, and it has all been very interesting and instructive. Maybe you could arrange to come out here, to see what war is like, what really happens. I have taken part in two operations. The first was with the Marines, near Da Nang. We passed through several villages with our tanks. Apparently the people there were allies. I always thought that, when soldiers went off to war, the girls came running up in the street, throwing flowers and kisses, and that the old folk waved their hands and uttered cries of encouragement. But here, the people looked on with an air of suspicion and bewilderment and stupor, while the column of tanks and soldiers made its way through their peaceful little villages, or through their fields of rice and their cemeteries.

One morning we sat on a hill-top and looked down, like kings of old, at the battle raging in the valley below, though it was not really a battle, just a wave of aeroplanes dropping napalm, 2,000-pound bombs, high explosives, phosphorus bombs, and so on, on everything that moved. Despite the fact that this was apparently a pacified sector. That's to say, they had first parachuted leaflets over the entire area, to warn all opponents of the Viet Cong to leave their little villages and their ricefields, and go to a refugee camp — something little better than a concentration camp, here. Unfortunately,

124

it seems that half the leaflets never reached their destinations. Most of the villagers were working in the fields when the bombs started dropping.

The following day, there had been a clash, and the Marines had suffered a few casualties. Three men suspected of being Viet Cong had been brought in from a nearby village. All three were over sixty-five, less than five feet tall, and barefoot: the enemy, theoretically. The Marines went mad with rage when they saw them, and uttered strange curses such as 'off the motherfuckers' and 'zap the slit-eyed gooks'. One soldier smashed the butt of his rifle into the face of the oldest (who must have been in his seventies), crushing one eye. The following day, after a night spent in the cemetery, we systematically burned every house in the village. The heaps of gathered rice were burned, the furniture smashed and burned too. The pigs were shot with rifles, the reservoirs smashed, the women and children herded forcibly into carts and led off to camps. I don't know how many of these peasants were pro-Viet Cong before the Marines arrived, but I'm sure they were all supporters by the time the Marines had left.

Last week, I was present at one of the worst defeats the US has suffered since the war started, when about eighty of our men were killed in the high central plains. The US Command refused to admit it was a defeat, and claimed unofficially that 475 North Vietnamese infiltrators had been killed during the battle. I was there when a reconnaissance party was sent out to make a body-count, and it found nothing apart from four recently-dug graves. The official score was finally fixed at 106, but it all goes to show how badly the war is going for the Americans, and how dishonestly it is being reported. Most of the papers give the impression that everything is going fine and that the Viet Cong are practically finished, but it isn't true. The Viet Cong and

125

North Vietnamese may not be able to gain a military victory, in face of the overwhelming US superiority in manpower and sophisticated weaponry. But even so, I am convinced that the US cannot hold out here for very much longer. Hope to see you soon.

X.

A later letter, typed out on sheets of airmail paper, continued:

3 march 1968

dear bea b.

first of all, please excuse any typing errors. i am sitting by the hotel swimming-pool and there are so many chicks in bikinis parading to and fro that it is a bit difficult to concentrate. plus the fact that the shift-key on my typewriter is broken so i cannot make capitals etc.

i expect you have been following some of the news about these latest setbacks in the vietnam debacle. i was not in saigon when the attacks were launched, i was in the montagnard capital, ban me thuot, where a good deal of fighting and destruction took place as well. the south vietnamese airforce dropped napalm on some areas of the town; when i think about it i cannot recall any other example of government forces bombing their own partisans. still, ban me thuot was a picnic compared with hue – apart from the massacre of a few missionaries by the viet cong, and that probably convinced the americans that right was on their side.

i spent a week with the marines inside the citadel of hue, and it was the most thrilling revealing week i have spent in vietnam so far. the americans call this a limited war so i would hate to think what they consider to be a total war. how can you improve on dropping 1000-pound bombs on a town, except i suppose by dropping 2000-

126

pound bombs. for a conservative like myself, the most tragic thing of all, perhaps, was the wholesale and wanton destruction of vietnams one fine historical city. it was as though someone decided to wipe out oxford, cambridge, edinburgh and westminster at one go.

i do not know much about political policy but i cannot help noticing that the americans here have a knack for doing everything wrong; if there is a sniper holed up in a house, the marines simply bring up a heavy mortar and flatten the house. the americans are ready to pour money and material into this great cause of theirs but they do not have the slightest desire to give their lives. it is easy to see that they do not think the vietnamese are worth dying for.

hue was a sad business. i am not crazy about dogs, but i think the gis here go rather far, the way they use every moving animal as a target. i have seen marines shoot dogs and cats just for fun, and skewer pigs with bayonets. they do not seem to show much more consideration for human beings. i was watching a young woman carrying her invalid mother on her back while two younger relatives were loaded with the few bundles of clothing and possessions they had been able to rescue from the shambles, when a marine held out his automatic rifle to me, saying hey how about getting in a little practice on them ... hue was a revelation to a lot of the marines because up till then they had not realized that there were other vietnamese besides those that lived in mud huts. hue is full of splendid houses, mostly far more beautiful than the ones back in the states, but the marines seemed to go mad when they went into these houses, and took everything they could lay their hands on — cameras, tape-recorders, watches, jewellery. i took a photo of one guy walking off with a tv set. the mercenaries in the congo have some excuse for looting because that is their main source of income. but the citizens of hue were supposed to be on the side of the allies. well, they certainly cannot be any more. for the north vietnamese army, hue was a complete success because they held on to the town for far longer than they had anticipated, as well as inflicting heavy losses on the americans, and in addition they gained a great deal of prestige by treating the citizens with respect. refugees with whom i spoke told me that the north vietnamese had behaved very correctly and never stole a thing while they were there.

I am continuing this letter a few days later. Meanwhile I've had this machine fixed. Talking about Hué, I forgot to tell you that I had a couple of narrow escapes while I was there. On one occasion, we had launched an attack on a school where two concealed Viet Cong were lobbing grenades down on us. The Marines had decided to gas them out, but since I didn't have a gas-mask I had to get into a classroom a little distance away. I was in this room with a Marine who didn't have a mask either, and I was showing him how to make one out of a handkerchief soaked in water. He was watching me from a couple of feet away when a bullet came through the window and struck him in the back. He fell like a log, but when they examined him they saw that the bullet had lodged in his bullet-proof vest without touching him. After I had left Hué I came across another guy from the same platoon. He asked me if I remembered the guy who had been hit in the back. When I said yes, he went on: 'Well, he was hit again the next day. Only this time the bullet went straight through his back and killed him.' Another time, while I was helping to carry a wounded Marine, a mortar shell burst a few feet away. When I came to my senses, I found myself holding one of this guy's feet in my hands, while all the others who had been there were writhing around on the ground, screaming. Of the six

of us, four died, but luckily I got off without a scratch.
I'll write you again soon, with more news.
X.

That is the sort of thing that a person could write, during those times. One tried to understand what was going on, but there was this feeling of wanting to be everywhere simultaneously, in time and space. The noises of war grated from all sides, in the forests, the deserts, the swamps and the towns. They were all fighting: Macedonians, Goths, Huns, Normans. The Burmese burned temples and villages: one side was fighting to pillage and destroy, the other side was fighting in defence of its fields and cows. That is how things have always been. War was inside them, within their bodies; and it was war that throbbed in the rapid movements of their hearts. The English fought against the Portuguese, the Portuguese against the Spanish, the Spanish against the Venezuelans, the Venezuelans against the Arawak Indians. There was neither peace nor victory for anyone, ever. And, somewhere in the centre of the city, a girl called Bea B. fought day after day against all the noises, all the movements, all the lights, all the words, all those fierce entities whose chief aim is to murder sleep.

*Ça qui ti voir li, napas li qui ti prend li;
ça qui ti prend li, napas li qui ti manze li; ça
qui ti manze li, napas li qui ti gagne baté; ça
qui ti gagne baté, napas li qui ti crié; ça qui
ti crié, napas li qui ti ploré?*

*— Ptit noir fèque coquin mangue: so lizié
qui té voir, napas so lizié qui té prend, so
lamain qui té prend, napas so lamain qui té
manzé; so labouce qui té manzé, napas so
labouce qui té gagne baté; so léreins qui té
gagne baté, napas so léreins qui té crié; so
labouce qui té crié, napas so labouce qui ti
ploré.*

Mauritian '*sirandane*'
(nursery rhyme)*

Occasionally the war grinds to a halt, and then there are
moments of amazing peace. Moments of silence and love,
broad reaches as calm as sleep. It's true, that did happen now
and then. It was all over, the same day: the noise's terrible
blows, the reflux of emptiness came very quickly, in one and
the same second, perhaps.

The girl called Bea B. walked the streets of the city at
night. As she watched all the lights coming on, like the phos-

*Translation: 'What is it that sees but does not grab? What is it that
grabs but does not eat? What is it that eats but does not get a beating?
What is it that gets a beating but does not yell? What is it that yells but
does not weep? — Little black boy steals mango. So the eyes that saw were
not the eyes of the one that grabbed. So the hand that grabbed was not the
hand of the one that ate. So the mouth that ate was not the mouth of
the one that got a beating. So the backside that got a beating was not the
backside of the one that yelled. So the mouth that yelled was not the
mouth of the one that wept.'

phorescent auras of deep-sea monsters, she began thinking that it was difficult to know just where the war was really raging. She walked straight ahead, her feet treading the cement of the pavement, and she forgot a great many things. Or perhaps it was the other way round, and things were forgetting her, had suddenly withdrawn from her presence.

Night had fallen, as it always did, at around six in the evening. The girl had seen the shadow advancing along the streets, had observed the ashen colour that crept over walls and roadway. Great holes had been hollowed out of the shop windows, and men's faces had become livid. The cars and buses had kept going, but it was no longer quite the same. It was no longer possible to see the people imprisoned in the metal shells, and it seemed as though everyone was at last going to stop pretending.

The girl had sat down several times, at a café terrace, on a bench in a public garden, on some church steps. Each time, she had smoked a Kent cigarette, blowing the smoke out of her nostrils. She had even extracted from her airline bag a little book bound in blue rexine, on which was inscribed:

'EZEJOT' DIARY

and in the light of the electric air she had written several lines:

Another day coming to an end. Today
I feel happy (!) I've run into Monsieur X
twice, and the second time he spoke to me.
We strolled along together for a moment, and he told me
what a long time he had known me. Later,
I lost my sunglasses in a café. Now I'll
need to buy a new pair. I came across
Danièle who immediately asked me why I wasn't
working at the paper any longer. Then she asked me
what I was doing, and I answered: nothing!!!

131

Monsieur X looks terribly like Errol Flynn in
Morgan the Pirate.

After that, she had watched the pigeons doing their dance-steps, a young couple fondling each other, and a man falling off his moped.

Meanwhile, the night gradually took over. The platform of the city's flat roofs moved away slowly towards the east, and the girl joined it on its voyage. She travelled with Monsieur X inside the earth's nacelle. They crossed many streams and rivers, mountain chains, deserts, steppes. They crossed empty lakes in which trails of bubbles were floating. They travelled in a spiral, then in a circle, then in a straight line. It was extraordinary, going off like this, completely free, through the darkness. From time to time, there were white flashes as one was passing through a station, and Bea B. tried to make out the names:

> MURMANSK
> ULAN BATOR
> TENOSIQUE
> LA CIOTAT
> CEDAR RAPIDS

or else when one was passing another train hurtling in the opposite direction, there was this great wave of iron and light that hurled its explosion against the windows, and Bea B. tried to make out the people's faces.

She also saw constellations, meteorites, nebulae receding at a tenth of the speed of light.

These were all things that could be seen, uncomprehendingly, simply while watching the night in the street. Monsieur X started up his big bike, and she climbed up on the saddle behind him and gripped his shoulders. The machine bellowed, tore its bulk forwards, and set the wind's wall moving ahead of them.

Then there was no more need to talk. One was enveloped in the night's thickness, one's movements dictated by chance. The bike overtook long lines of idling traffic, made a right turn, another right turn, and emerged into an avenue.

Next came a wide esplanade where there was nothing at all. Then Monsieur X stopped the bike, and it was good to sit on the ground and gaze at the night together.

This is what one saw, what one thought:

SHE

The blackness which travels thousands of miles in a single stroke, which covers the whole earth. The sky and the ground, two steel globes going to seek each other out, they are bound to collide soon, then a spark will fly. The esplanade, the beach? Suppose the whole world were covered with round pebbles? It is an island, or the hump of a sperm-whale, and, all around, the sea. I am here, I am not thinking about the others, I don't want to. They'll never come as far as this. So I am someone. To be someone: the globe, the sphere differentiated from the others. How is that possible? Monsieur X is myself. I never knew. I thought that Monsieur X was someone else. I have his hand, it is my own, I have a motorbike.

HE

One night after so many others, the earth has turned and it is night again. On the other side, at Wakayama or at Vancouver, well, it's daytime. But so what? It's quite extraordinary, a place like this, in the centre of a town. One is simultaneously with others, and far from them. One has so many things to say, or nothing at all. One knows everything, yet one does not. One can speak, one can utter words, one can look at oneself, too. When one is eighty-eight years old, one will recollect that on this occasion one had not been afraid. That will be good.

133

Then Bea B. turned to Monsieur X and said:

'What are you thinking about?'

'Nothing. And you?'

'Oh, nothing really, except perhaps, yes, I was thinking what an extraordinary thing the night is, just here, like this.'

'True,' said Monsieur X, lighting a cigarette, and Bea B. watched as the flare of the match lit up his profile for an instant.

'In daytime people move, at night-time people sleep,' said Bea B.

'At night-time people are blind,' said Monsieur X.

'When I was small I was afraid of the night,' said Bea B. 'I used to believe there were animals that sprang out of the shadows, demons, creatures like bats. I believed there was a wicked god named Tezcatlipoca, who disguised himself as a jaguar, and the spots on his skin were stars.'

'I used to believe that when mice died they turned into bats.'

'And then I believed that the dead used to come at night and look at you through mirrors.'

'And I believed they lived in tombs and so I was scared of cemeteries. So one evening I went out and spent the night in a cemetery, sitting on a tomb. I was very frightened, but I just had to know. Luckily, nothing happened.'

'And I believed that God lived in flames. So I lit matches to try to see him and talk to him.'

'And I believed that if one said certain words, if one pronounced them in exactly the right way as one said them, one would die. I can't remember any longer what the words were, but I was very scared of saying them accidentally and dropping dead.'

'And then there were the things that it was fatal to see.'

'And salamanders, I was really scared of salamanders, I believed they slid around everywhere.'

'And that kind of underwater seaweed, that coils itself round your legs and then you drown.'

'And scorpions.'

'And night moths.'

'And I used to be scared of people going mad, all of a sudden, just like that. I believed that my father might go mad and kill me.'

'And hands reaching out of walls.'

'The Devil, too. A few evenings, I called the Devil, and then looked around my room to see if he had come. I could hardly open a book for fear of seeing his face staring up at me from a page.'

'And I used to be afraid to stand at a window. I believed, I really thought that I might suddenly get the urge to jump out and plummet to the street.'

'I used to get the same feeling in cars. I used to say to myself, now if I grab the wheel and twist it and the car crashes before my father has time to — '

'You know, sometimes I used to get a sudden urge to kill people, and then I had to look away so as not to see them any longer, so as not to think about it any longer, because otherwise, I thought, perhaps the feeling would have been stronger than myself, and I — '

'The people never suspected.'

'No, they thought I was just another little girl, they didn't understand, they used to pat me on the cheek and stroke my hair, and then I closed my eyes and whispered to myself for them to go away quickly, quickly, for them to go away, and my hands were trembling and my whole body was soaked in sweat. In the end I was forced to run away so as not to have to kill them, and they laughed and said how silly to be so timid, and what a wild little monkey I was, and they never guessed what a narrow escape they'd just had.'

She smoked a cigarette, trembling a little because of the cold and the night. The esplanade stretched out in all directions, one no longer knew where one was, or who one was. The girl went on talking, as she sat on the ground beside Monsieur X. She said:

135

'It was the same at college, you know. I didn't want to see anyone. When the lectures were over, I used to go off without speaking to anyone. The other girls were trying out lipsticks and bursting out of their new bras, and that's all they talked about, that and the fellows they had seen around. They made fun of me, but I think that at heart they were a little bit afraid, they found me really weird. The professors, too, because I did everything they told me but I never answered when they asked me questions. So in the end they left me alone.'

'They were all ham actors ...'

'Exactly. They went through their old routine, there, and I just stared at them and wondered when they were going to stop talking and moving around, when they were going to quiet down. There was one in particular, I remember, Passeron, the professor of philosophy, he was a chap who had a lot of problems, I think, and he wanted the whole world to have problems. He gave lectures on responsibility, liberty, the myth of Er, stuff like that, but it was all words, hot air. From time to time he asked the students questions, and that made him very pleased with himself because he could demonstrate that everyone was an idiot and that nobody had understood a thing. He used to worry about me because of my refusal to answer, and at first he imagined I had problems like he did, then later he realized that it wasn't that at all, that they weren't the same problems, that I simply didn't give a damn, and then he got very cross.'

The girl lit another cigarette, and Monsieur X watched the flame from the match light up her profile. Cars were circling the esplanade, sounding their horns. The lamp-posts shone brightly. The sky was very black, starless, and the moon was swimming in the centre of a halo that looked like a swarm of flies.

'Yes,' said Monsieur X, 'it's funny how people can't resist hamming it up like that, even when they know quite well that nobody's going to be taken in.'

'It's like when I was working at the paper, you know, it's

incredible the way they all took themselves so seriously. They had political ideas, ideas of all kinds, each wanted to be one up on the others. And then they all wanted to give the impression of being in charge. And then they got so involved, with all their hates and sympathies and marital dramas and jealousies. The extraordinary thing, to me, was that they never seemed to realize what a ridiculous farce it all was.'

'Yes, it's like the whole thought-process – when I just look at people, casually, at a café terrace, for instance, or in the street, I see all these heads bobbing up and down, men, women, old, young, all these skulls. And they are all thinking about something. Then I tell myself that ultimately thought cannot be such an extraordinary process, it must surely be something quite trite, the same sort of thing as myelin or sweat, simply the activity of the brain, and that it wasn't worth writing so many books about thought, and that it certainly wasn't worth inventing so many metaphysical theories about such a normal activity.'

'Yes, when it comes down to it, perhaps everyone is thinking the same thing, and one day we'll know what it is.'

'Perhaps, but that will be terrible, because at that moment people will no longer feel original, they'll see that they are not superior but all alike, so they can no longer attempt to impose their way of thought, and then they won't be able to fight each other any more.'

'It's true –' said Bea B. She looked at the town surrounding the esplanade, the black houses divided up into little compartments, the rectangles of the lighted windows, the steeples, the towers, the skyscrapers, the pylons, and then the crevasse-like streets where cars festooned with headlamps and red lights moved to and fro, she looked at all that and she went on, slowly:

'It's true that, over there, they are fighting.'

And one could indeed hear in the distance the dull rumbling of the whole war. It reached the centre of the esplanade under the black sky: engine noises, cries, appeals, the belly-

137

rumbles of television sets, sighs, the whirring of cog-wheels, the gurgling of drains, the squeaking of randy mattresses, the zigzagging of neon signs, scraps of the conversation of bargaining prostitutes, slaps, theatrical rejoinders, the sounds of pinball machines and cash-registers ringing up numbers, prayers, manifestos, clarinets playing *Chippyin'*, string-basses playing *Wednesday night prayer meeting*, drums beating out *Little T*, electric organs playing *I'm gonna move to the outskirts of town*, harpsichords playing Buxtehude's *Preludes & Fugues*, bagpipes wailing *Lochaber no more!*, and the terrible gravel voices hovering over the microphone in the semi-darkness, screeching so loudly that the heart began pounding furiously in the chest and the hands grew clammy and sweaty, voices repeating: I love you! I love you!

... A living organism, in order to slow down its plunge towards the thermodynamic equilibrium of death, subsists on negative entropy in such a way that it seems to be attracting a current of negative entropy towards itself so as to balance the increasing amount of entropy that it produces during its life.
... − (entropy) = k *log* (1/D).

Erwin Schroedinger.

What formula could possibly bring sleep, when there is so much beauty, alive, on the move, everywhere? To the east, to the west, to the north, to the south, the city stretches out, sparkling. The light from the sky is white, the air hangs motionless, the earth is a circular plateau. The girl called Bea B. is making her way through streets towards the spot where Monsieur X is waiting for her. She walks quickly in the sunshine, like a dancer on tiptoe, and the light flows about her, giving a radiance to each hair of her head. When she passes by the window of a big store, she sees her slim supple body moving forwards with its white garments floating in the wind. When she walks in the sunshine she knows that her shadow is reaching out behind her on the pavement. When she walks in the shade, her face becomes clouded by a light dust, as though she were floating through cobwebs, one after another. She says nothing. She walks along the street, alone, swinging her arms by the side of her hips, treading an invisible pathway with rubber-sandalled feet. Her eyes cannot be seen. They are hidden behind heavy sunglasses, two big discs of black plastic that ring her face. Reflections glide over the polaroid glass, stretching thin at the sides of the lenses, elongated rectangular bubbles that continually take shape, then burst.

The cars' bodies are rounded mirrors, and the girl's own body swims slowly alongside the Buicks' black wings, the lorries' doors, the Citroëns' bonnets, the Mercedes-Benzes' hubcaps.

As the girl walks along the street she recognizes, in passing, all the familiar signs, all the inscriptions, all the old refrains: scraps of crumpled paper, old fag-ends, pages torn from newspapers, revealing for a split second the headlines

SENSATIONAL DEVELOPMENTS
FULL PHOTO COVERAGE

empty matchboxes, animal turds, human gobs, pebbles, hairpins, bus tickets. She recognizes the pigeons, the dogs, the flies. She recognizes the people, too, the men with their moustaches and spectacles, the women with their candy-pink skirts and their imitation-crocodile handbags. She passes through them like a kind of car with sealed shell and shining paintwork. She glides between their bodies, darting, hurrying, skipping round obstacles, constantly on the move.

The hard ground is drenched by the light from the sky, the white light. The buildings' high walls display their faces filled with windows and balconies. The whole world breathes in and out. Little clouds of invisible steam curl from mouths and nostrils. In the depths of bodies there exists a mysterious gland known as the thymus.

Thoughts, too, come and go. Hertzian waves speed through the air and bounce off sheet-metal panels. Then they infiltrate into antennas, and flow down into things like black boxes, where loudspeakers begin to vibrate. These are thoughts, spoken words. They fly fast. They dance. They say:

140

Today, today, weather fine, cloudless, limpid air, sun,
light breeze from the west, beautiful sea, tension
scarcely rising, heart beating at 96 pulsations per
minute, traffic conditions along all main arteries fluid,
fatal accidents 8 minor accidents 34
exact time 16 hours 8 minutes 27 seconds stop

The girl floats through the cloud of mosquitoes bred by
thought, through the shoals of millions of quivering fish, and
she too is a thought, a quick rational thought, a thought that
says:

'I am me, I am Bea B., I know the way'
'I am the sun, yes, I am alone and I shine, the sun'

She is there wherever things are astir, wherever there are
bursts of light and noise. She makes her way past great crossroads full of winking lights and car bonnets, she strolls along
streets lined with plate-glass windows, mirrors, slabs of imitation marble. She follows a bald man whose pate is shining in
the sun. When he crosses over, she crosses over. When he
turns left, then right, she turns left, then right. When he
stops at the edge of the pavement to light a cigarette, she also
stops and lights a cigarette.

Sometimes there are vast perspectives, and she watches the
boulevard shoot straight to the horizon, plunge to the centre
of the earth. She walks on the left-hand pavement, because it
is the sunny side of the road, and tries to think what she will
do when she reaches the end of the boulevard. Over there, in
the far distance, a cloud of mist and dust is floating and
dancing like the smoke from a conflagration.

So much beauty violence life. So many things, everywhere,
that kill words. She hears all the cries spurting from the walls
and the ground, she sees all the drops of liquid glistening in
the light, all the clouds of gold dust and powdered mica.
There are white mountains so high that the air crystallizes as

141

it settles on them, sending out icy networks of bristling threads. There are lines so beautiful that the nature of the design they ceaselessly trace will always remain a mystery. And there are words so long, so extraordinary that they go right through the mind like bullets, opening gaping wounds that bleed.

Whirlwinds hover over the ground, seeking in all directions with their mouths, twisting themselves round legs. Either the black tar is flat, so flat that a marble thrown by a child's hand would roll for two hundred years without stopping; or else it undulates beneath the feet, billowing forward in great vertical waves, liquid cliffs that will one day, somewhere, come thundering down.

The girl stays calm amid this chaos. She glides her lithe body between rugged surfaces, steers clear of crevasses and abysses. When the pavement's cement harbours a pile of gravel, or an open drain, or a banana peel, she knows what to do about it: she skips lightly over the obstacle, never twisting or breaking her fragile ankles. When a distant window throws out a beam of light so white that it could reduce the whole world to dust, she turns her beautiful matt-complexioned face towards it and shatters it with a single blow from the blueish lenses of her sunglasses. When the roar of an engine approaches in an explosion that rips the air brutally apart, she is not frightened and does not run away: she simply lets the noise envelop her, and her half-open mouth expels the noise in the form of a sigh,

'aaaah ... '

The girl journeys for a long while, like that, through the beauty of the city. From time to time she passes vast public buildings, stone towers three hundred feet high, towers of glass and concrete a thousand feet high, black steel pylons more than three thousand feet high. She walks through big department stores that are like ant-hills, through sites full of abandoned vehicles. She strolls by the side of muddy rivers in which barges are floating, she crosses over arched bridges.

She is far away, untired, with her silent engine and the soft cushions of her tyres. She propels her hermetically-sealed shell bordered by glass windows, and the wind whistles in the ventilators. Everything is present, absolutely real. There is nothing invented. One could never invent anything. The streets' corridors are inexhaustible, impossible to know them all by heart even if one spent centuries walking along them all from end to end.

The girl had never dreamed of so much beauty. It was like entering a vast hall entirely lined with mirrors, or like looking through a magnifying glass at a postcard representing

The causeway of the Passage du Gois (Vendée)
at night-time

Natural colours

but this time one was really there.

Somewhere in the city, right now, there is someone waiting. No-one knows who exactly, but someone. He is waiting behind the cement walls, in the waiting-halls of railway stations, in service stations with bright red petrol pumps. The girl walks towards him. As she threads her way through the dense crowd that throngs the streets, she knows that she is expected. Every screech of a brake, every blast on a horn means just that: 'Come quickly, come, I'm waiting for you.'

She goes round in circles, in the city, looking for its centre, and each time that she loops the loop she knows that she is a little closer. The city is also circling upon itself, a little like a wheel, a little like a propeller. There must surely be a centre somewhere, and that is what has to be found.

The city is designed like an 8, the one truly infinite sign. Bea B. no longer possesses an age, a past, anything at all. She no longer possesses a home. She lives everywhere simultaneously, everywhere where there are walls and roofs and windows and stretches of black roadway. As she moves on, she studies all the openings, the skylights, the doors and the fanlights. She had never in her life imagined that there could be

143

so many windows. They are so beautiful and calm, incised there in the great expanses of white wall. They are so deep that people will feel an insatiable urge to go on plunging through them. There are so many of them, and they are so motionless, that they could cover the infinity of space. Are there not more windows than stars? Are there not more windows than there are seconds in the life of the tree at Tula? The girl goes by in the street below, and she goes by each window. These eyes do not pass judgment; they are simply open, breathing the girl's form like a mouth breathes air: uncomprehendingly. Is that not extraordinary, calm, beyond imagination?

The air is transparent, neither too warm nor too cold. The air rests upon the earth, and the girl cannot see it with her eyes. But she sees it with her whole body, her skin, her nostrils, her lips. She drinks it in, with little sips, as she walks across town. Breathing is a quite astonishing business. With her mouth half open, the girl inhales a little air, and her chest swells; then she retains it for a moment, somewhere deep inside her, distilling it gently; finally, she exhales it through her mouth, and that makes a little invisible cloud impregnated with all the secret odours that are inside her body.

Occasionally, she passes a lorry halted at a red light, and inhales the acrid fumes from the exhaust, and that is like a tranquil drunkenness, the odour of death, perhaps, bubbling in the bloodstream. The girl breathes in and out as she walks, and that too is a way of thinking of something. She fills herself up from the air's great reservoir, now with her lips, now with her two whistling nostrils. Her skin breathes, too, the skin of her face, the delicate skin of her hands, the white skin of her belly concealed by clothes. She swims amid the white air, amid the light. At one and the same time she is a quivering engine consuming petrol drop by drop, and a kind of tree spreading leafy branches. The air is vast. She can see it, above the rooftops, stretching out its pale ceiling on which the clouds are painted. From time to time, a jet plane swoops

through the air, very high in the sky, leaving a grey trail behind it. Or else it is a helicopter. Or a bird.

Maybe Monsieur X is hidden in the air, diffused throughout it. Bea B. advances through his body, inhales his blood.
But she does not know that, yet. No doubt that is what life
involves: being drunk with air. (Each time one inhales, one
gets a little drunker.)

Bea B. walks up the endless boulevard, looking at all the
magical things. On her way, she passes hordes of magical
men and women who talk, gesticulate, smoke cigarettes and
lick cones of magical ice-cream. She is only just embarking
upon the story, the one that is told in a low voice, the meaningless story. The story that gets scribbled down on the pages
of an exercise-book with a black pencil:

> 'Once upon a time, during the present century,
> in a town, upon this earth, there was a little girl
> called Bea B. She lived alone, she had a grand-
> mother and a brother, and every day she met a lot
> of people. In the same town there was a little boy
> called Monsieur X. They went riding together on
> a mighty 500 cc BMW motorbike.'

In those days the whole city was reeling drunk. The crowd
went lurching and staggering down the streets, the cars
hurtled along the motorways, and the great white buildings
pitched and rolled.

But in those days the girl was unafraid. She walked quickly
along the pavement, striking the ground with her feet,
breathing through her mouth. She received back these millions of blows, they entered her body, sent sparks from her
nails, teeth, hair and eyes. The electricity surged through her
limbs, the radio messages penetrated her ears.

Never had there been so much movement, so much beauty.
The world had no desire to sleep, to die. Its energy burst
forth from all sides simultaneously, in the sky and in the

straight-limbed trees, as well as in the blocks of concrete and along the iron poles. The buildings' enormous cubes, all seething with life and noise, had settled their bulk upon the earth. The girl passed by their outside walls and heard all the human voices murmuring, talking, yelling, shouting, roaring like bulls. All these voices spoke of money, politics, love, goodness knows what. It was like the vast sigh of a prostrate woman, a breath that rasps the throat for months on end. None of all this could ever come to a halt. So much strength and toughness could never topple. The world was infinitely understandable, vast, open, full of things to eat, things to touch, things to love or hate, things!

It was never possible to say that there was NOTHING. The girl turned the corner round a ten-storey building, and there ahead of her was yet another street, yet another building. Each time that she put one foot in front of the other, she precisely filled the outline that awaited her. Above, below, in front, behind, to the left, to the right, there were THINGS!

That was not dream. It was not falsehood, or poetry. There was no little notebook with a blue imitation-leather cover on which was written in gilt letters 'EZEJOT' DIARY, no novels with beautiful nostalgic titles, no letters ending up

> I kiss you tenderly on the lips
> Eternally your devoted
> Henri

No, it was a peopled vastness shaken by convulsions, whining, pounding away. The crowd's convoys ascended, descended. Study the ant and you will know mankind. The streets poured forth their streams of wheeled machines, the sky darkened under its mantle of flies, bats, Boeings.

There were words, but they were no longer the words of poetry. They were no longer words such as: sinews, ponds, downpour, lucerne, forests, rustle, lair, fur, shrew, ret, wool,

146

gravid, sprout, compost-heap. These were brand-new words, words that exploded violently, that struck mighty blows, that uttered exclamations, that insulted, slashed, stabbed ceaselessly. The girl read them as she went along. All these words. Advertisement-words. The words STOP—BUS—JUNIOR—NO—PARKING. The words

MONTE CARLO

CANNES ←————————————→ VENTIMIGLIA

Building-words. Words as huge as mountains and as small as fag-ends. She read the words written on lavatory walls, the words engraved in the pavement's fresh cement. She saw that the manhole covers were embossed with the words

NATIONAL GAS AND ELECTRICITY GENERATING BOARD

She watched them flashing on and off at the summits of great scaffoldings, or else erecting the triumphal arches of their soaring letters throughout the city. Everything was in writing, but one had to know how to read. There were names of heroes, such as

KAZAKH-Stan

POLICE

EAGLE PASS　　Nobody

Malikah'orriya

O.A.

BICMAN

All these words that covered cigarette packets, matchboxes, postage stamps, vehicle side-panels, café doors, the buttons

147

of leather jackets, wrist-watches, the tabs of zip-fasteners and the clasps of brassières. All these words that shimmered, motionless, like beetles or shell-fish. The girl went all the way along the boulevard, reading out in a low voice the things that were written all around her, things that she would never forget. And the words too became drunk, shot their rays into space, lit up like stars, made noises, breathed.

The girl sat down in a café and drank a warm liquid from a white cup; she sipped the milky coffee through a straw and watched the plastic tube grow brown.

Or she smoked a Kent cigarette while watching the passers-by through her dark glasses.

She took an airmail letter out of her air-hostess's bag, and read it slowly to herself:

> Earth, one day in spring.
>
> I have carried sadness with me since the day I was conceived. Perhaps you and I were born at the same moment. For twenty years now, the light has been seeking me out. I myself, hidden in a pale ray, am a dim and feeble light. I live. I cling to you desperately, because you resemble the image of a living creature that I recognize as being a unique species of great value to the world. I want nothing and I want everything, and my everything harbours a mysterious force that sends me soaring up like a kite. Like a kite, I hunt the sun of which I am so fond. I am fond of the darkness, too.
>
> But what are you seeking? I have found you, and nothing else matters any more.
>
> I want to find you again by closing my eyes. What shell encloses you, in this vast ocean, and in what seaweed is your name entwined?
>
> Woman beyond all bounds, why do I not know the colour of those eyes of yours that have laid the world's heart bare?

I wish my arms were long enough to encircle the twisted trunk of an olive-tree, or the statelier trunk of an oak.

A yearning to roll with you on the warm sands, one day of a summer invented by ourselves.

Candles ... lit, extinguished. I am very fond of candles; torches, too.

To wander through the night, holding hands from fear of the heartbeats that are audible. Fear, too, of the day when people crossing the street will find me lying on the ground, covered in blood!

I have a crown to give you, whenever you would like it. I will crown you now, with paper and with words of praise, or make you queen for one night of tender caresses.

I would like to talk to you for a long time, with my hands clasped in your own, talk to you gently and sadly, like now ... Send me an answer, I beg.

DON

She screwed the letter up and put a match to it, in the ashtray inscribed

The Beer from Alsace — Mutzig — Mutzig

and meanwhile people continued to pass by.

Later, the girl got up and walked across the big room with its mirror-walls, listening to the music, a low-pitched thundering of The Animals' *See see rider*. She went up to a burly man wearing a black pullover, and asked him something. The burly man pointed silently towards the end of the bar, and the girl approached the door on which was written

TOILETS
TELEPHONE

She pushed the door and found herself in a sort of dark corridor. At the end of the corridor there were three doors on which were written respectively

GENTLEMEN   LADIES   TELEPHONE

She opened the third door and entered a deal-lined booth, in which a naked bulb was burning. Then she inserted a token into the black machine, unhooked the receiver and dialled a number. Then she had a telephone conversation:

'What are you doing?'

'Nothing — and you?'

'Nothing ...'

'You know, I saw you in the street, the other day.'

'Oh yes?'

'Yes, I didn't dare speak to you, you ... you were walking so fast.'

'I didn't see you.'

'You looked very preoccupied.'

'When was that?'

'Oh, I don't know, three or four days ago.'

'Have you seen anything of Henri?'

'No, not lately.'

'So what's been happening to you?'

'Nothing.'

'Are you working at something?'

'No, not for the moment. I saw an advertisement the other day for a dentist's assistant. You know, someone to open the door and so on, but I ... frankly, the idea didn't appeal to me.'

'And your grandmother?'

'She's fine, thanks. She wrote me last week.'

'Did you answer her letter?'

'Yes, I sent her a postcard with the picture of an aeroplane on it.'

'That's nice ...'

'And how are things with you?'

'Oh, pretty quiet.'

'Sophie?'

'She's fine.'

'Good …'

'Where are you?'

'You mean at this moment?'

'Yes.'

'In a café, in town.'

'Many people there?'

'Yes, quite a few.'

'Had anything to drink?'

'Yes, a white coffee.'

'Oh, good.'

'With a straw.'

'With a straw?'

'Yes, I like it that way.'

'Oh, I see.'

'It's funny, you know, I … I was thinking about reality, just a moment ago.'

'About reality?'

'Yes, I was thinking that maybe it is a good deal less important than people imagine.'

'What, reality?'

'No, things – I mean, seeing things. I was thinking that it was less important to see them than to hear them, for example, or to touch them.'

'You believe that?'

'Yes, well I think I do, yes.'

'Do you say that because you are on the telephone?'

'No, I was thinking – that perhaps it wouldn't be so terrible to be blind, that perhaps it would be far more terrible to be deaf, or anaesthetized. With silence following you wherever you go.'

'Well, maybe.'

'You know, when you are in a dark room and suddenly you

151

hear a cracking sound, you get a feeling of terrible reality, even the tiniest creak has that effect, whereas with a ray of light you don't even *see* it.'

'That's particularly true of dogs, they are always listening and sniffing, but they hardly ever look at anything.'

'Yes, my grandmother used to tell me that I was like a dog because I sniffed at the things that people gave me.'

'You know, there's a saying of Heraclitus that comes down to the same thing: if all things turned into fumes, we would learn to know them through our nostrils.'

'Yes, that's true. I love all sorts of smells. The different smells that books have, for instance, and the smell of bread, the smell of earth, the smell of upholstery in new cars.'

'The smell of wool.'

'Yes, that's pleasant. And touching things is pleasant, too.'

'Yes, some things are bristly, some are cold.'

'The things I like best are stones, glass, warm wood.'

'Sand.'

'Yes, when it's very fine.'

'And water is extraordinary stuff.'

'There are things that are unpleasant to touch, too, like rough fabrics, blankets, velvet. And then imitation marble, which looks like stone but never gets cold.'

'Things that make you sticky, too, like glue and jam and grease.'

'Ah yes. I'm always washing my hands because of that.'

'It's pleasant, washing one's hands. Perhaps it's on account of the soap, because at first it feels sticky, and then it all washes away with the water.'

'You know, I can never understand why people go to the cinema all the time. They should, oh I don't know — they should sit in darkened rooms and instead of a film one could distribute odours and noises, and one could give them objects to touch. I'm sure that would be far more interesting. Don't you think so?'

152

'Perhaps they couldn't stand that sort of thing? It might drive them crazy?'

'No, I don't think so, I think that when they left the place they would all write poems. Because there would have been visual effects, as well, you see, not sentimental stories like in all the films but lights bursting in their eyes, and curtains of smoke, and images flashing on for a hundredth of a second at a time, and words too, nothing but words being shouted or mumbled right into the microphone. I can't understand why people always think that reality is basically what the eyes see. Anyone would think they have cameras instead of eyes, and boxes of colour-slides instead of brains.'

'Yes, it's funny.'

'Right, well, I think that's all I had to say to you today.'

'You see, we kept it up for quite a bit.'

'You think so?'

'Sure. I didn't time it, but it must have lasted five or six minutes.'

'Not longer?'

'But that's a lot, you know, on the telephone.'

'What about the voice?'

'Very good.'

'Really?'

'Oh yes, you've made a lot of progress since last time.'

'Good!'

'Of course, there are still too many pauses. On the telephone, that's quite out of the question, you know.'

'But I have to stop and think occasionally, don't I?'

'Sure, but you're supposed to go on saying something. That's indispensable, otherwise the person on the line gets the idea that you've gone, which is annoying.'

'OK, I'll remember.'

'And how about gestures? Do you make gestures?'

'No, I can't manage it. I've tried, but I simply can't gesticulate in front of a machine.'

'You're wrong, you know, you should gesticulate. You

153

should say, for instance, I'm going in that direction, and then point with your arm, to show where.'

'But what's the point, since you can't see?'

'No, you don't understand! It's the telephone. The *telephone*. It's not just any old machine. It's like television or radio or one's own car. If you want to understand the meaning of ritual you have to believe in it. Otherwise, you remain an outsider. Do you follow me?'

'Yes, perhaps you're right—I really must try.'

'It's not just any old thing, the telephone. It's a machine for, umm, making one's confession. There you are shut up in a booth and you are speaking to everybody. Understand?'

'You mean, when I've learned how to telephone with the right voice and gestures and so on, it won't matter any longer whom I telephone?'

'In the end, no, it won't matter any longer.'

'So, in other words, I could even telephone without having anyone to talk to?'

'Yes, even by dialling numbers at random, then there is no-one on the line any longer, no telephone, nothing any longer. But that's an ideal state of affairs, of course. I don't even know whether anyone has ever achieved that yet.'

'You're quite sure that that's the way to go about it?'

'I think so, yes. You see, if you really want to not just win the war but exist within it all the time, knowing what's going to happen, when it's all going to break out, then you need to be aware of what you are doing. You have to have a total insight into machines, into all those gadgets, radios, telephones, cars, aeroplanes, cinemas, ballpoint pens, washing machines and radar screens.'

'It's terrible, I—'

'And the only way is to understand what they are concealing, what it is that they have there in their innards.'

'And you, what are you studying at the moment?'

'Oh, I'm still working on small things. Yesterday afternoon it was a cigarette.'

154

'What brand?'

'Peter Stuyvesant. To help me, I substituted kef for half the tobacco in it.'

'So?'

'What?'

'So what effect did it have?'

'That wasn't the point. I mean, it wasn't for the sake of beautiful dreams or whatever. But kef cools one down, and then one can concentrate more easily. I smoked that cigarette right down to the filter, and the best thing of all was that in the end I forgot that I'd been smoking. Perhaps one day I'll succeed in smoking without cigarettes.'

'Well, it all sounds like a big joke –'

'No, really it isn't. At least, it's not meant to be. I think it's the only way of fighting against everything that is around us. You see, Bea B., there are too many things, there are too many things.'

Then, since no more vocal sounds were coming out of the receiver, Bea B. started listening to the distant humming that vibrated against her ear. She listened for quite a while, breathing steadily in and out. She looked at the booth's white wall a few inches away from her face, the thickly painted wooden wall. People had written many words on the white wall, with ballpoint pens, with fingernails, with the edges of coins. Words, numbers, letters, and the same kind of zigzag designs that electrons leave on the vastness of the photographic plate.

Then she replaced the receiver on its hook, and the black machine made a whirring tinkling sound, and the thought came into her head that one day, perhaps, she would be able to telephone like that, from a booth, to the planet Saturn, or the centre of the earth, or her dead grandmother.

Dear XX

I am writing to ask you just one more thing. I don't know how to put it, and probably there isn't any answer, anyhow, at least not a definite answer. I don't know how to ask you this. I could ask you WHO AM I? of course, as though we were playing some children's game. Or I could describe one of my dreams to you and ask you to analyse it. But that would not be the truth. I could compose a poem like the one I did the other day on a piece of paper with a ballpoint pen:

> The infinitely flat earth, lake of mud, river,
> waveless sea, sky, sky of earth, blazing grasslands,
> road, grey asphalt road for cars to drive along.
> Rooted.
> Immovable.
> There is just a single cry.
> What does it say?
> It says
> I AM ALIVE
> I AM
> That's what it says.
>
> Faced with the immensity of time, with lake of
> mud, river, sky, road, always the same cry
> and it is not easy to hear what it is saying.
> And it is not TO LIVE! TO LIVE! but perhaps
> TO LOVE! or TO DIE!
> From deep in the throat.

Faced with indifference, pool of dead water amid
impassive vegetation, cold body between the sheets
refusing with closed mouth and eyes
It hurls itself forward
Smashing its way
It is yet another cry
It says:
Slut! Filth! Trash!
Disgrace!

In the stifling black night, forests of sounds, vain
dreams, world turned upside down preposterous
shadow of the intelligible, mane growing inwards,
hairs that have already invaded throat and belly,
There is a light
the tip of a cigarette
the reflection from a storm-lantern
the eye of a cat

Straight rigid cry, hit, cat's eye, gleam, droplet,
point, hole, tower, stone, word, noise, taste, skin,
being, being,
tigers, tigers,
ticks that I let loose upon you
demons that are my sentence of extermination
for me, for you, for all,
to burst through the sky, the skin, indifference.
Ho! Ho! Houa! Houa!

Sometimes I put together poems like that, on scraps of
paper, and then I burn them. It is curious, watching a poem
burn. The flames spread quickly, and one can watch the
paper twisting and the words becoming paler and paler and
vanishing. When I do that, I lean over the piece of paper and
smell the odour of smoke and heat. A burning poem releases

a great deal of heat. And then I try to read the final word, you know, the word that one sees stirring last of all amid the flames. I have read *morning*, and *notebook* and *America*. Those are the words that I want to remember for a long time. I'm telling you all this because basically I don't know the question I mean the real question that I want to ask you. I don't know, either, whether there are answers to questions. Perhaps when one asks a question one is simply asserting something in reverse, and that's what annoys me. WHY DO PEOPLE ALL WANT TO EXPRESS THEMSELVES? They are so intelligent, all of them, and there they are, trying to keep things together. They all want to do something. You see, they don't want to disappear. They want to assert themselves. I wonder why? With all their sports cars and poems and music and love affairs. They would all like to conquer the world, persuade the others, convince them; so they juggle with words, or put blobs of colour on canvases, or devise objects. Children are like that. Old people are like that. What really makes me sick, though, is that I am like that too. They spend their whole time fighting each other, and then they say: I did this, or: I am far lovelier than you are. At school, the girls were all like that, wanting to show off everything they had, wanting to be noticed. When they had beautiful breasts they wore tight sweaters, and when they had beautiful eyes they put mascara on their lashes so that everyone would see that they had beautiful eyes. When I was working at the paper, it was just the same. They all wanted to be noticed, you know, they treated themselves like detergent powder, trying to find the package design that suited them best. That's how I let myself be taken in, little by little; at the beginning I wanted to do as they did, I thought that I too could find the right box for my detergent. But it didn't work. I couldn't stand — I just couldn't stand people looking at me and judging me like that, on the basis of the box design. So then I began to lose my grip on things, and that was terrible because no-one wanted to help me, the people were all happy to have found

159

someone inferior. But it was my own fault if I was miserable as a result, because that meant that fundamentally I hadn't completely abandoned the idea of expressing myself and asserting myself.

Basically, that's what I wanted to ask you, whether you think it's possible? Whether you think it's possible to succeed in not expressing oneself at all? Perhaps, whatever one does, one is always seeking that one thing, to be ONESELF, to hurt other people, to dominate the world. Even when one says nothing, one is saying something. Even if one managed to write, if it were possible to write, like this: ▬▬▬▬▬ perhaps that would be just as violent a way as the others of saying AS FAR AS I'M CONCERNED, I EXIST, I THINK THAT, etc. You know that phrase of Descartes: 'I wish to believe that no-one has existed before me.' That's what is so terrible, having to witness war, having to watch this whole farce, the individual fighting to impose himself on others, it's enough to make one sick, one longs to disappear, to stop being anything at all, and then one becomes conscious that one is acting that way, with all one's condemnations, because one wants to be different, and then everything goes rotten and it's no longer possible to be lucid. This desire to assert oneself is such a painful process. When I see others making the effort, my heart bleeds for them. They would do anything, anything at all, just so that people will listen to them.

I remember this fellow, a couple of years ago. His name was Pepe. He was a gipsy, and played the accordion in front of café terraces. He used to dress up like an Argentinian gaucho, and he wore ear-rings. He was very tiny, this fellow, a dwarf really, and he used to play this absolutely incredible music to these people drinking glasses of beer. He always played the same tune on his accordion, just three notes with a funny kind of rhythm like the noise of a train engine. I found that absolutely astounding, because it wasn't really music so much as noise that he was producing from his accordion, a noise to say that he was there. And at the same time I felt very ashamed for him, because no-one was paying attention, and people were giving him money to go away and make his noise somewhere else. So now, you see, each time I think about art, about human suffering, about the need to assert oneself, or things like that, I think of Pepe busy playing his accordion in front of people who don't give a shit. And then there are all those people who kick up such a fuss, who all want to talk at the same time, who want to invent brand-new things, who want to change the world. Perhaps the only way of changing the world would be to suppress adjectives, or else for people to give up trying to express themselves. But what I am saying is silly, because in fact I can't see how that would be possible. Women ought to be beautiful naturally, and not seek to seduce and bewitch, and men ought not to seek to dominate any longer. You know, I look at couples in the street. It's such an extraordinary pantomime, such a blatant provocation. People don't like to be happy for its own sake, they get their happiness from destroying other people. Their eyes are as hard as steel, and the women want so much to be admired. There's no way out. And everything is like that. You know, XX, I look at a book, for example, and I see something extraordinary, something that holds my head under water until I think I am going to drown. I am so, euh, it seems so sensational to me that people are capable of inventing things. That people can take a sheet of paper and write what they think, just like that, without being ashamed. The world is so beautiful, XX, so terrible, made up of so many things already, so much life, so much space, so much time. So what would make it possible to believe oneself capable of adding anything new to it? What would make it possible to stop looking at it and listening to it and start *writing* it? What would make it possible to forget the world just long enough to write a sentence, not even that, a word, a mere syllable. It's as though one were sleeping with eyes wide open, I don't know how to put it, as though one had forgotten that sun, sky, sea, noises and odours exist. Some people consider it naive for others to express themselves through a car, by driving it along the motorways at 120 miles an hour. But isn't it just as naive to believe that one can assert oneself better by writing a poem or acting in a play? How I would love the war to stop, if only for an hour, so that I could get some rest. It would be so nice if the war stopped; one could go to the beach, for instance, sit down on the sand and look at the sea. One would listen to the sea. One would no longer need to repeat the tragedy's gestures and words, one would no longer be part of the show. Or rather, for once one would be within one's own vision, and then one would no longer fear or hate anything. And above all, if it were still necessary to express oneself one would do it with easy things, and all those forms of expression would be not for conquering but for becoming a part of a whole. With pebbles, for example, with piles of dust, with caresses, with little gurgles. It would no longer mean: To hell with you all! I am the only one! I love! I loathe! I love! No, it would mean that the beach slopes gently downwards to the sea, and that the waves have travelled all the way from the island of Zante, or Pariparit Kyun, or Corpus Christi bay. It would mean that the beach is a space-ship heading for the sun, or that my name is written somewhere in some book, the Anabasis, or the Chilam Balam, or Selfridges catalogue for 1955. Yes, I would really like the war to end, so that I could start studying birdsong and learn to recognize the trails of hares. There are so many things to do and to learn, here. Only, I can't do anything, because of the noise and the eyes, because of the walls I have to keep building to save myself from being killed. Still, we can make an effort, if you like. We could start by forgetting about names and signatures. There are too many signatures everywhere. People spend their time signing everything everywhere. They sign walls, trees, pavements, horn blasts, cigarette smells. Every time they see something they whip out their ballpoint pen and sign it. Every time they have an idea, while they are sitting talking at the café, they pause for a moment and look at you with shining eyes, and they SIGN! Using a felt-tip pen, they write on the idea, in block letters:

MULLIGAN
NAPOLEON
LOUIS FALCHETTO

and their aim is never to be mistaken, never to be lost, never to fall. They have suits of solid armour, and axes, whole quantities of axes. Come, XX, perhaps you are the one person who can do something, if you choose. We can roar through the city, or across plains and mountains, on your mighty 500 cc BMW. We can try to abolish names. Perhaps there are places still untouched by the war, I mean *places within*. Let us go and watch the iguanas, maybe they have something to teach us. I know a place where there is a tree growing by the edge of the sea, with its roots embedded in a wall, and with odd-shaped branches that skim the surface of the water and have a pungent odour. I know a hill called MOUNT BORON and a hill called BALD MOUNTAIN. If I ever get to know, even for a moment, why it rains and how the wind blows, perhaps the war will stop. And I don't like war. I like peace.

XY

> *As for the definitely polycalic or con-*
> *federated colonies, ... they often include as*
> *many as two hundred nests, each of which*
> *may contain from five thousand to five*
> *hundred thousand inhabitants, and they may*
> *occupy a circular area whose radius is two*
> *hundred yards or more. Dr McCook, a dis-*
> *tinguished and highly conscientious observer,*
> *tells us of an enormous city of* Formica
> exsectoïdes *in Pennsylvania which covered*
> *an area of fifty acres, and consisted of sixteen*
> *hundred nests, many of which measured*
> *nearly three feet in height and twelve feet in*
> *circumference at the base. Comparing its*
> *volume with the dimensions of the insect,*
> *McCook calculated that it was relatively*
> *eighty-four times the size of the Great*
> *Pyramid.*
>
> Maurice Maeterlinck.

Then across the city, a city filled with tremors of the death that must come to it one day. All these great buildings that are too white, too beautiful, that have too many windows; all these roofs that are too high, festooned with antennas and wires. All these roads that are too long, stretching endlessly ahead. Evening was approaching, and the girl called Bea B. was returning home because she had found nothing. She was sitting in a bus that had electrically operated doors, watching the walls of the houses as they rushed past on the other side of the window. Then she got down from the bus and started walking through the slowly dying city. The sun had disappeared behind the clouds, and the sky was grey. Historic buildings, frozen vertically to the ground, stood there while pigeons fluttered between their colonnades. Along the streets, shop windows gradually assumed a steely, slate-grey hue. The surface of the pavement was leaden. Trees protruded their wintery trunks from the cement, and manhole covers sealed hermetically the mouths of the subterranean channels.

The girl went on and on, surrounded by this incomprehensible beauty. She saw the vast wall areas soaring upwards, white cliffs sparkling with unbearable brightness. She walked along the bottom of a sort of deep valley hollowed out of the rock by thousands of years of water and wind, or perhaps by a few hundred hours of bulldozer. She passed countless street-lamps, strange long-enduring trees made of cast iron. Sometimes she crossed the asphalt roadway, the old black river, patched and worn, imprinted with the grid left behind by the soles of shoes and the treads of tyres. Chiefly, she looked at the polished metals, the tinted windows, the blocks of reinforced concrete, the networks of electric wires: all those things which signified that she was not walking here, or anywhere else, but that she was walking upon time itself.

This is how it was: gigantic blocks of cement standing upright and pressing their thousands of tons against the earth, miles of roads and railway lines, forests of masts and telegraph poles, lakes, great cubes of glass, shores of nickel, plains of corrugated iron. No landscape throughout the world had ever been so vast and deep. There had never been such high mountains, such vertiginous canyons. Never, so much iron and stone, so many transparent and opaque substances. All the violence of the universe, all its energy and power had converged upon this place and traced their pattern there. As the girl walked through the city, in the early evening, she did not feel at peace. She saw the pyramids defying time, and all the arches and windows keeping the sky's vault at bay. Beauty was not gentle, did not sing with a woman's voice.

Beauty had set out to challenge silence, its muscles were tensed for the onslaught upon empty space.

At one moment Bea B. passed by a great white building. She saw that it was floating on the ground like a giant steamship on the Arctic ocean. It glided silently over the surface of the sea, driven by an invisible engine, carrying its cargo of rectangular windows to America. It vanished, very quickly, yet very gently, and the girl read out the name painted in big black letters across its stern, the tragic name

TITANIC

It sailed straight ahead, slicing through the steel-blue waves with its enormous bulk, noiselessly, smoothly, motionlessly. And there were others like that, huge aircraft-carriers, blind-snouted submarines, oil tankers, banana boats, freighters with holds full of coal, canal barges, factory-ships propelling their inferno over icy oceans.

All these monumental structures were fleeing together over the grey sea, carrying their insect populations towards unintelligible destinies. Nothing was secure, nothing penetrated the earth with the sharp-clawed fingers of roots. The earth itself flowed ceaselessly underfoot, like a tide of mud; whole esplanades were drifting towards the horizon, slabs broken off some huge ice-floe, with long black fissures running through them.

A little farther away, a glass and concrete tower trembled on its base. Watching it, the girl realized that it was trembling from fear and hatred. Making enormous efforts, the tower strained upwards towards the clouds, pressing down against its four cemented pillars. But the sky was drifting far away from it, and that is why it was trembling: because there was nothing left for it to support. Neither its efforts nor its pillars were of any use; so fear and anger entered its body, and emptiness rushed down its stairways and plunged down inside its lifts. How much longer could the tower last? To all intents and purposes it was already disintegrating where it stood, like a tree eaten away from within, collapsing in a cloud of white dust and with a noise of splintering glass.

No-one suspected for a moment what was really happening in this city. Bea B. saw the people's faces, and their hands, and their shoe-encased feet. They came and went, between the gigantic blocks, they walked in the shadow of the great walls, they even lived inside the flats with their identical cells. When they were hungry they ate, and when they were thirsty, or wanted to urinate, they entered some brightly lit café and said:

'Waiter! A half of lager!'

Or alternatively:

'The toilets are on the left, at the back, huh?'

When they felt a twinge they went to the dentist; when they felt like hating they watched a sports match on television, or thought about Hitler or Westmoreland; and when they felt like loving they thought about Gary Cooper or Barbara Steele.

Meanwhile, all around them, the great silent edifices trembled from fear and hatred, and glided very fast and very gently over the Arctic ocean.

It was all quite extraordinary. Emptiness was the cause, the black emptiness that surrounded the world with its fatal liquid. The girl scanned the sky and the low clouds, trying to see the sun, but it had disappeared behind the cubes of the houses, and only the light was left. Perhaps, if the sun had been there, things would have been different. Perhaps she would have been able to turn her face towards it, drawing her hair back from her face, feeling the heat settle upon her cheeks and mouth, like the palm of an open hand an inch or so away from her skin. Perhaps she could have thought very fast, while her eyes filled with tears, and said:

'Stay with me, Monsieur X, stay here, I don't want to be alone.'

And then the colours of the red dresses and the blue cars

would have been genuine, not simply illusions of cone-like and rod-like cells. Perhaps the walls and street-posters would have ceased to absorb all but one of the colours of the spectrum, and the world would have become a single immense rainbow, a single gigantic jelly-fish.

The girl called Bea B. was crossing the city just as it was on the point of crumbling into dust. She could feel beneath her feet the kind of dull vibration, the distant rumbling that announced the end. The menace was not yet visible, but already one could hear the gallop of its approach. In what form would it appear? Would it be a cloud of locusts in the sky, unheralded, or a cloud of tiny flies? Would it be a rain of fire? A second sun, but this time a black sun stabbing the earth's surface with its rays of nothing? Would it be made of water? Of air? Of stone?

Suddenly, Bea B. saw them. They were there in the street, at the windows of houses, inside the shells of cars. The men, and the women, and their children, who would one day destroy the city.

The white buildings as tall as mountains, the towers, the poles, the highways, all these had sprung straight from human skulls, the imagination's simple images, ancient dreams come to life. Then these things had been abandoned, left all alone upon the earth amid stretches of cement and tar, and thus delivered up to fear and death. They had remained upright, pointing skywards, heavy fragile nacelles incapable of soaring away. Huge soap bubbles quivering in the atmosphere, streaked by blue reflections that turned green, then red, then orange, then yellow, then white: after they turned white they would explode.

The earth shuddered beneath Bea B.'s feet. Not the solid fertile earth that nurtures plants and weeds, but the flat surface imagined by mankind. The great white walls wrapped around iron skeletons were resting upon this soft sludge. It only needed a ten-year-old-boy, for example, or a twenty-one-year-old girl, eyes flashing with anger, to say aloud:

168

and it would all be over right away. That is why the metal towers and the skyscrapers and the TOTAL service stations were so afraid.

The whiter they were, the higher and the more beautiful they were, with their concrete ramps and their serried ranks of window-panes, the more they became the towers and sky-scrapers and TOTAL service stations of fear. That is how things were.

The girl walked quickly along the streets, between the giant draught-screens. Her feet struck the ground. She followed with her eyes the lift cages that rose slowly behind transparent walls. She stretched out her hands to touch the imitation marble, still warm with daylight, around the door-ways. She watched out for the rays cast by electric light bulbs. In the depths of the supermarkets' hiding-places she saw riches of every kind: tin cans, gaudy cartons, bottles, plastic bags. She saw them screaming with mouths wide open. She saw their hearts beating: a word written in blood-red letters, striking repeated blows in the centre of a white circle.

The Supermarket was ablaze with the light of two hundred neon tubes as she entered and walked very quickly between the display shelves. She saw terrible things, very soft objects in satin cases, violent objects, silent objects, objects that had no name. She picked them up, then put them down again. There was a huge nylon basket filled with thousands of rec-tangular boxes fashioned from polished tin, with a picture painted on one side, and the words, written in black letters:

SARDINES IN OLIVE OIL
COMAC S.A.
MOROCCO

She took the cold smooth tin, the beautiful oblong sculpture, and she thought that nothing so beautiful had been made for

169

centuries, and that nothing remotely resembling it would ever be made again. She took it with her to the far end of the shop and paid for it with some coins. Then she left, and started walking through the streets once more, the tin resting at the bottom of her airline bag.

The girl busied herself with things like this as she fled through the city, to keep fear at bay.

The city trembled from its constant efforts to speak. The words were stuck inside it, inside its walls, inside its deep throat-shaped wells. Bea B. heard the words forcing themselves up the vocal chords, rumbling such deep vibrations that no human syllable could ever represent them. The words swayed to and fro at the brink of every mouth, upsurges of lava that the earth had kept in check for centuries. It was just that: words heavy with time and space, bringing with them all the power that the world had stored away. Around the white cliffs that sparkled with a million panes of glass, the roads split, joined up again, then split once more. Steel girders soared skywards, the angles of the roofs were as sharp as iron spear-heads. Clouds of smoke clung to the sides of the building, curled along the balconies, and dispersed like a pale vapour into the cross-currents of air. Birds flew into these frozen ramparts, and died. Fists thudded into these glass doors, faces smashed against their own reflections. And the noise of the pent-up language sounded gaspingly from the depths of matter. No doubt the sea, the great viscous reservoir, was to be found somewhere far, very far beneath one's feet, beyond the slab of cement and tar, beyond the pipes and cables. But it was not in the sea that speech originated; nor was it in the grey sky, nor the air, nor the deserts. Speech was born in these vertical blocks, lived in their cavernous depths, constructed its words from concrete and steel.

The girl moved on up the street, looking at the words that were at last visible. They were not really words, like those that hang in shop windows and mean: 'Come, come, buy, quick, quicker!' No, these were the words of an unknown language, something greater than man or woman, something that one understood immediately without any need for explanations. Blows, perhaps, heavy-fisted words that struck hard, tons of bombs and violence, storm-clouds, cliffs engaged in confronting the sea, or snowy peaks engaged in moving through the air. There was so much force, here, in this city, that no-one would ever again be important. Beauty does not exist. What does exist is force.

Impossible to love such things. One could love the shade, or the sun, or the trees with their rustling leaves. But one could not love these mountains. One could talk about water, or silence, or the round pebbles to be found on beaches. But one could not talk about these mountains. One was beneath them, eternally beneath them, a speck of motory flesh moving about at the foot of these calm masses. Death prowled around the great buildings but could not penetrate them, for it was their function to be impregnable and to repulse time with their gigantic flanks.

The great towers rose up, neither living nor dead, with their eight hundred windows on each face. The giant flippers soared straight up from the ground into the sky without ever touching each other. The pyramids displayed their tiers. The stretches of wall formed semicircles, or else undulated like the bases of eucalyptus trees. There were enormous arches resting on the ground. Pylons of black iron, cables as thick as tree-trunks. Series of balconies revolving above the giddy void, right angles, sharp blades, darts, opaque discs. Three hundred feet above the ground the wind blew eternally through great empty esplanades. Indistinct striations opened fissures like lidless eyes in the white façades. Needles huge enough to absorb a thousand lightning flashes bristled from the tops of the towers. Wherever she went the girl could see nothing but cement, steel, glass and sheet-metal.

No, it was no longer fear. One could no longer feel fear before so much beauty. It was something else, something more powerful, more universal. Something opening up above

171

her head, then suddenly rending space and carrying it far away. Those were the consequences of language: after the manner of a hurricane flattening forests and transforming the earth into a desert, after the manner of the wind.

Bea B. walked among the giants, looking at their words that stood erect upon the ground. She was not really walking upon the earth: she was gliding along these immeasurable toboggan-runs, guided despite herself towards the unknown goal, empty of thought or desire, while the void gaped beneath the soles of her shoes. The bridges were so long that they spanned entire arms of the sea. The tunnels intersected outer space between two galaxies. The motorways, jammed with vehicles, crept along like boa constrictors, each curve of their body thrashing slowly across the plain at 500 mph. A four-engined jet plane flew for hours between two white mountains pierced by windows. In the south, cloudbursts discharged torrents of sooty water. In the east, at the same moment, the setting sun flooded with its light the glass dome where two harsh words shone forth:

GULF   LIFE

Then Bea B. realized that she was in no ordinary place. She was walking in the *city of time*. These enormous words hanging in the air, these plains of asphalt, these cliffs, were more than simple objects; they were whole centuries looming heavily out of the history of mankind, bringing with them the whole of knowledge. When she understood this, quite suddenly, a sort of dizziness swept over her. It was as though a fissure had opened savagely in the grey sky, allowing a glimpse of the night beyond. The towers, the roofless columns, the iron and concrete structures, and all the other things that seemed so new and so pure were in fact thousands of years old. They were bones polished by time. There was no way of escaping from this spectacle. They told all the stories that make up history, they made long ancient gestures heaven-

172

wards, they thrust their roots down as far as the earth's centre.

Bea B. caught a glimpse of the crowd scurrying along in the shadow of the walls, and beside them the cohorts of cars rolling along in their slots. The immobile buildings displayed their flat frontages. They knew. They had always known. A cloud of ashes floated over them, each particle gliding past the windows. The earth was fragile, its substance merely cinders. Strange tremors ran through the ground, weird shudders of life. And the white towers continued to shoot up. The iron constructions proliferated as far as the horizon. They covered farther plains, farther valleys. Even the sea had been encroached upon by floating platforms. Was there a single free space left? Bridges joined the buildings to each other, soaring above the broad fields of sand. Ponderous aeroplanes crisscrossed the city on their way from one airport to another. Giant ships got under way. Nothing but blocks, huge blocks everywhere! Men lived imprisoned in these caverns. They thought that they could live for the moment, they imagined that they were still the masters. But they died quickly, crumpled in a corner of their cells, and meanwhile the tower of stone and cement had become larger still, a little higher still. Language was passing overhead, above them, above her; the giants were talking to each other as they raised their menhirs. They spoke sentences that lasted for centuries, containing adjectives that lasted longer than the oldest man alive.

Now night was setting in. The sky became a dirty white, then grey, then ashen. But the girl was not tired. She continued to walk along the streets, between the great slabs of buildings. As the shadows thickened, so the walls seemed to grow less dense. A kind of drunkenness welled from the cemented cliffs and the window-panes and spread through men's bodies.

Bea B. had forgotten all that, the looks, the sounds made by shoes, the reflections on car bonnets. In her airline bag the

173

tin of foodstuff clinked against a bunch of keys. Bea B. wanted to visit all these places, from top to bottom, all these corridors and cells. She pressed her hand against the cement surface of the walls, she touched the iron railings. She paused in front of entrance-ways and gazed in at the vast imitation-marble halls lined with mirrors. She entered two or three buildings, taking the aluminium lifts that climbed silently up to the fifteenth floor. Then she came down again immediately, pressing all the buttons on the way. The lift doors slid aside slowly, to reveal identical landings.

In the street the cars continued their endless vibrations. Lights came on, one after the other, and started glowing steadily. The great towers projected lakes of shadow against the ground, but their summits were so high that they were still gleaming in the sun.

Everything was poised motionless, there, in the twilight. Like primordial rocks overhanging the sea, or iguanas with spiky crests. Bea B. paused for a moment, too, while the night closed in rapidly. She sat down on the front steps of a building and concentrated on becoming very tall and vertical, like a tower. The prongs of television aerials sprouted from her skull, and her skin turned smooth and white and cold. Thousands of windows opened up across her belly, her back, her face, surrounded by spiralling balconies. Then she got up, and her legs buttressed themselves against the stone-clad ground, steadying the scaffolding of her bones right up to the top of her body. Her mouth contained no more words, no more sentences, nothing. Her eyes were two searchlights scanning beyond the horizon, beyond even the sky's sphere, beams stabbing the starry blackness of outer space. And in the place of her heart there was an odd sort of lift, an aluminium box that rose silently and went on rising ... The girl called Bea B. remained like that for a long time, standing there among the towers, in the night, in company with all the lighted street-lamps.

It now began to be known and talked of in the Neighbourhood, that my Master had found a strange Animal in the Fields, about the Bigness of a Splacknuck, (an Animal in that Country very finely shaped, about six Foot long) but exactly shaped in every Part like a human Creature; which it likewise imitated in all its Actions; seemed to speak in a little Language of its own, had already learned several Words of theirs, went erect upon two Legs, was tame and gentle, would come when it was called, do whatever it was bid, had the finest Limbs in the World, and a Complexion fairer than a Nobleman's Daughter of three Years old.

Jonathan Swift.

At night, airport buildings are white. There are fifty suns shining together in the great empty halls. From all sides simultaneously the light flashes as sharp and bright as a razor blade, and sparks fly: from the glass walls, from the plastic floor-tiles, from the ceiling that is a single transparent slab. Soldiers at war, like Monsieur X and Bea B., for example, are bound to find themselves there sooner or later. You remember where it is: at the end of the motorway that plunges straight through the night, climbing, descending, turning gradually in great banked curves. At the end of the road, one sees this sort of fortified castle rising out of the strident plain, bathed in light and looking just like an aircraft-carrier at anchor.

The glass doors slide back as the girl approaches them, and

175

she enters the cavernous hall. There is no-one there. There is no shadow. Nothing but light, bouncing to and fro between the walls, its waves colliding in mid-air. No matter how hard one may look in corners, under baggage-trolleys, in table recesses, there is never any shadow to be seen. Light streams from everywhere at once, a strange white glow that serves no other purpose than to illuminate itself.

The girl continues through the great grotto, saying nothing. For a long time now she has wanted to speed through the night along the motorway, and enter the airport, like this. Anyone who wants to know the war's origins, its ebb and flow, its history, must of necessity visit all these extraordinary places, these railway stations, hospitals, canteens, morgues, slaughterhouses, casinos, bars, cut-price shops, butchers' cold rooms, banks, petrol depots, churches, Social Security offices and airport buildings. Once inside them, one begins the search for all that is mysterious, unknown, for thought itself. One looks at all this light that hurts the eyes, one listens to all these noises that echo through the plastic labyrinths.

Bea B. walks the whole length of the great hall. A row of gleaming counters lines one wall from end to end. Above the counters are red circles, golden stripes, blue panels, white panels. Flags. And then, writing:

PAN AM   LUFTHANSA   IBERIA   ALITALIA
LOT   KLM   BEA   JAL   GARUDA

crazy words, scraps of mute words that flash on and off. The counters are empty. The vast brightly-lit hall is full of empty counters. Bea B. sits down in one of the red imitation-leather armchairs facing one of the counters, and studies the posters and bits of paper fastened to the wall. Monsieur X remains silent, too, as he smokes a cigarette. Bea B. studies the advertisement-ashtray that has PAN AM written on it in big white letters, together with a caricature of the world and its meridians. She notices that the ashtray contains three crushed

176

stubs and some ash. Then she picks up her red plastic travel bag that has TWA written on it in big white letters, and takes from it a little blue vinyl-covered notebook that has 'EZEJOT' DIARY written on it in big gilt letters, and writes very slowly:

The dreadful silence that accompanies me everywhere.

Then, since she has nothing more to say, she closes the notebook and stows it away in her bag. The hall surrounding her is rectangular, made of great slabs that rest upon each other. There are aluminium pillars rising to the ceiling. The air is white, cold, silent. All is calm. Occasionally, a noise of thunder can be heard coming from somewhere outside in the night, but it stops almost as soon as it starts and there is no way of telling what it means. Occasionally, too, a woman's voice echoes through the loudspeakers, but she says things of little significance, full of names of towns or people. For instance:

'Monsieur Joëts is requested to report immediately to Channel Two control point, thank you.'

'Air India flight 136 destination Cairo, Bombay, New Delhi, departing at 0130 hours.'

Or:

'UTA announce a delay in their flight 1841, destination Abidjan. Provisional departure time is now 0345 hours.' But Bea B. is not listening. She never listens. No-one is calling her name, the woman's voice is not speaking for her. Bea B. simply looks at the smoke rising from Monsieur X's cigarette, and at the ash that has fallen into the ashtray. The time does not pass quickly. Outside, the night is an opaque sea pressing down with all its weight upon the plastic cockpit. The enormous room is higher than a grotto, but there are no bats hovering. Everything is bright and clear, there is absolutely no mystery. The war is very near, now, but there is no longer any fear. The girl is there, sitting in the middle of the room,

177

without speaking, without thinking. *And there is nothing apart from what she sees.*

She knows that she is at last involved in reality, in the truly harsh world. There are no glaucous swamps to be seen, nor troubled skies. No earth, nor stones. No trees, no folds of flesh, no signs of sorrow. No, there are only these panels riveted to other panels, these cubes and spheres and lines. And there are words to be seen: written words in rows on huge luminous frontages; gigantic words written in letters six feet high, EXIT 1, EXIT 2; tiny words printed on the back of airline tickets, words like ants, so small that you have to hunch right over them in order to read them out.

Then she says:

'You know, it's nice being here.'

'Yes, it really is an extraordinary place,' said Monsieur X.

'It's so beautiful, so pure, here, like, I don't know what — a museum, something like that, no, even more beautiful, an immense cinema screen.'

'Yes, and then there's nobody around at this hour.'

'Yes, that's true, like an empty department store. You know, I've never seen such a beautiful place before. When I was small I used to enjoy wandering through the supermarkets because they were just like this, white, with great empty corridors, and metal objects gleaming on all sides.'

'Yes, there are a lot of extraordinary places like that, but people don't pay attention, they don't know how to.'

'Did you notice the ceiling?'

'Yes.'

'And that great white wall over there? And the glass doors with the metal knobs? You know, I used to dream of living in a place like this, I used to tell myself that one day, if I had money, I would have a supermarket built specially for me to live in. Or a cinema hall, with all those armchairs and balconies and passage-ways. I wonder why people go on living in rooms with little beds and little chests of drawers, with a

Gauguin reproduction in one corner, when they could all live together in places like this.'

'Yes, that's true, communal houses would be a good idea; people could take over town-halls, too, for instance.'

'There are so many extraordinary things around,' said Bea B.

It was true. There were many extraordinary things. There were sliding doors that were noiseless and very gentle; there were electric clocks that recorded 01 12; there were great illuminated notice-boards crowded with numbers and signs; escalators that started moving when you passed through two yellow eyes; carpets of royal-blue nylon; Coca-Cola vending machines; huge mauve-tinted panes of glass; book-stalls full of novels by Hemingway and Chad Oliver; sparkling aluminium trolleys rolling along silently on rubber tyres; dimly-lit bars with music and low-slung armchairs; electrically-lit arrows pointing upwards, downwards, north, south, east and west. It was inexhaustible. Maybe one was in another world where time and space no longer existed. One was floating over the earth in a gigantic abandoned aircraft-carrier, bound for unknown atolls.

Bea B. remained seated for a long time in front of the empty counter, watching, and running her fingers along the edge of the plastic table. Monsieur X smoked several cigarettes, stubbing each one out in the publicity-ashtray. There was no need to talk; soon, no doubt, one would never talk again. One would no longer murmur all those phrases into another person's ear, inhaling a faint whiff of the odour of skin and hair. One would never again say, in a strange husky voice:

'I ... I love you, I'

'I'm afraid'

'I don't ever want to die'

'You are so beautiful, oh so beautiful'

'Make love to me'

'I – I never – never – want to be alone again'

There would be no more need to flee. Because everything

would be so soothing, here, everything would be so pleasant that there would no longer be anything else to hope for.

Suddenly, Bea B. heard a noise approaching her. She heard it coming from the far end of the deserted hall, sending echoes ahead of it. It was the noise of shoes walking, one after the other, rapping the soles hard against the glazed tiles. She turned round in her seat and saw a policeman advancing slowly, his hands behind his back. The man in black walked towards her, his eyes like ink blots in his white face. Bea B. turned her head away, because she was frightened. But she could still hear the sound of the measured steps advancing straight across the hard floor. Bea B. pretended to read her airline ticket, but her hands trembled. She listened to the squeak that each shoe made as it started to leave the ground. As the policeman passed behind her he stopped for a moment. Bea B. waited, her heart pounding. Then the noise moved away again, as the shoes continued their journey towards the opposite end of the hall.

It had become dangerous to remain seated. Bea B. got up and started making her way towards the rear of the airport building. She hesitated for a moment because there were two alternative directions: the toilets and the lift. Monsieur X pressed the button for the lift, and the two metal doors slid open. The hermetically sealed box was empty. While the lift rose, Monsieur X lit a cigarette. The smoke rose, too, making little clouds.

Up above, the airport building was empty. Bea B. found herself on a sort of balcony overlooking the hall. She could see the perspectives of roof and walls, the white chasm receding towards the horizon. Down below, on the glazed floor, the policeman was beginning a half turn.

Bea B. started walking quickly along the corridors. After crossing a dark work-site full of building debris, she came out onto a terrace, under the night sky. The air was black, and a cold wind swept the walls. Monsieur X leaned over the guard-rails and looked downwards. He could see the main runway gleaming dimly in the night. Out here, too, it was extraordinarily beautiful. The ground was flat, a desert of tar. Over an area of twenty-five acres there was nothing. Nothing but these flattened black sheets under the sky, and the sound of the wind. It was rather like the sea, silent, grey, blending into an invisible horizon, something that one could look at for centuries on end. The world had been sliced into segments by a scythe blade of magnetic steel, the world had been broken in two, and no-one was able to put the split halves together again. The wind swept quickly over the sheets of tar, without finding any dust. Far away, close against the night sky, the sea's waves broke into foam, inaudibly.

The war had reached this place, too. The flat ground vibrated in the wind. Something was lurking around, something that willed people to lose their eyes, their mouth, their ears, their parcels of nerves. Emptiness had hollowed out its pocket, emptiness had thrown open its vast room, so that the girl might lose her way inside these spaces. It was as though, after so many centuries, the sea had suddenly retreated, revealing an endless beach that was stark and silent and lonely, its surface lifted skywards by the wind to form an airborne beach, so that all distinctions blurred in the swirling sand.

Bea B. glanced around the airport, and found she could no longer think of anything else. Her mind soared above the flat ground, covering the expanse of tar like a shadow. She fell, but horizontally, skimming the ground, concentrating all her energies on speeding through the night at 200 mph; the whole of this deserted silent space was filled with the call of violent air, with openings, with all that was urging her to renounce words, to enter the great empty room.

Series of beacons, blue, yellow, red ones, were afloat in the freezing sea. The girl looked in amazement at the luminous colours daubed on the ground, until suddenly she realized that this was the war plan. Electric light bulbs had been screwed into the asphalt to mark out the labyrinth's paths, and it was impossible to avoid them. For the first time, perhaps, the drama was unfolding in its entirety: there was no more beginning or end; there was no more waiting or tension or fear; everything stood out clearly, comprehensively, after the manner of a diagram sketched on a sheet of paper. After the manner of a huge picture etched into the cement, showing all the gateways, all the crossroads, all the possible routes that one could take.

Thought had ceased frittering itself away. It was no longer groping its way along, like the caterpillar that uses all its antennae and all its feet as feelers. With a single leap it had taken wing and was gliding through the sky like a sparrow-hawk. It was gliding through the cold wind, taking photographs of the earth's history.

It made the head swim. The girl had to grip hold of the iron handrail to save herself from falling over the edge of the balcony onto the apron below. Down there, in the distance, she could see the silhouette of Monsieur X darting along the rows of light bulbs, in the middle of the airfield. Then she suddenly understood the way that the fighting had to be carried out, this time. She ran to the other end of the terrace, and made her way down the control tower's iron stairway. Her steps reverberated in the dark like detonations. At the bottom of the tower she found a door on which was written:

NO ENTRY

On the other side of the door the great tarred runway lay spread out in perfect freedom. The corridors of blue and yellow bulbs spurted their colours right ahead of her, as they rose gradually skywards. She began running with all her might, battling against the wind. She ran between the rows of bulbs, and her feet stumbled against the bits of gravel embedded in the tar. Sometimes she changed direction, and there was a new row of blue and yellow light bulbs. The wind carried with it the smells of kerosene and rubber. Perhaps she was dreaming. Death would loom up, as it always did, and this time it would have the form of a metal aeroplane cleaving space with its outstretched wings, crushing the ground under its dozens of tyres. It would bear a name, something like BOEING 727–200, or LOCKHEED SUPER CONSTELLATION L1049, or SUD-AVIATION CARAVELLE, or DAKOTA C47, or TUPOLEV 134, or perhaps CONVAIR 990 CORONADO. They were the ones that had to be fought, fought with all the rage that one could summon up. The only way was to hurl oneself upon them, shatter their fuselages with a single butt of the head, rip off their jet pods with one's teeth. It was too late for play-acting. The war had started, and this was one of the fields of battle. Another way would be to run forward with a box full of nails, and then watch calmly as the huge tyres explode and the long duralumin cylinder tips forwards, gouging its own grave from the surface of the earth.

Bea B. fell breathless to the ground. Monsieur X said something, but his mouth was filled with the roaring of the wind. Pointing at the yellow line painted along the strip of asphalt, he shouted:

'THIS IS IT! ...'

'WHAT?'

'THIS IS IT! ... THIS IS WHERE THEY TAKE OFF! ...'

Then they lay flat on their faces, on the ground, and peered up at the runway stretching into the far distance, stretching to the other end of the world. The blue and yellow bulbs shone steadily over the greyish sea; the lights of great beacons pierced the night. For a very long time nothing happened. The only movement was that of the wind as it swept the ground. Then, after several hours, there was a sort of deep thundering noise at the other end of the runway. Very far away, framed against the sky, a dark mass approached slowly, winking coloured lights. The girl heard the noise swelling in the night like the roar of a jaguar. She pressed herself against the ground and closed her eyes. Her heart started beating very fast. There was a long pause, then suddenly she heard Monsieur X shout:

183

'WATCH OUT! ... IT'S COMING! ...'

The noise of thunder vibrated underfoot as the DOUGLAS SUPER DC8–63 began taxiing between the ground-lights. Not very fast, at first, swaying over the runway in the deep gloom. Then, at some mysterious signal from the control tower, it unleashed the full fury of its jet engines and hurled itself forward, shuddering.

The girl heard the noise approaching, sounding exactly like ground-swell bearing down upon the cliffs, and she raised her head. What she saw transfixed her to the ground, left her incapable of movement: right in front of her, at the end of the corridor of blue light bulbs, the DOUGLAS DC8–63 was looming out of the night, devouring the asphalt with its giant wheels, its immense pale wings covering the ground. The colour of mercury, it glowed weirdly in the darkness, casting its red and green gleams alternately to left and right, and left and right ... It hurtled towards the girl at a dizzy speed, puncturing the wind with its blind snout, sucking the cold air in through the four gaping mouths of its air-scoops. It was coming closer. The girl watched it grow bigger and bigger, spreading its colossal wings ever wider apart until they covered the whole horizon, and the noise of thunder travelled ahead of it, filling the sky, filling empty space as far as the stars, and the utterly deserted sheet of tar began undulating beneath the girl's belly, while the platinum wings spread, spread, and the night opened around the DOUGLAS SUPER DC8–63 with a strange sparkling glow. It was coming closer, gliding along its rails, between the lines of blue ground-lights, at 25 feet a second, 30 feet a second, 65 feet a second. This was the biggest aeroplane that the world had ever seen. It stood, motionless as a skyscraper, a few feet away from the girl's face, with its blind snout and its wings that hid the sky completely. She wanted to cry out, but her voice was absent; her voice, her thought, her life, all of her was in the screeching of the jets about to make their onslaught on the air, in the efforts that the wings made as they strove to tear the wheels

184

away from the glutinous runway. Then everything happened in a fraction of a second: the DOUGLAS SUPER DC8–63 vanished, as an avalanche of iron and flames soared over the girl's body. She heard a terrifying din that seemed to rupture her ear-drums. Her eyes clouded, while the fiery blast hurled her body backwards and sent it rolling over the gravelled surface.

DOUGLAS SUPER DC8–63

There is not that much time left, now, for getting to understand things, Monsieur X. I want to hurry because by now time is beginning to run out. Perhaps even now I won't have time to understand. It's sad to think that maybe one will not have understood what was going on. That's even sadder than missing one's train. I would have liked you to help me, but that's not possible. I have gone too far; it is for me to understand, not for anyone else. What I mean is, this war and so on was just a bad dream, and you can't enter my dreams. Even I can't enter my dreams. They exist on the other side of me, in a different compartment. Still, I believe I'm right. And I'll tell you why. I saw it written in big black letters on white paper: there is too much beauty, too much gentleness, and the world will soon explode. How can one manage to go on living under such conditions? But the question does not come from within, it comes from outside. That is why it is so difficult to answer it. That is why what is happening seems like a dream. You see, if, euh, if it were a problem of glands, or some sort of maladjustment, oh I don't know, that kind of romantic situation, anyhow, well that would be easy enough, I'd just take Lilly Add-a-Bee vitamins, or I'd go and consult a psychiatrist, or I'd go and live on Cocos Island, in any case I'm sure there would be some remedy or other for my difficulties. But it's not like that. This is a movement that comes from outside. However hard I try to hide or get away, it always materializes. All around me there are forces that I do not understand. Shops, windows, buildings, crossroads, airports, roads, motorcycles, everything is impregnated with

186

force, everything seeks to crush and conquer. It's because of the words, Monsieur X. It's true. It's the words inside me struggling to fight against the words outside, and they are going to lose the battle. That's why I'm in such a tremendous hurry. I want to say all my words before they have destroyed my mouth, I want to see everything before I lose my eyes. There are some people who say that basically that's all a sham. They give a smug little smile and say 'Bourgeois class, bourgeois problems.' People have always got some explanation to trot out for everything, they are all so brainy. For some of them, the explanation lies in sex and obsessions and so on. For others, the explanation lies in the class struggle. For others, the explanation lies in metaphysics, Zen, the Vedas. They are all so civilized. They explain, and then they go off down the street, they drive their cars, they use their telephones to make telephone calls, they drink their whisky, or else they smoke their ganja, and they are happy. And meanwhile, all that beauty and all that force is accumulating in the machines, in the walls of the houses, slowly, and everything is trembling, about to crumble into dust. But they don't know this. They have no inkling of what is going to happen. But I do see it all, and I am afraid the whole time. Well, not exactly afraid, no, but I get a heavy choking feeling at the bottom of my throat, something like a goitre. You know, even when I was small I used to spend my time looking at things as closely as possible. I always noticed immediately what was wrong with anything: a crack, some tiny detail, the first smut of decay. It's the same, today. When I walk along the street and see the people's heads with eyes protruding from them, when I see the cars and roads and bridges, I hear all sorts of odd disturbing things. A low noise, a tremor, a peculiar rustling sound as though there were termites gnawing away everywhere. I have no idea what it is.

Monsieur X, there are powerful forces everywhere. At night they gather in the darkness and swell up. And when day comes they burst out. It is extraordinary the way everything seethes with life, even things that look dead. There can be no more peace and quiet for anyone who has begun to perceive this fact. It becomes impossible even to close one's eyes and listen to Handel. Because that other music with its unremitting noise is far more terrible, far more beautiful. It has even become impossible to talk meaningfully. It has even become impossible to take a little blue notebook and jot down one's thoughts, because it is as though one no longer had the time to think. Naturally one still has desires and ideas and so on, but it is as though external forces had already uttered them and realized them in anticipation, and then one feels oneself trapped by the whirlwind. How I wish I could understand the plan, you know, the pattern of things. I know it is there, somewhere, but how to see it? I know that society doesn't just drift along, that there is a secret way of knowing everything that is going to happen. But I cannot manage to guess that secret. Without a doubt, all these mysterious forces have a direction, are working towards something. But it is like a vast labyrinth with countless false openings, countless wrong directions. You turn right, thinking that you are headed the right way, wind your way through a whole series of corridors, and eventually, when you feel sure you must be almost there, you turn yet another corner and find yourself back where you started.

There are so many things, too, Monsieur X. So much energy everywhere. Everything is so much there, present, alive. What is the point of dreaming when there are so many things? It is a jungle of sorts, filled with millions of different leaves, millions of insects, fruits, caterpillars, roots, snakes. That is why there are so many noises. And in a jungle one can't just wander aimlessly: one needs to be able to recognize everything around one, taste things with the tip of one's tongue, sniff the spoors, know all the ways of the water, of fire, of the air. I want to learn to walk through the streets of the city like that: knowing that there are fatal forces everywhere, dangers and poisons everywhere.

188

I'm frightened, Monsieur X, and yet I love it all. I am no longer alone. I am surrounded by friends and enemies. They lie in wait for me, spy upon me all the time. I must learn how to make their acquaintance, and then perhaps I will know what is going on. I must learn to recognize every category of screw and bolt, every category of nail. Sheets of tin-plate, sheets of cast steel, sheets of cast iron, sheets of zinc. I love plastics: some are smooth, and cold as water, some are the colour of chocolate. I often go to look at the nylon fabrics that they sell in shops: some of them are like gossamer, with designs of fruits and flowers on them, while others are opaque and heavy, like soft glass. Every category of cement, concrete, stone. There are new materials invented by man, transuranic elements: neptunium ($Z=93$), plutonium ($Z=94$), americium ($Z=95$), curium ($Z=96$), berkelium ($Z=97$), californium ($Z=98$), einsteinium ($Z=99$), fermium ($Z=100$), mendelevium ($Z=101$), nobelium ($Z=102$). There is the white steel that glitters on automobiles and on railway carriages. There are strange liquids fizzing inside bottles, which all have to be sampled in turn. In supermarkets I have seen thousands of identical little pasteboard pots containing thick cream or yoghourt or cream cheese. That whole scene is really extraordinary, you know. And, and what's more, I have seen thousands of tin cans containing different kinds of meat, or vegetable, or fruit in syrup. Yesterday I bought one which had written on it:

> Libby's
> Fruit Cocktail   (Cherries artificially coloured red)
> in heavy syrup

And all those tons of paper. And all those ballpoint pens that write in red, and black, and blue, and green, and violet, with tiny tungsten balls that leave a thin dribble behind them as they roll round and round. And all those cigarettes in their little pasteboard boxes, all identical, containing yellow tobacco

189

and black tobacco, with filters made from cotton and coal and toilet paper.

There are so many things that vibrate, that talk, that move. There are so many machines everywhere. Electric razors, electric billiard games, electric mixers, fans, refrigerators, electronic calculating machines. There are so many engines. SAVIEM, SOGIC. The power of engines. Heat, aluminium. Pistons, camshafts, valves, spark-plugs, carburettors, jets, selector switches. Enclosed in gleaming bonnets, snarling with their 105 genuine hp, pressing down upon the wheels. So many tyres and wheels. The other day, I saw a very beautiful wheel. I looked at it for a long while, so that I would never forget it. It was a very high, very wide wheel belonging to a lorry, and it was surrounded by a fat tyre of black sculpted rubber around which was written UNIROYAL, 6 50 R 20, 10 PLYRATING. But the really magnificent thing about this wheel was its centre: a six-branched star radiating from the hub. In the centre of the star, a circle fastened by ten bolts. Each ray was fixed to the wheel-rim by a big square-headed bolt. So I stood for a long while looking at this sort of six-branched star, and I saw that each of its arms was swelling with strength and energy, that it was pressing against the rim as though with a hand. What I'm trying to say is that this star of steel embodied such perfection, such real beauty and power, that it almost seemed to be the centre of the world, the nucleus. The wheel was motionless, pressing down upon the roadway with the lorry's whole weight, and its six arms opening out like a star shone with force and calm violence. I shall never forget it. That beautiful peaceful wheel, dominating space, indestructible. Ever since that moment I keep on trying to see it again in the street. But the lorry has vanished. Perhaps it was a sign. Perhaps this wheel might teach me something, an attitude, an idea. Perhaps it was the magic word which stops wars:

WHEEL

That's what I am seeking, Monsieur X. I am seeking words and signs capable of helping me survive. In the matted forest I am seeking friendly plants, and boulders, and snakes, and friendly birds. I want to rediscover the ancient legends and tell them to you, so that you in turn can tell them to others.

For example:

LEGEND OF THE FIRST CIGARETTE

In olden days, men were not acquainted with fire. They lived in shadow, and they resembled bats. During that time, there was a very beautiful woman called Pall Mall. She was afraid, because everything was dark, and there were not even any stars. So one day she took a sheet of newspaper and filled it with dust and smoked it. But it was no good. So she tried with dog's hairs, but that was no good either. And then, one day, she had the idea of rolling her own long tresses in the paper, and she began to smoke that. And the smoke was so smooth and gentle, and it spread so much warmth and light, that the rest of mankind wanted to do the same. But since all women did not have golden tresses like Pall Mall, all sorts of different cigarettes resulted. There were some with black hair, others with red hair, others again with grey hair. It is since that time that men are no longer afraid at night, and that they take pleasure in inhaling the smoke of cigarettes in which their women's hair is smouldering.

Or else:

THE MYTH OF THE BLACK SEDAN

The world has not always been there. But the moment that it was created, with all its streets and all its motorways, this big black limousine appeared and started to prowl around. This astonishing vehicle is very beautiful and very big, but no-one has ever been able to say what it looks like because it kills all those who approach it. All we know is that it is a very long black car, *with no chrome at all*. Its whole body is of a dull hue, even its windows are opaque, and no-one knows who is driving it. It prowls, day and night (preferably at night, when it can switch on its blinding white headlamps), along the deserted streets. It moves noiselessly, and those whom it encounters are later found squashed flat on the asphalt, with tyre marks stamped into the throat and sex, peculiar Z-shaped marks.

And then, again:

THE MYTH OF MONOPOL

It is he who runs everything. He has armies of leather-jacketed cops patrolling the town, armies of cops who carry big rubber truncheons and keep fierce dogs on the leash. No-one knows precisely who MONOPOL is. He lives in fortress-palaces of a sort, by the side of the sea, or on the tops of mountains. He also lives in town centres, and he has huge glass and concrete structures built, and people are obliged to go there and buy. He has hordes of slaves, all dressed exactly alike and all thinking exactly alike; he has fleets of new ships and planes and cars that sparkle; he lives with a lot of very young and very beautiful women who have green eyes framed in black mascara, and long slim legs. No-one has ever seen MONOPOL, because he stays hidden behind his concrete walls, and then he is never in the same place twice. He simply spends his whole time putting up these palatial buildings, and handing out orders to his army of cops and slaves. He owns factories where millions of people work, but his riches never suffice. He loves gold and silver, hoarding it in great silent vaults guarded by his cops. He loves war, too, because his slaves kill each other with the guns he manufactures. And he loves power, because he is the only one who knows what he wants and how to get it. There are people who want to slay MONO-POL, and so they hurl grenades through his shop windows and under the wheels of his cars. But MONOPOL is invincible. He has many bodies, many lives. He is everywhere at once, behind the plate-glass mirrors, listening in to telephone conversations, on the other side of the television screens. He knows everything that is going on. Maybe, one day, MONOPOL will cease to exist. But not until every stone, every window-pane of his gigantic warehouses has been ground to dust. Not until the whole earth has burned fiercely for a year on end, so that everything is destroyed, down to the very roots.

All such myths are there, around me. I listen to all these stories: those that the street gives birth to, with its shifting crowds and convoys of vehicles, and those that form in the sky as the Thunderbird streaks past with screeching jets. The myths inscribed on blank walls, with all their magic symbols, PSU, SFIO, PAN, PRI, PC, US=SS, LIBERATE PRAGUE, CADA ESTUDIANTE ES UN CHE. There are so many words reverberating everywhere, so many incomprehensible words, so many guttural cries. So many god-words and demon-words, on walls, on the pages of newspapers, carved into the doors of latrines. They do not seek to communicate. They say nothing. Their one aim is to leap upon me, bruise me, hammer at my head and throat. These are warmongering words, in a rage to conquer the world, flashing with a blueish gleam from the depths of plate-glass windows: BRANDT Chemical Co., WINSTON, SALEM, *Frill*, Airborne, UNITED FRUIT. They flash and wound with their sharp stings, they give fatal electric shocks. Monsieur X, I see all these pitiless weapons, everywhere, slicing through the air. Perhaps, one of these days, the words will strike me down. Perhaps they will stab me in the back while I am walking alongside a wall, perhaps they will rip through the back of my neck and smash my spine. Or perhaps they will confront me, and blind me with a single glaring light from their flash-gun. There are so many beautiful, dangerous things, Monsieur X, all determined to conquer. The world is streaked by the rays of all these objects, and all I can do is try to slip safely through the hail of bullets. It is no good my trying to understand them, to interpret their life, to tame them: they burn my hands, they are sometimes so hot that my eyes mist over as I look at them, and sometimes so cold that my thoughts freeze over and grind to a halt. Never has the forest contained so many splendid, malevolent things. Never have there been more terrifying tigers, more poisonous snakes, more pullulating insects. No tree has ever borne such a wealth of beautiful, succulent fruits: in their aluminium boxes they lie steeped in their own thick syrup, gorged with sugar and perfume. It is true, Monsieur X. There are millions of new stories that no-one has ever told, yet. Profound stories that whirl ostentatiously between the cities' walls. Such true, such powerful, such speedy narratives that the mind succumbs before ever having understood. Stories about dark glasses, for example, or stories about leather belts. Stories about stainless steel knives, stories about wrist-watches, glasses, electric light bulbs, tanker-lorries, mirrors as vast as cliffs, transistors that speak for months without stopping. There are long-drawn-out stories that last

194

for years and years, while the building sites raise their scaffoldings of planks, and the old cement walls fashion a fresh
barrier. There are stories so rapid that one could tell a
hundred thousand of them in a single second, sparks in the
light switch's sealed box, explosion inside the scorching
breech, smashing of the nucleus in the cyclotron, typewriter
key striking the letter K, bullet leaping from the pistol's
black barrel, clicking of the great electronic calculating
machine as it multiplies the figure 17 632 411 722 006 181 by
the figure 2 225 034 999 216 000 074 926 and produces the
result 2 391 332 723 367 206 974 223 821 175 777 035 117 606.
In the midst of all these, I am reduced almost to nothing. I
try to hear the myths, but it seems fruitless. All these stories
are talking at once, and I have only my brain to absorb it all.
And yet, Monsieur X, I know that that is what has to be
done in order to survive. I suspect, now, that I know what we
all should do. It would be a great help to me if you would co-
operate with me. What is needed, once and for all, is the
preparation of a new bible, one that will speak of our new
gods and our new calamities. A big blank book, you see, in
which one would write everything down, just like that, simply
by listening to all these stories whirling around us. One would
write down the creation of the world, starting with a huge
building site and the noise of pneumatic drills. There would
be steamrollers lurching over the waste ground, and then
the motor-pump sucking up the lake of mud. And then there
would be the cranes turning this way and that in the wind,
and the concrete-mixers revolving their great drums full of
sand and cement. After that, one would write down the birth
of plastics: the rivers of vinyl gliding slowly over the earth,
the great sheets of dacron as immobile as ice-floes, and this
whole intense glacial light, these cliffs of mica and bakelite,
these jungles of cellulose.

Another thing that should be told is how woman was born,
emerging one day from her brand-new nylon sac, with sleek
skin and hair and breasts and belly, then how she wrapped

herself in her white plastic raincoat, and how she set off on her undulating journey between the stores' opaque windows. One should repeat all these stirring glowing accounts that whirl around me all the time, these stories screamed by engines, exploded by jukeboxes, murmured by neon tubes. These stories destined to last for centuries. There is not much time left, by now, Monsieur X. Soon the eddies will be so strong that they will tear me away. Soon the light from all the lamps will scorch my eyes, and the moaning of the turbines will penetrate my head and make me speechless. There are not many days left, now. The words are aiming their bursts of machine-gun fire around me, and it is a miracle that I have not yet been riddled. One day, perhaps, I shall encounter the great black limousine that crushes those it finds, or else I shall cross the path of the Thunderbird, and its jets will reduce me to ashes. One day, perhaps, I shall vanish down an endless tunnel where streams of excrement flow. I think all the time of the lightning flash that will appear on the horizon, above the city, with its umbrella-shaped cloud and its millions of tongues of fire that will eat away flesh and nylon. I think, too, of the madness that will erupt in an immense supermarket, and of the rivers of blood that will flow between the white counters. When I think of all that, I am afraid, and long to find the words that dissolve dreams.

Good-bye.

Bea B.

P.S.   Story of the silly cat.

It was a very stupid cat.

One day it fell asleep on the balustrade of the balcony.

Then it woke up. While it was yawning and stretching its paws, it lost its balance, and fell from the third floor.

Never saw anything stupider than the expression on that cat's face as it started falling.

To understand the acumen shown by so-called primitive peoples in observing and interpreting natural phenomena, it is not, therefore, necessary to assume that vanished faculties are being exercised, or that a supplementary sensibility is in play. The American Indian who detects a trail by means of imperceptible signs, the Australian who unhesitatingly identifies footprints left by some member of his group, proceed exactly as we do ourselves, when we are driving a car and judge at a glance, from a slight shift of the wheels' direction, a fluctuation in the engine's pitch, or even the apparent intention of a look, the right moment to overtake or avoid another vehicle.

Claude Lévi-Strauss.

When separate pains grip two parts of the body at the same time, the keener of the two dulls the other one.

Hippocrates.

The girl called Bea B. was poised at the edge of the great river of vehicles. It was exactly midday, in the centre of the city, and there was this immense boulevard stretching from one end of the earth to the other in an unbroken straight line, thrusting the buildings' chalky cliffs aside, then squeezing them together again. The girl was not there simply by chance. For a long time now, she had wanted to make her way to this boulevard and stand there at the edge of the pavement, watching the river of vehicles flow by. Months ago she had

197

started to hear the noise coming from the back of her room, the steady sound of the flowing river, a deep rumble that made the window-panes vibrate. It never stopped. Night and day she had listened to the distant rumbling, and tried to see where it came from. She had looked at all these flat roofs, all these walls, all these valleys of streets, but the noise came from farther away, as though it were issuing from an invisible cavern or even the very bowels of the earth. It was frightening. At night, if one looked in the direction of the noise one saw a sort of halo of rosy light hovering in the sky, and one imagined abominable things.

That is why the girl was there, this midday, poised at the river's edge. Standing on the pavement, beside the pole with its eternally winking yellow light, waiting. The sun was high in the sky, while on earth the shadows were very short. Bea B. was not alone: other people were waiting, wordlessly, on either side of her. Bea B. gave them a furtive glance and saw that they were ordinary folk such as one sees every day, matronly women carrying imitation-leather bags, and men wearing suits in various shades of anthracite. Some bespectacled, others not. From time to time a gap opened up in the flood of cars, a few seconds of empty space between the bumpers. Then the cluster of men and women charged onto the roadway and crossed over, swinging their arms energetically.

Bea B. did not cross over. She remained standing on the edge of the pavement, waiting. Her right shoulder supported the strap of the red plastic bag that had TWA written on it in fat white letters. The girl waited, almost motionless, beside the iron pole. She saw the people stepping onto the opposite pavement, across the boulevard, and immediately the river began to flow again, with its rumbling of thunder.

It was very hot. The sun was so high that it was scarcely visible, a white star vaguely lighting up the hazy sky. Below this star, upon the earth, the boulevard was the centre of the universe. Aeons of time ago, a cataclysm had opened up this

198

valley amid the blocks of buildings, and now the river flowed, flowed without respite. The river of metal came swooping from both horizons at once, with two unswerving currents passing each other endlessly, one to the right, the other to the left. Bea B. tried to see the place where they originated at each extremity of the boulevard. But the air was shimmering and all that could be seen was a sort of grey cloud that looked like dust or ash and blended with the sky. Then she decided that it was impossible to know, that the double river had neither beginning nor end, and that it simply flowed like that, eternally, from one end of space to the other. Perhaps at each extremity the boulevard was swallowed up by a flaw, plunging to the very centre of the earth before gushing out again through another flaw. Or else perhaps there was a vast circular esplanade in the remote distance, a terminus around which the river swirled in a giant whirlpool before sending its waters racing back in the opposite direction.

So the floodtide of cars flowed through the lunar valley, and the noise of their engines submerged everything. In front of the girl, the mass of metal and rubber swept forward rapidly, gliding over the black roadway with its thousands of wheels. It was a majestic, powerful movement that was taking place effortlessly alongside the pavement. Each car followed the one in front without stopping, casting a reflection of garish light as it passed, each car like a scale on the skin of a great snake. There were thousands of them, hundreds of thousands, all identical, rushing along the valley, welded to each other by a tiny buffer of scorching air. The girl's eyes jerked in their sockets as the cars passed, but her glance never lingered for more than a fraction of a second on each transient shape. There was no time. There were too many things to see, there was too much speed. She looked at the river as though she were a television camera, letting the luminous blobs flicker on the line-streaked screen. The wave of metal rolled on continuously, minute after minute, filling space with its steady motion, urging forward its flock of chrome fixtures and bonnets, parading its thousands of windscreens and glittering windows.

It was like a train hurtling through an empty station, or like the dream in which one is falling, with eyes wide open, down the side of a grey building with a hundred million storeys. But this was even more terrible because it was happening in broad daylight, under the sun's harsh glare, in the centre of the world. The people on either side of Bea B. had also stopped, and were staring vacantly as they watched the river go by. No-one here had anything left to say. Thought had soon been driven from the world by the movement of all the cars speeding along the boulevard. The noise had annihilated truth, and words. The uninterrupted power had annihilated will. The motion of the two opposing currents as they glided against each other had split the world in two, and it was no longer possible to speak of time or space. It was a vision from beyond life, total and brutal, a vision from within life.

With a relentless roar the broad river sped simultaneously towards the opposite sides of the earth. It sped onwards in an absolutely straight line unbroken by whirlpools or rapids, with a single grand motion that swept straight through the landscape. Its steel body glided over the black ground, gradually wearing away the asphalt until it dispersed in the air as an impalpable dust. The engines raced, and the girl heard each one distinctly as it whizzed past, in the brief moment before the sound was swallowed up again in the general din. Sometimes the strident sound of brakes and horns or the grinding of changing gears unexpectedly filled the air. This composite noise flowed along with the river, a liquid sound like pebbles rumbling against each other, or like an invisible cataract. The noise never died down: it lasted hours, days, years, centuries. The noise pounded at the ears with all its weight, compressing the ear-drums like the depths of the ocean.

The cars followed each other so quickly that there was no

time to notice their colours. They glided in unison towards the horizon, towards the little cloud trembling at each extremity of the boulevard. The wheels all turned together, imprinting hard upon the tar the little zigzag patterns of their rubber tyres. They were waves of iron and glass, long undulating waves sparkling with lights, sweeping inexorably forwards ...

No-one could cross the river. Farther on, perhaps, there were great iron poles supporting a red lamp that glowed from time to time; then the people had to leap onto the roadway, men wearing anthracite-coloured suits, and women swinging imitation-leather handbags from the pendulum of the right arm. They were bobbing up and down, perhaps, pumping their arms strenuously, in the gap that yawned briefly between the bonnets. But here nothing could halt the river's flow. The windscreens swept onwards against the blasts of air, broad plates of curving glass with dormant windscreen wipers that reflected the rays of the sun. Bea B.'s eyes could just take in the lightning arrival of the headlamps and chrome-plated radiator grilles followed by the windows, metal panels and wheels. It was the same image projected repeatedly, endlessly, flashing past, taking shape and vanishing in almost the same moment. To the left and the right, the girl could see white walls rearing up, receding towards each horizon, and beneath them the torrent of cars coming and going. Sometimes great tankers drifted along among the moving mass, and she watched them loom out of the far distance like giant tree-trunks riding the floodtide. The river of steel ran along the cement-rimmed channel, its hard waves glinting in the sun, but it was not really a river: it was a flow of red-hot lava shimmering its way through the city while the earth quaked and rumbled. It was also a glacier on the move, bearing down its blocks of drift-ice and its tons of earth and boulders, grating ceaselessly against the tarry surface, hollowing out its valley through the mountains of buildings. Nothing could stop it. The sluice-gates had been opened, one day, at each end of the earth, and the raging flood was pounding the ground, wreaking havoc along its path. Slowly, as the years went by, the city would open up, the highway would become an esplanade, and the esplanade would become a desert. The rounded wings, the bumpers, the shatter-proof windscreens continued to forge ahead, chipping fragments off the pavement kerbs and flattening lamp-posts on their way. Sometimes, somewhere or other, the wall of a house would collapse in a cloud of dust, and the debris would be immediately swallowed up by the river. Or else a helicopter would suddenly appear overhead, buzz above the boulevard for a while, then vanish elsewhere.

Bea B. stood quite still, contemplating the scene. Her eyes and ears were filled with beauty, her skin was perspiring in the sun. She witnessed the onrush of each metal shell, she heard the roaring of each engine hurtling forward at 4,000 rpm. It was extraordinary to remain motionless, like that, watching the river of cars pass by, at midday. This made it possible to understand a whole lot of unknown factors about war, about beauty. It made it possible to become increasingly cold and static, like an iron pole. The river had launched its solid body full of din and gleams, and was advancing implacably from one edge of the world to the opposite one, then back again. It possessed thousands of wheels and plate-glass panels and headlamps, thousands of sheet-metal bodies, doors, radiator grilles and windscreen wipers, but they were always the same ones. The stream of vehicles came from the end of the horizon, emerging without respite from the centre of the dust-cloud, yet nobody noticed. The cars advanced, huddling together like a herd of buffaloes, trampling the earth under their identical tyres. And this meant many things that were both strange and simple, as for example: truth is the cohesion of the crowd. Or else: 1 vehicle = 1,000 vehicles. Or again: FROM NOW ON, I WANT TO KNOW THE SURFACE OF THINGS. And this could also mean: today, midday, traffic conditions on the ring motorway remain fluid. An accident is reported at the junction with Exit 18. Heavy traffic build-up along the outer boulevard ...

Nothing, then, could halt the river's progress. It marked time, it hollowed out its bed in the city, it plunged under great cement bridges with echoing arches. It pressed on relentlessly, expelling its thousands of joule-seconds. There was so much power, so much warmth and truth in this place that it seemed as though nothing else could exist. The straight road was stretched taut beneath the vault of the sky, all its pent-up energies straining to be unleashed. The girl felt the road's scorching breath, mingled with exhaust fumes and dust, brush past her face and hair. She felt the long-drawn-out vibrations that made the ground shudder, sent tremors up her legs and clutched at her solar plexus. And she could hear the unbroken tattoo, like low thunder, that heralded imminent storms and floods. The sensible thing, of course, would be to get away, to climb on top of a high building and cower on the roof to escape the tidal wave. But that was not possible, for she was incapable of wrenching her eyes away from this spectacle of furiously spinning, onrushing movements. She could think of nothing else. Her feet seemed glued to the edge of the pavement. The streams of sleek metal flowed by her, a moving rampart that had sealed her body within its prison. The wind churned up by all this motion blew steadily. Flashes of sunlight bounced ceaselessly off the moving surfaces, exploding the same star across each windscreen. The odours of burning petrol, of rubber, of tar rose continually in great jagged clouds, and no other odours were imaginable. Bea B. struggled to breathe this air, and her heart beat very hard in her chest, under the nylon brassière.

Just a few feet in front of her, the two opposite currents passed each other indefinitely, then receded towards the boulevard's two outlets. The cars' shells slid together blindly, melted into each other, then separated once more. This process repeated itself ten times a second, while the engines' noises blended briefly, swallowed by the coagulating mass.

Bea B. made an effort to understand what happened during the moment when the cars met and passed each other; but doubtless there was nothing to understand. The two streams came from the two ends of the earth, each along its half of the roadway, moving symmetrically as though a gigantic mirror were positioned somewhere along the route. This aimless arrival of waves that flowed against each other resembled nothing so much as a flattened circle. On each side of the river, the pavement's thin strip also receded towards the horizon, with all its pillars and posts and all its men and women. But the latter were of no importance. They were the vague witnesses of a more powerful movement, as they stood there for hours on end, waiting for a safe moment to launch themselves across the road. Sometimes they died, felled by a single blow, like trees, or dismembered by the vulcanized wheels. For a brief moment a few eddies and a few bubbles would show that the flow had been obstructed; then the current would sweep everything away, down to the last smear of blood and sliver of glass, and the river would resume its journey, roaring hoarsely, as before, and hurling its waves of metal against each other.

The girl remained there for a long time, watching the river of cars flow along the valley, in the centre of the city. She watched the wheels with their chrome-plated hubcaps, spinning furiously as they passed by. She watched the ventilators slice through the air with a whistling sound, and the radio aerials sway like whips. With smarting eyes, she watched the distant shimmering of the river, near the horizon, where the dust-cloud hovered overhead. Clinging to the iron pole with the winking yellow light on top, she concentrated all her attention on the majestic and terrible spectacle of the two streams of metal endlessly meeting and passing each other. She even tried to see the empty space, right there in the centre of the roadway, that separated the two opposing streams. It seemed to her that this space must surely be filled with powerful eddies, scorching whirlwinds, while the con-

204

trary currents passed each other at an ever-increasing speed. She began to think that, if she wanted to understand things, she should perhaps take up position on that spot: stand there in the centre of the road, while the two tornadoes of steel whetted their blades in a shower of sparks; stand there and wait, more alone than a cop in the centre of a crossroads.

She saw again the white dome of the sky suspended above this whole scene, and it too was like a river, with ice-floes floating through its vast valley. Perhaps the distant star that shone in the depths of space was the motor that drove everything, and one day, after many centuries of warmth and life, these valleys would be motionless once more, sand-covered highways strewn with charred carcasses. Vultures were wheeling in huge circles, very high above the rumbling river, keeping a look-out for these scattered remnants. Bea B. felt a kind of dizziness come over her, and she had to cling to the winking pole with all her might to save herself from falling under the wheels of the passing vehicles.

Suddenly a car stopped in front of her, alongside the kerb. It was an ancient American model, a massive black machine with an enormous bonnet, and wings like a fish's fins. A man opened the front door and shouted something, but his voice was drowned by the noise of all the motor-horns that had started screeching behind the halted car. The man opened the door wider, and Bea B. could see that the seats inside were upholstered in red. She went up to the gaping door and climbed inside the car, which immediately pulled away, belching a cloud of exhaust. Bea B. looked around and saw that there were five people in the car, the driver and another man in front, and a woman and two men in the back. The American car sped silently along the immense boulevard, following the flow of the traffic. The girl slumped back in her seat. Slowly, she felt the dizziness recede and her strength return. The man sitting by her side leaned towards her:

'Where are you headed?' he asked.

205

The girl took a little time to answer.

'Anywhere ... Just let me out anywhere ...'

'We rescued you in the nick of time,' said the driver, a thin man with close-cropped hair. 'In another moment you'd have been under the wheels of the cars.'

'It's the heat,' said Bea B.

'Do you feel all right now?' said a voice from the back. Bea B. turned round. First she saw the woman who had spoken, a young woman with black hair and a very pale face. Then she glanced at the two men sitting in the back with the woman, one on either side.

'Do you feel better now?' repeated the young woman.

'Yes, I feel better, thank you,' said Bea B. But her voice was feeble.

'Here, drink this,' said the man sitting beside her. He took a small bottle from the glove compartment. Bea B. uncorked the bottle and took a sip of the liquid. The bitter taste brought a lump to her throat.

'What is it?' said Bea B.

'Drink it, it will do you good,' said the man firmly.

Bea B. took another sip, then handed the bottle back.

The man at the steering wheel spoke without looking at her. He was weaving his way through the traffic, adroitly overtaking the cars in line ahead of them.

'It's a recipe of Starrkrampf's,' he said. 'An infusion of marijuana in alcohol. It creates all kinds of energy.'

The pale-faced woman gave a laugh and said in an odd husky voice:

'Careful! She'll begin to think we are dope-fiends!'

Bea B. gazed ahead, through the blue-tinted windscreen. She felt like sleeping. Outside, the scene was snowy, deserted, agitated by spasmodic movements.

Suddenly she saw that the sun was very low in the sky.

'What time is it?' she asked anxiously.

The man driving, who looked rather like Monsieur X, glanced at his watch.

'Six o'clock,' he said.

'Six,' she repeated.

'Where are we going?' said Starrkrampf.

'Where do you want to go?' asked Monsieur X. Bea B. suddenly realized that the question was addressed to her.

'I don't really know, I —'

'Are you on a trip?' said the pale young woman, pointing to the airline bag.

'Yes, I'm sort of travelling around,' said Bea B.

'Well, that's fine,' said one of the men at the back, 'so are we.'

'Perhaps she's hungry?' said Starrkrampf. He leaned over towards Bea B. and touched her arm. She gave a start.

'Are you hungry?' repeated Starrkrampf.

'No, no,' said Bea B., trying to stay awake. 'I, I think maybe you'd better let me out, over there will do ...'

'We can't just abandon you like that,' said Monsieur X. 'You'll be all right with us. Won't she, Geberckx?'

'Sure,' said Geberckx.

'I wouldn't mind going to that drive-in cinema,' said the pale-faced young woman, who was called Alexandra Tchkonia.

'Not now, later,' said Geberckx.

After that, nobody spoke again. The big American car flew over the grey city as it raced along the circular motorway.

It was night, by now. The black limousine had been travelling through the city for a long time, doubling its tracks along the motorway, turning left, then right, then right again. Occasionally, red lights shone through the darkness, and Monsieur X brought the nose of the car to a halt in line with an intersection, drumming on the steering wheel with the tips of his fingers as he waited for the light to turn green. Hunched forwards, with her shoulder against the door, Bea B. looked at the walls of the buildings, and the patterns of lights, some of them stationary, others moving. Beside her, Starrkrampf was sitting with arms folded, listening to a muted voice on the radio. At the back, Geberckx and the other man were asleep, their heads lolling. They were both in need of a shave, and their faces were drawn with fatigue. Alexandra Tchkonia was smoking nervously; her white face looked even whiter now, gleaming under its black wig in the dark.

At long last, the American car turned into a vast car park that had a box-shaped snack-bar in the centre. Monsieur X stopped the car near the snack-bar and got out. He came back a few minutes later, carrying packages of sandwiches and bottles of beer. Everybody ate and drank rapidly, in silence. Then they visited the washrooms, one at a time. When it was Bea B.'s turn she took her bag and walked quickly towards the neon-lit structure. The cold air helped to wake her up. She decided that when she came out of the washroom she would turn left, and keep going left until she was out of the place. But Alexandra Tchkonia must have suspected something because when Bea B. emerged she saw the pale-faced young woman waiting for her. The girl hesitated.

'It's too late for you to go, or too early,' said the pale-faced young woman. She took Bea B. by the elbow. 'Come on, the others are waiting.'

Bea B. opened her mouth to protest, but no words came out. So she walked towards the American car. When she had settled herself once more on the red imitation-leather upholstery she simply thought, very briefly, 'I am not afraid.'

Monsieur X gently turned the ignition key on the dashboard, and the powerful engine started throbbing. The headlamps were suddenly ablaze, and two white beams shot straight ahead, illuminating the car park, picking out conglomerations of cars and advertisement hoardings from the darkness, and lighting up the red stars of cat's-eye reflectors. With the same slow gesture Monsieur X shifted the gear lever upwards and engaged first gear. Then he eased his foot off the clutch pedal and the black car started moving. It passed silently between the parking lanes until it reached the street. There, Monsieur X rotated the steering wheel three times, the American car swung round gently, and the wheels bumped as they went over the edge of the pavement. The road was bright with lights. Many other cars were racing along, their engines screaming. Clinging close to the walls, pedestrians were walking along in small groups, lingering in front of the white shop windows. The American car got onto the roadway and began picking up speed. Monsieur X smoked a cigarette as he drove, holding it in his left hand while steering with his right hand. Reflections slid over his lean face; his eyes stared straight ahead like headlamps. Bea B. saw all this as though in a dream, a new dream that was longer than the others, one in which she knew neither the beginning nor the end. It was strange, driving along like this at night, in this big American car, with Monsieur X, Starr-krampf, Geberckx, Alexandra Tchkonia, and the other man whose name she did not know. It was like letting oneself be carried across the sea in a ship, listening to the sounds of the engine and watching the coast's reflected lights very far away on the horizon.

The American car criss-crossed the city for a while, skirting a whole number of identical streets and avenues. Then suddenly Starrkrampf looked at his watch and said:

'Ten o'clock. Time to go hunting?'

Monsieur X did not reply.

'Well, are we going?' Starrkrampf repeated. He half turned towards the rear seat.

'Sandra?' he said.

'What about her?' said Monsieur X, jerking a thumb towards Bea B.

'She is with us,' said the pale-faced young woman, 'we'll give her a demonstration.'

'Whereabouts do you want to go?' said Monsieur X.

'We might try the south motorway,' said Starrkrampf.

'Isn't that a bit risky?' said Geberckx.

'We haven't been out since the other evening,' said the other man in the back.

'Yes, but —'

'And anyhow, all we need do is go a little farther on, this time, that's all.'

'OK, let's go.'

'Let's go,' repeated Alexandra Tchkonia.

Monsieur X said 'OK' once more.

The big car leapt forward. From that moment onwards they limited their conversation to occasional terse remarks, while the car glided through the streets. Bea B. noticed that their faces had become serious, with eyes staring fixedly through the windscreen. The wind whistled along the sides of the black panelling, and the engine gave out a dull hollow roar like an aeroplane. From time to time they passed the little bottle around, each taking a gulp from it, or they lit cigarettes. Or else they rapped out brief phrases that sounded like orders:

'Left, here.'

'Straight ahead now.'

'Watch out.'

'Left here, then right.'

'Squeeze right for the approach ramp.'

'There you are.'

'That's it.'

'OK.'

'Watch out, the toll-booths are about a hundred yards ahead.'

A kind of white wall pierced by six archways suddenly loomed up, in front of the car's bonnet. It was a triumphal arch made of cement, rectangular, illuminated by floodlights. Above each entrance a green light shone brightly. The road ran straight up to the construction, splitting into three parallel channels marked with broad yellow stripes. At the end of each channel, there was a sort of undulating carpet made of rows of iron pipes embedded in the tar. The American car shuddered as it drove over the carpet. It continued its slow progress until it reached the porch. On the left was a glass-walled cabin with a man in a black uniform inside it. At the far side of the porch a red light gleamed and a metal barrier blocked the way. When the car came to a halt under the cement arch there was a click and at the same moment an automatic machine proffered a pasteboard ticket, the light ahead turned green, and the metal arm lifted. Monsieur X took the ticket and propped it against the windscreen. Then he let in the clutch, and the car passed through the toll-gate.

On the other side stretched the motorway. It lay spread out in front of the car, as broad as an airport runway, plunging straight ahead into the night. This too was a river, icy and stark, a black river flowing between lines of stunted shrubs. Once on the motorway, the car quickly picked up speed. It seemed to be floating, and its four tyres glided over the asphalt with a slight tremor. The two headlamps pierced the thick night, throwing into sharp relief all the yellow geometric designs, the dotted lines, the stripes, the metal panels with the figure 100 on them, the arrows, the circles, the triangles. The signs all arrived in a flash, surging out of the night with their bars and hooks, and they talked, they talked all the time. They told stories about speed and death, stories about accidents, when the overturned carcases blazed in the centre of great pools of oil. The girl looked at the never-ending line of yellow dots that came rushing sinuously between the car's front wheels. Then she looked at the night's solid mass, as motionless and black as the sea's lower depths, with only a few phosphorescent glows traversing it. By now they were parsecs away from the city, travelling through space between one star and another. Everything was silent and calm. No-one inside the car spoke. Monsieur X was scanning the road ahead, his hands resting lightly on the steering wheel. Starrkrampf was sitting perfectly still, listening to the radio. In the back row Alexandra Tchkonia went on smoking her filter cigarette, leaning forwards now and staring over Starrkrampf's shoulder. Geberckx and the other man were finishing off the contents of the little bottle. They were all waiting for something. The American car speeding along the motorway was now inhabited by a strange intensity that may have been an electric current or else a sense of hatred. It was difficult to pinpoint. No doubt it emanated from the compression of the engine and its low throbbing, and from the friction of the black coachwork against the air's layers. It also emanated from the signals lit up by the headlamps, from all those hooks and crosses that sprang out of the darkness and hurtled at them at a speed of over a hundred feet a second. At long intervals the dark mass of a lorry appeared on the crown of the road, and then the American car overtook it and passed it effortlessly. Or else, for no apparent reason, the road slewed round in a long gentle curve, and all the occupants of the car were tilted sideways by the force of gravity.

The black limousine drove on like this, along the motorway, for a long time. There were many bridges, bends, steep gradients, luminous signs. There were petrol stations as big as towns, lit by giant neon tubes.

At one moment Monsieur X said simply:

'The police.'

Everybody sat up. Bea B. was horrified to see, just a few yards ahead of her, the menacing shape of a black car that seemed to be floating along the road. She also saw something perfectly extraordinary, the golden star rotating on the car's roof, the revolving searchlight that sent its flashing message of danger and fear in all directions. The American car gradually overtook the police car, as Bea B. watched the star grow bigger. Now she could make out the filaments inside the bulb, each time that the pivoting searchlight pointed its plexiglass hood in her direction. Her heart began beating very fast. The pale-faced young woman in the back had stopped smoking. She, too, was watching the star. Monsieur X

212

reduced speed slightly, and the American car edged slowly past the police car. Just for a moment Bea B. could see the black profiles turned towards her from behind the windows. But nothing happened. The patrol-car remained behind and began to dwindle away into the night. Monsieur X glanced at the vanishing star in the rear mirror, then said:

'I don't like that.'

The pale-faced young woman giggled nervously.

'If they only knew what we were up to!'

'I don't like that,' repeated Monsieur X, 'we'd better turn off at the first exit.'

'Yes, that's safest,' said Starrkrampf. 'In any case, there's nothing worth hunting on the motorway.'

Monsieur X accelerated. When he saw the sign announcing the exit, he turned the steering wheel slightly; the car moved over to the shoulder of the road, which suddenly broadened ahead of them, and then the car was descending a steep banking slope. At the end of the ramp there was a toll-booth, a white concrete cabin with a barrier attached. Monsieur X lowered the window and held out the ticket and some money to a man in black, who took it without speaking. Then the barrier lifted, and the American car was off again.

Now they came onto a road bordered by trees, and a bridge. The car passed under the bridge and began cruising along the road. They were in a very broad plain stretching flat under the black sky, dotted with occasional thickets and a few hills. The road went straight across the plain, between lines of poplars. The car was riding the crest of the road, with headlamps blazing. Bea B. saw that the car's other occupants were straining forwards in their seats, staring intently into the space lit up by the headlamps' beams. They were waiting. Something was going to happen, something terrible, but the girl could not bring herself to guess what. She, too, watched the road ahead, her eyes smarting from fatigue, her mouth full of the bitter taste of Starrkrampf's tincture. Very occasionally a pair of headlamps would come into view at the

213

other end of the plain, and the girl watched them come slowly closer, floating over the dark earth, veering left, then right, sometimes flashing dazzling beams at them. The American car travelled on like this for a long time, and no-one any longer had the slightest idea where they were. Then, all of a sudden, Monsieur X said in a muffled voice:

'There!'

At the same time he dimmed the lights. Less than a hundred yards away, the outline of a man appeared at the side of the road. Then everything happened very fast. Monsieur X switched off the lights and gripped the steering wheel hard. The engine began snarling more loudly and insistently as Monsieur X accelerated. Through the windscreen Bea B. could see the road rushing towards them at a dizzy speed, although the black surface was only just visible in the night. The verge struck the wheels with great thumps that jarred the car's frame, and flying gravel stung the doors and windows. The outline of the man walking by the side of the road grew bigger and bigger. It seemed to float in the misty air like a stunted shrub. The car continued to hurtle along the verge of the road, ripping away lumps of earth and crushing the grass flat. Monsieur X hunched himself over the steering wheel and shouted something, but his voice was so hoarse that no-one could understand him. Fascinated, Bea B. watched the grey outline running desperately, just ahead of the car. For a split second, she had a vision of the man as though suddenly illuminated by a flash-gun, a motionless figure wearing a grey overcoat, the back of a neck, black hair, two hands hanging down at each side of the body. Then there was a dull thud, followed quickly by a sort of hunh! that rose from the ground. Not a cry; rather, a violent movement of the diaphragm, and it was perhaps the pale-faced young woman, or Geberckx, or the fourth man who had uttered the sound, or else it was the girl herself, unconsciously, and the big American car continued bumping over the grass verge for a few seconds. Then it swung back onto the road, and began

214

speeding along once more, effortlessly, almost noiselessly, in the centre of the night-shrouded plain. This happened some time or other during the anonymous war, when people used their cars to go man-hunting in the night.

Bea B. listens to the malediction of Monsieur X:

'Let him who has ears give heed, for the moment has come
to say all these things. The movement and the noise are dying
down now, the machines are stilled at last, and in this silence
I can write down the words I know, the final words perhaps.
He who seeks to know is fated to stand rooted to the ground
like a tree, his eyes rigid. Fear has entered into him and petrified his muscles, turning him into a statue. Let him who seeks
to learn renounce idle chatter and make his ears deaf to the
sounds of songs and sweet music. In the kitchens of flats that
resemble concrete cells the television sets, too, are talking all
the time; but I no longer hear their words, I no longer see

216

anything through their portholes but millions of little blue dots moving continuously from right to left.

& I am alone now, with the words I have to utter, attempting to penetrate the cells' steel walls.

What I say is the truth. I do not lie. Year after year you have been hearing nothing but the truth; everything around you proclaimed it. But you did not want to listen. You have preferred to keep your ears and eyes closed to the spoken and written word, you have closed the door to thought. That is why it is too late, now, and why you are entering the kingdom of shadows, by my side.

Everything around you showed you the right path, but you refused to take it. Cursed be speech, since it has been unable to convince you. Cursed be the intellect, since it has been incapable of understanding the truth.

& indeed, speech was no longer speech but the frenzied clatter of machines. Words were no longer words but merely witless insects dancing in the lamplight. There were thousands of languages, millions of them, even, since each person spoke his own private language: futile noises that conveyed nothing, that had nothing to convey. It would have been better if every woman had torn out her sons' tongues at birth, it would have been better if she had punctured her children's ear-drums, rather than that they should be false to truth.

But they were all born with unmaimed tongue and ears, and for centuries now they have lived in the midst of noise. Their futile words have swept over the earth like a cloud of locusts, obscuring the sun's brightness and turning the fields into deserts.

The storm has been gathering its clouds and sparks for centuries on end, and today it is about to break. Power in all its forms is contained within the sphere that hangs, the colour of molten metal, above the world. One cannot utter so many words with impunity. One cannot make so much noise without fearing lest one day, after having travelled through the crystal labyrinth, the noise's terrible echo may suddenly

217

return, ten times as loud, to shatter the ear-drums. I know it is coming, I can even hear its arrival. But I cannot halt it. Nobody can halt it any longer. The vengeance of objects and noises is raising its whirling funnel in the sky. Let those who are able to run, flee fast. Let those who have ears listen.

Beauty has been invented by the tiny-minded. Together, they have raised the pretentious monuments that defy space and time. For centuries on end they have been creating their towers of stone and cement, their squat breakwaters that keep the sea at bay, their tarred roads that bisect deserts. They have done all that and more. They have invented panes of glass with bottomless reflections, great walls of liquid colour that sparkle with light and life, mirror-cliffs that a single pebble hurled by a single hand could smash to smithereens. Inside these cages they have stored their wealth, their priceless treasures, mountains of gold-dust and precious stones. And these treasures comprised mountains of corpses and rivers of blood. Century after century, this eager throng has been constructing its machines with their gleaming engines, their wheels, their crankshafts. Forces of energy were broken down, then imprisoned in vast ovens. Sweet sap flowed from all the trees, the earth was disembowelled, rivers of mud were diverted from their paths. So much labour, so much power, everywhere!

I am going to tell you what I see. It is a terrible vision, like that of the bone beneath the flesh, a vision that traces its fiery pattern across window-panes and cement slabs alike. It is a vision that I see not only with my own eyes but with all the millions of other open eyes. The camera lenses are focused on the scene, with apertures wide open. I shall try to say with words what everybody *sees* with their eyes, even if I die in the attempt. There are so many words flying in from all directions: how to pierce this thick cloud of insects? I shall try, I shall try.

The riches are enclosed in concrete buildings. Food lies waiting in the halls of gigantic stores. I can see tons of meat,

218

rice, fruit, sugar, salt. Inside the tin cans, food is bathing in its own blood. The light illuminates the mountains of food, makes it all gleam fabulously. Flashes of icy light stream over the cellophane wrappings, the plastic containers conceal many flavours, the glass bottles are full of yellow oil. All possible riches are housed within the aluminium bins inside the white stores. But no-one can get at them. They are very far from the mouth, and they glow dimly, like unreachable planets.

Hunger gnaws at the stomach. A long-drawn-out sound can be heard coming from somewhere inside the earth, a rumbling sound that never ends. It is the sound of hunger. Stares shatter against the plate-glass windows, stares shoot their darts vainly against the reflected tins of food. The human floodtide advances, swirling in huge eddies around the stores. It tightens its circle gradually, pressing with all its hands against the doors and windows. How much longer still? How much longer will this great human mass continue to endure hunger and craving? The living waves break against the white walls. Already the first cracks are beginning to run along the plaster, then quickly fanning out across the surface of the concrete pillars. The façades of the newly-completed buildings are already crumbling into ruin, their windows have already become black holes through which life is leaking, escaping fast.

Beauty is awe-inspiring. It wears a great black breastplate that sends out sparkles. It is cased in iron and bronze, like a samurai. It stands alone in the middle of the sandy desert, like some herculean dynast. To vanquish, to vanquish constantly, that is beauty's aim. All its arms, its daggers, its shields, are massed and ready. The anonymous waves roar down upon it. I do not want to know who will emerge the winner. I do not want to witness any of this. But torrential forces gush endlessly from the grottoes, pour from the mouths of garages, fill the highways and byways with their myriad wheels and headlamps and wings, sweep onwards,

219

leaving ruin in their wake. Might and power have emerged from the ironworks that fashioned them, and now, after a long march, they are rounding on themselves. Enough. At all costs, not to see all that, not to hear all that any longer! But I am nothing. I am merely a mouth full of words, building sentences at random. And these words, too, have become knives, filled with a lust to destroy and kill, like all the others. There are other voices around me, above me. Habbakuk, Micah, Amos, Obadiah. Joel: Proclaim this among the nations: gird your loins for war. Let all the men of war approach and mount! Forge swords out of mattocks, and spears out of bill-hooks. Let the weak say: I AM STRONG.

Nahum: Woe to the murderous city! It is filled to the brim with falsehood and violence. Pillage is rampant within its walls.

The sound of the whip, the shattering din of wheels; horses galloping, chariots bounding forward. Horsemen charging, swords flashing, spears sparkling; and a multitude of wounded, great piles of skeletons; there are corpses past counting, and men stumble over the bodies of their own brothers.

Draw water for the siege. Fortify the ramparts, tread the clay, build brick-kilns, fashion them into powerful resources.

There, fire will consume you, the sword will cleave you, they will devour you like locusts. Multiply, then, like locusts. Multiply like the jelek!

Your merchants are more numerous than the stars of the sky. The locust destroys, then flies away; your princes are like locusts, your captains are like hordes of locusts swooping down onto the hedgerows as the night grows cold. When the sun rises they vanish once more into the unknown.

Jeremiah:

'My bowels! My bowels! I suffer in the very depths of my being. My heart is tortured. I can no longer remain at peace; for, oh my soul, you have heard the sound of the trumpet, the sound of the war alarm.

220

Destruction upon destruction is foretold. The whole earth is devastated. My tents are destroyed, my flags ripped asunder with a single blow.

How much longer shall I see the standard wave, and hear the trumpet sound? For my demented people does not know me. They are demented children who do not understand. They are apt at doing mischief, but they have no skill in doing good.

I look at the earth, and behold it is empty and ravaged; and at the heavens, and their light is no more.

I look at the mountains, and behold they totter, and the hills tremble on their foundations.

I look, and behold there are no more men, and the birds of the sky have fled.

I look, and behold the fertile earth is a desert, and all the towns are razed.

Hasten away, children of Benjamin, escape from the centre of Jerusalem, and sound the trumpet in Tekoa, and raise the signal of alarm upon Beth-haccherem: for evil is watching from the north, and great destruction lurks.

They say: peace, peace. Whereas there is no peace.

I harken to all these voices that trace their neon signs in the night, and it is true that there is no longer peace. External forces are about to unleash their might: they are impatient and poised to leap. They are inhuman forces, born in molten steel, in the interior of explosive machines, in stone, in fire, in the terrible heat concentrated at the very core of things. These thousands of forces are everywhere. Human flesh is a soft fabric into which claw, hook and bullet will plunge. Human flesh, so warm and tender, soon to be consumed by fire. The gutters lie waiting for the streams of blood, the deserts of sand have turned their plains into vast sheets of blotting-paper. Do not linger. Flee! But there is no escaping. It is late now, the gates are closed, the lights have been extinguished, all is dark.

There are no colours any more, there can never be any

again. The blues of the unfathomed deep, the verdigrised madnesses, the purples of sensual pleasure, the grey deaths, the pearly lustre of eyes, the bronze-hued flights, the white white skies, the plains of mud, the torrents of blood, all the colours shall be black, black do you hear, black! For the earth is criminal ...

The foolish folk were living inside the war, and did not know it. They thought that war was something alien, something that happened very far away, in forgotten countries, in savage forests, or else in the depths of the sinister valleys that fringe the earth. They thought that war was like the murmur of a storm brewing far beyond the horizon, and that they thus had the time to number the hairs of their women's heads and write poems about the death of their pet dog.

But they were living in the midst of war. They were living at the very centre of the massacre, they, their women and their dogs. Each day the fearful whirlwind forms around them, each day the nameless forces hurl themselves furiously at each other. Forces that are bent on slaying sight, on slaying thought. The forests are alive with electricity, whole towns are ruins of stone released from gravity. With their oak beams and their steel bars they strike, yell into ears, gnash at eyes, rip nostrils. Strange foreign cities with murderous walls! Killers, killers, killers, all killers, the walls, the smooth plaster surfaces, the gold bricks that echo the grating of fingernails. Killers! All objects rush headlong at me, while volumes ripple, grow hollow with dizziness and change shape. Angles alternately sag and bulge, reflections dissolve into rain. Sounds seethe along the pipes of organs, then burst forth. Inside the white stores the objects glow with hatred, and the mirrors reflect back the arrows of looks. Words come to birth deep in the throat, words bristling with stings and mandibles, words that pour forth relentlessly. They leap from the pages of books, from the loudspeakers of television sets, from magnetic tapes, from gramophone records and from the darkness of cinema halls. And none of these words mean peace, or love.

222

All around, the soulless mass constructs its ramparts and builds its prisons. It raises its immense walls, its towers, its pyramids. Then it loses its way within this new labyrinth, and slowly the walls start closing in! The crazed mass lays out its highways from one end of the earth to the other, yet violent death overtakes it! The mass itself, with the flickering flame of a single match, has lit the raging fire that is consuming it. Beware! Danger! Danger ... But I can say nothing, since I myself grew up with those same flames.

My curse is that I am one when I need to be a million. My voice is senseless. What is one voice against an entire army? My body will be trampled underfoot. My gullet will be throttled. A single cry has no more importance than a single scale on the skin of a boa constrictor.

I can see the hurricane of luxury and beauty bearing down. I am inside the temple, and the wind is carrying me away. I know only what is coming, what is already happening. I did not guess this, nor did I dream it. I did not hide at the back of a windowless shack to drink tonga. Quite the contrary: I lived out of doors, I opened my eyes to the light and I listened to all the noises. It became obvious. Already the air's lower layers are drawing aside, a few seconds before the explosion. Already the colour of the sky is changing, and the thunder's whitish ideograms are scattered far and wide. Something is coming now. Something has travelled in a streak through continents and centuries and is coming now. Something has run like a shiver over the skin of a thousand generations, and is coming now.

The very ones who spoke to you of peace and gentleness were themselves at war, although fear kept the knowledge from them.

Once the armies are locked in combat, the earth will explode. The deflagration will not be savage, and may even simply take place without anyone realizing it, very gently. Perhaps destruction will arrive like a fire that kindles slowly, twig by twig. Or like a steady flame from the sun, shooting up for millions of miles without flickering. And it will gnaw and rend mercilessly.

I hate those who have confidence in their name. Madness is not an alien thing; hatred springs from within men, and they destroy each other without realizing. It is happening at this very moment. Look around you, watch the war in action. Listen to the war being waged along the highways, in the airports, in the immaculate buildings, in the underground passages, along the esplanades littered with thousands of abandoned vehicles, everywhere, in the city, over the sea of cement, over the plain of cement, on the mountains and in the sky of cement. War has glorious names of victories, resounding names like Super, Parking, Videostar, The Animals, Molybdenum, Steel, Zeiss, Chrysler, Flaminaire, Honda. It has names that are already murderers. Its iron and concrete workings are mausoleums, and its gigantic stores glowing redly with merchandise are fortified castles with raised drawbridges. I enter the great white hall, walk over the plastic flooring that the light strikes harshly, and look for the four pillars where I must place my four bombs. The rustle of silver as the water gushes into the baths and mosaic swimming-pools, the soft, limpid water lovelier than the air, purer than the air; yet the baths will drown the women who fall asleep in them, and the fountains will spurt blood into their basins. Gases pour from exhaust-tanks and float above the streets like a fog; lungs are corroded, soot-stained.

There are too many things, I tell you, and the weary masses are close to exhaustion, There is too much richness, clarity, music; there are too many words, adjectives, adverbs, participles. There is too much movement.

The colour red is intense and suffuses the sky from end to end. Even the shadows are red. How to survive, bathed always in this blood, when I would have been perfectly content with blue, or with green if necessary? Sharp sounds pierce the air like arrows, but they are far more deadly. Deep sounds continually shake the ground and split walls apart. In fortresses with countless windows, anonymous monsters devour paper and human flesh, monsters who are always demanding more paper, more identities. Each day, in the streets, words unfurl: new words, new crimes. Skulls are filled with images that multiply and grow more beautiful every second. Every second, movement devours speed. All around, girders rise from the building sites, weaving their iron towers foot by foot upwards. The cemeteries have tombs that look like railway carriages. The clouds have come so low, today, that the lightning-conductors are gashing their undersides. The night, traversed by millions of volts, is whiter than the day. Underground, the sewers ferry their stinking rivers towards the stinking sea. Mouths wolf down tons of cream and cheese, tons of meat, bread and tinned fruit. The tide of cattle flowing through the gates of the slaughterhouses never stops. Machines flatten the hills, explosions disembowel the mountains, sending their entrails of sand and clay gushing out. It is permanent war, the war of all epochs and all places. Why should it, how could it, ever stop, since the hands work to produce what the intestines destroy? How to halt the flow of words, how to squeeze them back once more into their mute matrices, when language itself is simply life and death?

Yes, all the objects upon this earth that for centuries on end have been stretched, compressed, suffocated, imprisoned, are doomed to annihilation! For whole centuries the elixir of life was kept imprisoned within its curved wall of glass, and the glass itself was imprisoned by the light, and the light by its circles of air, and the air itself by the weight of the infinite that pressed down upon it like a hand.

Men are waiting all around the white buildings, waiting in a circle around the mountains of gold and nourishment. Many children are waiting, too, watching with eyes dazzled by desire and hatred. By the edge of swimming-pools filled with clear blue water, dust-streaked men and women wait patiently for a chance to quench their thirst. Sugar, salt and oil sparkle from the depths of the great stores. Hunger and

225

boredom send their waves surging through the crowds besieging the doors. But soon the polished plate-glass windows will shatter spontaneously, and the avalanche of riches will smother mouths and eyes. Beauty, when it has become ugly, is able to destroy itself spontaneously.

So much opulence, so many crimes! A black gas has seeped inside the soul and eaten it away, the fatal gas that is the effluvium of charnel-houses and shanty-towns. You have been breathing it all the time, it had entered your bloodstream while you were still in your mother's belly. Each sip of water, each scrap of food that you took was a little more poison in your body. When you opened your eyes for the first time you saw it immediately: the endless desert, the violence, the ravaged scar-marked skin. But in your determination to forget the sight, you have scattered your words in reckless profusion, and you have sought refuge at all costs: some deep grotto, a woman, a child, no matter what. But it was impossible. No-one gets away, just like that. One stays put, a machine like all one's fellows, geared to kill and steal and smash.

Hark now, I am speaking to you! I tell you that I have needed to close eyes that are deep within me, and cursed be those who constrained me to do so! What have I done? What gift of mine has helped to change the world? To save myself from ever entering the world, would I not have done better to kill the woman who was carrying me, by kicking her to death from within her belly? But this malediction of causeless couplings of people and events was already laid upon my forebears. There was nothing I could do about it. The war had started centuries ago, constructing its criminal temples and cities, building its walls from stone and bronze steeped in violence.

In those times I did not yet exist, my mother was eternal and I roamed obscurely in the depths of jungles. I was submissive, and I waited, inhabited by a new athletic desire: that the blood-drenched corridor to life should open up. Heavy as lead, I awaited the world's raging fires. I felt tinglings of hope stir in my knotted muscles, and it is ever since those days of herculean childhood that I have forged a straight path and lived life to the full.

Then I saw a woman coming towards me, a woman so beautiful that it was as though life had never previously existed on this planet. She was walking alone along the cement-lined street, in the midst of the violence and chaos. She did not see me. She glided effortlessly over the ground, as though upon wheels, parting the air and the light as she went. The sun lit spangled reflections across her body, setting her hair and clothes on fire. She advanced in silence, encased in iron and nylon, striking the ground with her hard heels. Her long legs passed perpetually through space, and her transparent eyes looked straight through my own, like headlamps. One day, by chance, I saw this woman walking away into the distance. I saw that there was a magic force alive within her, as within all women, a force that I would never understand. This was her way of proclaiming nonchalantly that violence was beautiful, and that therefore a universal explosion was imminent. I was unable to follow her. I was unable to speak to her, or to the others. I was unable to kill her. Instead, a sudden shiver ran through me, a sort of fever. I sensed that this woman was the war's figure-head, gliding safely through the scenes of battle while slaughter raged around her. Her water-repellent skin was moulded to her flesh like a breast-plate, and her garments clung to her like a second skin. She was coasting aimlessly along, sparkling brightly, a beautiful new car with windows raised. Let him who knows her speak to her, let him rip her belly open and read her smoking entrails. She is called Bea B., or else Beauty Lane. She is also called *Bothrops atrox*. Let him who knows something about her, or about any other woman, speak now. Perhaps the war's mechanism is still inside her body, perhaps it could be torn out. Speak! Speak! But no-one speaks. Each day, each year, I pass the glittering body of *Bothrops atrox* bound, no doubt, for the far end of the labyrinth to beget her foetuses of dynamite and guncotton. She must be stopped! Her skin must be stripped off, and air and water allowed to filter through her body. But the air is absent and the water is imprisoned within pipes and taps.

Ku! Listen! You dwell in Alahiyi, o dreaded woman! There, in Alahiyi, you dwell, o white woman! No-one is ever lonely in your company. You are very beautiful. No-one is ever lonely in your company. You have shown me the way. I shall never again be sad. You have set me on the white path. You have set me down, there, in the middle of the earth. I shall stand upright on the earth. No-one is ever lonely in my company. I am very beautiful. You have placed me in the white house. I shall be inside it when it starts to move. No-one will ever be lonely in my company. In truth, I shall not be sad. Unhesitatingly, you have decided things for me.

Listen, woman of steel, listen to me. Give your perfect engine a few moments' rest, stay still for once. One word from you, a single word, and maybe the war would end. Give your orders. Then you will rise above the swirling eddies of flesh and bone, clad in your veil of light, and you will be queen.

But her painted mouth never utters a word, and her eyes glint behind the lenses of her Polaroid glasses. Around her, the world is tensing its stomach muscles, voiding an endless stream of new things, unknown objects, from all its secret orifices. Heaps are mounting skywards, mountains of gold and beauty. Second by second, they proliferate upon the earth in all the gaudy splendour of their aluminium casings, their wrapping paper, their coloured buttons, their plastic-coated surfaces, their networks of wires. Machines, boxes, cylinders, reels, all made for her. The tons of new goods inside the stores and on display in their windows and showcases. There is not enough flesh for them, there are not enough noses, mouths or eyes for them. There are not enough thoughts for all the words that swarm constantly in the air like clouds of buzzing insects. There are not enough roads for all the wheels.

Ceaselessly, night and day, they are born: tinned pine-apple, tinned ham, fruits, vegetables, perfumes in their little square bottles, Onyx, Tabac, Arpège, Old Leather, Chanel, Ma Griffe, liqueurs with their magical colours, Drambuie, Misty Islay, alcohols that are white, green, yellow, boxes of chocolates from Cadbury's and Lindt and Bahlsen and Fry's, white sugar in thousands of tiny crystals, tobacco packed in the thin tubes of cigarettes, Carmen, Philip Morris, Mekong, Alas, Newport, Camel, Gitanes, W, Peter Stuyvesant, Marcovitch, Craven A, Krung Thong, Pall Mall! All this wealth is spread out there in front of me, and their glitter dazzles my eyes! The thousands of little bottles containing iridescent liquids, the tubes full of pink or mauve lozenges that conceal microbe-killing agents; the thousands upon thousands of aerosol bombs and ballpoint pens and women's stockings and fabrics and soap tablets and razor blades! All shining with their fierce power, with their beautiful vulgar colours: vast deserts of paper as white as salt, simmering oceans of perfumes, atmospheres reeking with poison for the mass slaughter of flies and mosquitoes! I walk through the labyrinth filled with facile mysterious objects. I pass through clouds of silver, I float upon waves of orange-flavoured liquids streaked by streams of tiny bubbles! All the objects are making their noise in unison, and I can hear their deep refrain pulsing with many varied rhythms. The world is offering its own blood for sale! In identical mineral-water bottles the ice-cold liquid is waiting, bulging against the metal capsule that grips with a scalloped rim. On the painted labels the living names are bulging, too: Pschitt, Schweppes, Coke, Fanta, Barilitos del Doctor Brown!

The end is near. Let those who have ears, listen. Let those who have mouths, taste. Let those who have eyes, see. Let those who have skin and nerves lie prostrate and travel along the thousands of tiny paths.

Depths beckon everywhere. Everywhere, bottomless chasms open up, doors yawn. There are more souls than there are grains of sand along the beach of the Great Black River. The warriors are like flies. They are like the bacillae inside a single drop of water, and there are oceans of drops. All is permeated by truth and life. Human knowledge is not so vast as the number of objects offered to its scrutiny; the number of words is vaster than language itself. Thought, limitless thought, stretches in all directions. The most secret dreams are marked out perfectly clearly, perfectly visibly. The mysteries are not inner mysteries, they do not hide in the depths of grottoes, they do not slip by, on the other side of windows, as shadows do. For all these things are happening on the surface, thrusting their myriad roots up towards the atmosphere, and reality has a million eyes!

Those who wanted to explore the depths, those who looked backwards, those who longed to rip the masks off all the faces were out to conquer the heart, all of them. With their gimlets, they bored through the bony shells and ogled the magma. But what they now saw was terrifying: for at the bottom of the well, what was shining was *still the surface*.

No more symbols. The jungle had written everything into the structure of its leaves. The snakes had written their whole history, of cold and sun and venom, on their glistening skins.

I say to you also: there is nothing that is invented. The reservoir of substance is immense, frontierless, existing from all eternity. Objects create those that create them: then they kill them. There are so many people. So many things. Life has so many claws, hooks, nails, eyes, cog-wheels, camouflage. And there is no escaping from it all. The earth cannot carry this weight much longer; it has started to crumble, and the cities are crumbling with it. I can see roads exploding under the pressure of passing tyres; the steel walls of factories glow red like furnaces. Men choke in the perfume-saturated air, women asphyxiate themselves by clogging the pores of their skin with creams and lurid colour schemes. Intelligence is a wall rearing miles into the air, ready to strike. It is too late for anyone to throw himself in front of a moving railway engine

230

and tackle it. The giant words written in thousand-foot-high letters batter away continuously. The roots tighten their grip around the blocks of stone and shatter them. There is so much light: white, harsh, bouncing off the ceilings, flooding from the floor and walls, pouring from the sky, the sea, the volcanoes. It devastates the ground methodically, slicing space with the strokes of its great scythe. The eyes that look at it are scorched, down to the retina, and the light penetrates the body to destroy individual thoughts. Let those who have dark glasses put them on, for the great fire that is kindling will rage ten thousand times more fiercely than the flame that leaps from a blowlamp; the light will be so intense that by contrast the day will seem like night. There will be so many riches stockpiled in the shops that desire will no longer exist, and whole populations will die of hunger in the streets.

There they all are, the accursed objects. Ranged along the length of the supermarkets' corridors, come from the farthest outposts of the universe, all their names being proclaimed in unison:

```
Lifebuoy      Paic
Palmolive     Pax
Safeguard     Sunil                         Exciting
   Lux        Breeze        Isinis          Dolce Finish
Cologne       Tide          Arpin           Majorque
   GL         Laden         O.B.A.O.         Saskia
Dogne         Persil                        Gerbe
              Omo                           Bafix
              Ajax                          Le Bourget
                            Martens         Supp'hose
   Gibbs                    Danone          Top Liberté
   Colgate                  Leon
Vademecum                   Miam-miam
Dentol NH4                  Balkan
Kolynos Ice Blue            Gervais    Elizabeth Arden
Email Diamant               Pykovsky        Novessence
   Sanogyl                                  Lanvin
              Rexona                        Lubin        Dim'up
       Cashmere Bouquet                     Trim         Kayser
              Dédoril                       Caron        Burlington
              Cadum                         Gemey        Escapade
                                            Eye Liner
                                            Canoe Dana
              Nilsol                        Bien-être
                                            Pompeïa
```

231

Substances! Substances! Glowing, soft, fragile, inflammable, just like smoke-clouds. Red, black, other intense colours. It is they who do the thinking, now. It is they who invent the histories and religions and sciences. They move, they entwine. Rhovyl chlorofibre, Polyamide, Rhodia 100% polyester, acetate, Gama, Skaï Kreon, ACSA acrylic fibre, Leacril, acrylic Dralon, synthetic polyurethane, textured Brinyl polyamide, Masulyne, Mérinovyl, Clévyl, Flanyl, Dropnyl polyamide 66, Terital, Tercryl, Viscose, Fibranne, Crylor, expanded Vinyl.

Destruction is already near. It will soon strike. This is written in the centre of all crossroads where the crowd is to be found tightening its running knot. It is written on the lanes of motorways, as well, where ridiculous metallic insects dart along at 75 mph, and it is written on the wings of aeroplanes. It is painted on the tall buildings' white façades, on the dusty panes of endless rows of windows, in the railway stations, the hospitals, the post offices. It is written; but no-one wanted to read the message. Everywhere were signs that foretold the advent of war, but no-one wanted to heed the signs. Various noises, various kinds of music, walls of words and ideas all arrived at the speed of a galloping horse. Alarm sirens echoed through the empty air, the lights all changed to red, hoardings collapsed with a single thud, but the cars continued to speed along the roads, and the crowd continued to tighten the knots of its anguish.

Destruction is near. This is how things will come to pass.

First of all, there will be signs in the sky and on the earth. Great silent aeroplanes will slice through the clouds and crash into the ground with their 137 passengers. Green gleams zigzagging above the horizon will illuminate the trees like searchlights. The sun will shine in isolation in the centre of the ether, like a naked bulb dangling from its cord. And circles of light will swim around it for hours on end, and all surfaces of iron or glass will start to sparkle. The sun will dazzle the eyes, burn the skin, frizzle the hair, dry up rivers and seas. There will be many other portents in the sky as well, mushroom-shaped clouds, lightning flashes tracing their patterns of rigid colourless fissures over the city, flights of gulls, flocks of vultures, swarms of gnats. When you see these things, know that the time is near.

The sea will churn up its waves, and the swollen rivers' muddy waters will overflow their banks. This, Hewandam has proclaimed.

There will be other signs. Over the surface of the earth, the slab-like roofs will bristle with antennas, and the air will resound with the continual passage through it of mysterious waves. Images and sounds will dart tirelessly between the four invisible walls, like flights of bats. Above the cities, as far as the eye can see, immense reddish haloes will appear, and sparkle night and day, while clouds of gas inflate their fluorescent domes.

There will be other, far stranger, signs: in the dark streets you will see great red letters light up like lightning flashes as they wink on and off above doors and shop windows. The words will advance in file, then erase themselves, then re-appear once more. Terrible insane words casting their hooks wildly, words which will say such things as

SHLAK! SLURP! KWIK! BOOPS!
PFFTSHSHGONG! RÔÔÔÔ!

and you will know fear. For no-one escapes these words.

But there will be yet more signs. Along the avenues that stretch from one end of the earth to the other, there will be lines of stationary black cars, burning their fuel away with deep throbbing sounds; the traffic-jams will last for years on end. The engines will suffocate in the hot air, the motor-horns will rend the sky, together, with their piercing shrieks! Terrible reflections will be seen on the cars' shiny panels, and tyre marks will streak the roadway's tarred surface. Behind each vehicle, a black silencer will spew forth its asphyxiating

233

gas: thousands and thousands of twisting tubes suspended beneath the rear bumper, intermittently belching out blueish clouds that the wind will be powerless to dispel.

Remember these signs well, for, in truth, when you see them appear you will know that the end is near, and that the war has started.

That is not all. I see the statue of Moloch-Baal, and his belly is a fiery furnace. Goyayota is not dead, and Hinupoto is on the prowl everywhere, claiming his bowlful of female blood. Their signs originated in the depths of history, together with murder and insanity. All the long-forgotten voices will return, one day.

I hear the cries of Cuauhtemoc and Condorcanqui. I hear an anonymous song that goes something like this: 'I was conceived during a night of torment ... The wind and the rain were my cradle ... Nobody takes pity on my misery ... Accursed be my birth. Accursed, myself.' I hear many other songs, other refrains. They make so much noise around me that I no longer know who I am. I want peace, I want to be alone. But it has become impossible. What is to be must be. The mountains must collide, and the crowd's hollowed eddies must swirl around the doors of all the cut-price stores. I shall do my utmost to destroy all these riches, all this beauty, for they are like a treacherous swamp. I want to rediscover the face I used to own, rediscover silence, forget the directions indicated interminably by the great yellow arrows by the sides of roads. Let those who understand, rally to me, let them smash the hoardings on which the names of war are written. Let them smash the shop windows, let them liberate all that pent-up energy, before it is too late. But it is already too late, and the forces have begun to liberate themselves unaided!

Therefore look closely: the signs are there. They have appeared. The ditches alongside highways are littered with inert carcasses leaking water and oil, their windows shattered. And these shells house incongruous white shapes like statues carved from ice, frozen in grotesque postures. In the white upturned faces the eyes have stopped working, are wedged between the eyelids' shields. The tiny cubes of fragmented glass scattered along the black tar of the roadway are gathered up to fashion strings of beads.

I know that the war has started. I am among those who realize this fact, and that is why I am afraid to walk the streets. There are so many signs everywhere. How to ignore them? How to avert the eyes, how to set one foot in front of the other? Every hour of every day, I read in the newspapers about how the battles are progressing. The blurred photos show faces that are staring directly at me; hovering on the other side of the screen of tear-gas, they call for help and wave their arms around. They are nameless. They are nothing. Their acts do not count. What counts is the endless procession of their faces, one after another, each trying to convince or dominate. The sentences display their words in heavy type, filling the pages of newspapers. Meaningless sentences, but in huge quantities, armies of them, dizzy litanies. AMERICA. 'Is there no room left in the world for.' SOS. The countdown has begun. Is dead. The revolutionary forces. Terrible accident. Da Nang. Taos. To be sure, one will bear constantly in mind that the one precept, in the matter of truth, is to eschew systematic negation even in the presence of facts that have every semblance of being intractable. It will be recalled that, as Geo has observed so succinctly.

The signs are present. They are legion. This morning I saw a blind man tapping his way along. The other day I saw a fairy pass by in the street; she was silvery-haired, wore a pink cloak, and was briskly wheeling a child's pram in which a little beige dog was sitting upright. Then she was gone. I have seen hatred blaze in the eyes of a motorist who believed that someone else had stolen his parking space. I have seen the city walls reaching almost to the heavens, unyielding walls built to last a thousand years. In all the shops and stores, hands are reaching out towards the gaudy containers. I have heard the telephone's strident jangling, and a mouth cry hullo! into the black bakelite capsule. All this has a meaning of some kind, it is all held together by wire and string and other bonds. It all moves according to a fixed order, and that order is: destroy! Every ten seconds a new machine gleaming with polished chrome appears on the scene. Novelty destroys: it swells up into the air, between the walls, like cigarette smoke. Every ten seconds a new idea is born, struggling, trying to fill space like a gas. There can be no more waiting. People are no longer content to wait. Movement devours itself, movement consumes its own inventions. Woe to all that moves! For all the meshed speeds are accelerating towards each other, and the moment of impact cannot be far off.

There will be many other signs, for those who have the wit to read them. They will appear every day, every hour, even. They will be written on clock dials and on the pages of telephone directories. Little barbed signs, little ciphers, to mark out a flare-path for the war. There will be frenzied hours, followed by hours of exhaustion. There will be explosions of such sudden and fearful violence that it will be like the moment when an earthquake erupts and buildings evaporate. There will be plaques, yet heavier and more menacing plaques, commemorating peace, and the desert will seem to cover the world. Listen to me: what will you do now that everything around you is turning into a *sign*?

There will be exquisitely beautiful, utterly desirable women, giant women standing naked against the walls, and the rivers of sperm will never rise high enough to cover them. Alien women with metallic bodies and white hair and long slim legs sheathed in fishnet stockings. If you should see such a woman, know that the time is near.

For these women there will be new abodes, new machines. Their glittering eyes impart a red glow to the piles of gold and food. The earth will clothe itself in all the fabrics, some of them soft and smooth, some of them rainbow-hued, some that look like leather, others made of chemicals. The ground will be a carpet of yielding furs, fountains of limpid water will flow, the night will blossom with red and blue stripes in zebra patterns. These women will arrive in armies, bearing grotesque and frightening names like Ronixa and Eve and *Bothrops atrox* and *Natrix natrix*. They will attempt to save the world, making a rampart of their transparent bodies. Their breasts will be shields, their warm, navel-adorned bellies will be armour plating. Their slender hands, adorned with nails that are painted pink or mother-of-pearl or gold, will try to keep fear at bay by tearing and strangling. Their lips will utter words in a thin lilting voice, snatches of words to sing. There will be no ideas or feelings present in these warm waves that will ripple gently towards the enemy, only goodness. But the enemy has no ears, he is incapable of hearing your women's voices.

They will have eyes, too, not eyes for looking or comparing, but speckled stones that will radiate light; their calm fires may scorch your inner being, or else they may permeate you gently with their symmetrical, fresh, powerful fountainheads. They will no longer be machines that see, or keyholes, or revolver barrels, but your own eyes, exiled from their sockets and staring at you. When you see these women close to you, when you pass them in the street, when they suddenly appear on the cinema screen, you will feel even more forsaken, for you will know at once that they are the final rampart, and that war lies just ahead.

Blood will flow. But these strange women love blood so much that they wash their lithe bodies in these red rivers. They will take the barbarous riches in their hands, they will wrap bright cloths around themselves, they will sprinkle gold-dust on their hair. There can never be enough water and milk and perfumed oil to bathe their arms and thighs. They are there, they are already there. They have come to conquer the world, immense women as tall as buildings, as vast as railway stations, their eyes as brilliant as the sun, as deep as the ocean. I watch their slow arrival, as they walk down the avenues with great supple strides that shake the earth. Their hair floats in the air, blends with the air's molecules, forces its way down my throat and chokes me. Their breasts are hard like metal spheres, their sexes smoulder like volcanoes. Sweetness sends out its acrid cloud, perfumes strike down. Beauty comes like a liquid wall, overflowing, smashing its way through. No-one at all has any inkling how this force was born. It is a force that burns slowly, like a phosphorus bomb, or else spreads out in a sheet of flame, like napalm. The forces of beauty are more terrible than crime, because no-one is capable of resisting their hypnotic gaze. Perhaps this is a long-contemplated vengeance; or perhaps all the desires that the centuries have accumulated, all the fits of passion, are reversing their outward course and re-entering men's bodies. There is too much thought. There are too many palpitations, too many tremors. Too much noise is rolling through the sky. The swollen cities are exploding. There is too much sweetness, terrible sweetness. Perfumes turn into poisons, caresses tear the skin away, delights that have suffused the flesh a million times suddenly rend it with pain, and one can hear the scream well up in the throat.

There is too much consciousness: that is what I wanted to say to you. Showers of arrows, hails of bullets spurt from eyes, eyes watching from every corner, bent upon destruction. They know too much. The eyes have vanquished the gods, have raked the depths of space, and now their gaze is returning from the long voyage, fiercer and emptier than before. Listen to me: let those who have eyes, pluck them out! Let them hasten to snap the thread of their gaze, for their gaze no longer belongs to them. But it is too late, far too late. The gaze has returned and begun its perforations. In the depths of space and within the earth's confines it has found nothing but huge mirrors. It has shattered against impenetrable surfaces, it has dispersed in ten thousand directions. Faster than light, it leaps from one mirror to the next, and each ray is like a metal splinter from an exploding shell. And I am not alone.

I am soaring aloft with the others, fast, very fast, striking out and stabbing at random.

War is when a whole world is gripped by violence. It is when there is no longer any silence or repose. It is when the towns are perpetually ablaze; when the machines open and close their valves inexorably. War is 12,000 revolutions per minute, 65 feet per second, multiplied 30,000 times, Mach 2, G6, 2000 ASA, separated, hashed, cut into tiny pieces, crushed by piezo-forces of 10^6, star at 12,000°, stress produced by 10,000 blind megajoules, suns of 100,000,000 blind phots, magnetic fields of 800,000 incomprehensible gauss, chasms, chasms splitting the world in every direction. Millions of men, women, children, rats. They move in unison; I see their cohorts advancing up the streets, I hear the shrill small cries rising from their throats. Where to go? The world is a raging Sahara, black with long palisades. Where to sleep? Soon there will be only a single language, only a single thought. I feel the fringes of the whirlwind passing close to me, as the spinning wind draws me towards its vortex. Nothing can withstand whirlwinds. When you see the wind appear you will know that the moment has come, that there is nothing more to be done. The moment when everything will be violent, when everything will be absolutely alive. This is the way it is. Nothing can withstand total life.

Soon, the cities will explode. In a flash they will consume whole centuries of energy and thought. A great cloud shaped like a jelly-fish will spread slowly in the sky, while a reddish glow lights up the horizon. So do not imagine that it will be a sunset like all the others. We are inside the tall furnaces, and the incandescent heat rises slowly, degree by degree. The light widens its beam, discharges its flux through an unseen breach, demolishes the ramparts, flattens the armoured doors. On childish faces the dark glasses melt instantaneously, and the boiling cellulose encrusts the empty eye-sockets. The colours of things are charred, and soon there will be nothing left but two rival vastnesses of black and white. Photographs

239

should never have been invented. Now they are taking their revenge, and it is the whole world that is becoming flat, smooth, rigid in its absurd posture. On women's bodies the clothes have stuck to the skin, nylon and silk fused with the living cells. The redness of their hair is that of flames. The asphyxiating odours of lavender and jasmine have seeped through the pores. The round-flanked cars have set their violence in motion; they are speeding along the endless motorways, seeking to kill, for that is their sole motivation. Long sharp knives have sprouted from their wings, and their black tyres are like the jaws of the sharks around Port Jackson.

In the stores, the merchandise is exploding. All the brand-new, gleaming, sumptuous objects are bursting through the great windows, cascading into the street. The hard-edged tins of foodstuff are splitting skulls, the bottles are gashing throats with their jagged ends. The crowd is milling around the streets, drunk from looting, drunk with food. The banks are burning like barns, mountains of twenty-dollar bills are heaped up in the courtyards, and men are drenching them with petrol and setting a match to them. Tons of documents have been dragged up from the cellars and are carpeting the streets with their old torn leaves. The books, all the books, are being hurled into great glowing furnaces, and the chimneys belch out columns of black smoke night and day. All the words produced by useless thought, printed in little black characters on numbered pages. The bibles, the novels, the dictionaries, the cook-books, the history manuals, the atlases, the philosophical treatises, the manifestos, the propaganda speeches. the long interminable poems that spoke of the colour of the sky, the colour of the sea, the colour of the green eyes of a woman called Rosalind Lind. You have written these books, you have sought to immobilize your thoughts on the white pages of books; and see how these words are smothering you and choking you. They descend upon you like swarms of flies, and they devour your lips and eyes. You had wanted to remain ignorant of the hatred of those who starved to death for nothing, you had simply wanted to build empires of thought, great iron towers balanced miraculously upon the ground, without paying heed to what was lurking in the shadows. The armies of servants are in revolt. They are streaming through the city, razing buildings as they go.

There is so much money everywhere. The merchants have hoarded their treasures for centuries on end. They have bought and sold everything: lands, flocks, forests, women, children. Over their counters, inside the cement blockhouses, they have sold everything in existence, everything that lives. They have sold wars, and soldiers' corpses, they have sold passions, desires, dreams. They have conquered their vast domains, they have built their concrete strongholds, they have invented cities and underground tunnels. They have sold the searing bomb and the healing bandage. It is they who have pronounced the malediction; it has never ceased filtering from their fortresses. They have sold language itself, they have made words out of letters as tall as mountains, they have covered the earth with paper and ink, to dominate, to conquer. And behold the malediction is rounding upon them, for their strength is ebbing away. The great white department stores stand in fragile isolation among the plains of car parks. Just a little dynamite at the base of their four columns, and they would soon be reduced to dust. A single spark in their warehouses, a match thrown into their fuel-tanks, and they would soon be burned to a cinder. Let those who have matches, come. Matches are good for more than kindling the tips of cigarettes.

In the streets, and along the deserted esplanades, sinister black buses are prowling. From time to time, mean-faced men pour out of these buses and fan out through the streets. They wear black metal helmets with chin-guards, goggles, gas-masks. They are encased in belted leather jackets. Their black uniforms shine in the light. Their fists grip long truncheons of weighted rubber. They carry sub-machine-guns and automatic pistols. They advance in serried ranks, shields raised, and their boots trample the bodies that their truncheons have felled. Occasionally they dart onto the road-way among the burning vehicles, and hit out. But it is as though they were hitting out at empty space, as though they were trying to shatter water with their clubs. When you see these armies appear in the streets, you will know that the great stores and office buildings have begun to tremble on their bases. You will know that all the words have begun their ravaging re-entry into human heads, and that all the riches have begun exploding. When you peer from a high balcony and see a group of black-clad men set up a machine-gun post and fire into the crowd, you will know that the war I am tell-ing you about has just begun. When you see helicopters swooping over the city to pick up the bodies of the victims, you will no longer be able to say: joy, sweetness, light, beauty; only: war, war.

Perhaps so far the war is simply within myself. Perhaps there is nothing of the sort abroad in the world, and the forces I am telling you about have never existed. I am surrounded by so many voices, so much noise, that it is difficult to understand.

The other day I saw an extraordinary landscape in which each detail, each outline was crystal clear. Black rocks, and others that were red, yellow, green, white. A little farther on, there was the sea with all its rippling waves. It is true that when I looked at all this I could see no signs of war. The scene was very far away from my dreams, at the other end of the earth, full of an immense mute peace. Nothing was happening in this place; I mean, nothing menacing or de-structive. Perhaps it was a vision of the world from the far side of war, and that is why there were no signs to be seen. The storm had passed, sweeping over these smooth surfaces with-out finding anything to destroy. I have seen many other such things; and I would like you to see them too, as though through a dog's eyes, not hoping or expecting anything.

And I have watched the girl as she stands there, waiting for the bus. Her eyes are calm, scarcely flickering between the rows of lashes. In front of her, in the street, the roaring flood-tide of cars and lorries. But she scarcely notices it, as her eyes gaze into the far distance, straining to glimpse the greenish dome that is rolling towards her, bearing in front of it, in the centre of a yellow bubble, the figure 9.

There are these flashes of peace and silence amid the clouds. Every ten seconds, without a sound, they light up the whole sky with strange patterns that are very soft and very white. These lightning flashes are within me, passing through me in quick succession, like the coldness within heat, or like the heat that lies at the heart of coldness. It must be due to them that there is war but no massacre. They appease violence, because they travel in the same direction.

Once and for all, here are the things I like:

> trees
> plants
> pebbles
> women's hair
> the eyes of animals
> the noise of rain on tin roofs
> the winking lights on cars
> Tonala pottery
> cold-water taps
> night sounds
> summer lightning
> plain cigarettes
> the pyramid of Palenque
> oranges
> spiders
> towers
> the Menez Hom
> girls waiting for buses
> deserts
> electric light bulbs
> the ...

These are my own lightning flashes stabbing the night now. But I know that they bear with them the whole weight of violence and money and hatred. And that is why I no longer desire to read poems that speak of these lights, poems that neglect the world in favour of a woman, a bird, a seed.

The other day, too, I saw these three little Arab children playing in the dust. They were shouting as they played. Since it was morning, I said 'Sbah el kheir' to them as I passed by. They stopped and looked at me but did not answer. Then I went away.

Another day, I saw the squashed corpse of a dog on the road, and a pack of starving dogs devouring it.

I have seen a letter that had this written on its pages:

'There is something I remember, though I don't know whether I can bring the image of it to life. It was in some town or other, where I happened to be, and I was in this house of assignation. One could go upstairs and come down again without being seen. The façade, the inside walls, the staircases, the doors were all grey. An anonymous house. On every floor of this huge building, in every room, were people making love. Passports were taken away in the front parlour, and returned on leaving. In each room, the same music, the same drinks. To get out of the place one had to walk along an endless corridor that led into a windowless courtyard. The door opened and closed again unaided. An elephant's trunk. The sense of despair that permeated this house, representing such total flight and abandonment by so many men and women, continues to haunt me to this day.'

It is all this, you understand, all this put together. All these things appearing in an endless stream, happening constantly, smothering me. Not just myself, but the others too. It is all this that goes to make up war; life is breaking loose, demolishing walls. Beauty, gentleness, suffering, passionate love, pity, hatred, indifference: there are too many feelings. They bounce from wall to wall, trying to find a way out, a window, a drain, any kind of hole. They proliferate by cellular division. Great waves, great shudders, swamps of fever and doubt. Permanent eruption flowing from all its craters, the boiling lava spreading its successive folds wider and wider. All these words, cries, appeals, 'I love you!' 'I want!' 'Down with!' 'Long live!' 'Drink!' 'I think!' 'Eat!' 'I believe!' 'I am!' 'Buy!' 'Smoke!' 'Invest!' 'I dream of!' 'It's mine!' 'Kill!' 'Kill!' 'Kill!', all these explosions that shake the air, these stars of flame, these actions that rip and grind and saw, these continual creations such as newness, progress, money. I cannot hold out any longer. No-one will be able to hold. No-one will escape unscathed. The movements, the noises, the lights. Food rams itself down the throat, exquisite flavours burn and gnaw. Winged outlines glide overhead, and in the factories the machines create forms of ever greater beauty, a hundred of such forms each second. The slaves work night and day to bury the world, ideas are objects made of glass or steel, ideas are black telephones, ideas are liars. On all sides, words are hammering and bursting, words seeking to destroy themselves, words that enter the ears and drive men mad.

Hear me out. Perhaps the war is only within myself, perhaps it is just a feeling among so many others, a vile feeling itching to hurl its grenades among arms and legs. Perhaps my words are merely further accursed noises, a few tins of preserved food on the immense counter. You put them into your nylon basket and then you go to cash-desk no. 3 to pay for them, and the little calculating machine gives a little hiccup and spits out a scrap of paper on which is written:

War	12
The world is absurd	06
Everything is beautiful	10
One day we will all be free	24
Malediction of Monsieur X	04
Total	56

Perhaps people die so that the earth shall not crumble beneath the weight of feet. Perhaps it is ordained that sooner or later everything must finish by becoming desert.

& yet, even if all this is only within myself, by the same token it is also within the others. I have seen all these signs around me, and I have understood that what had to be said, here, contained more than my own thought, more than the words of my own language. I was unable to see what needed to be seen, because I lacked a million eyes. If you too should see these signs, all these signs, prepare to wreak death and destruction, for only fire can halt fire. Accelerate the machines for inventing things, until they break down. Race your motorbikes and cars until they explode on the roads. Launch your giant words, fashion drums to compete against the thunder. When the stores finally burst apart and pour forth rivers of nourishment; when the blood finally flows over the linoleum flooring; when all the lies finally fuse together and become truth; when violence finally appears upon the scene, and many other things besides, and men are killed, not by truncheons or sub-machine-guns any longer, but by the walls of their own houses, or die bombarded by the rays from their television screens: then, true peace might come. Not the peace that marks an interval between two wars, nor the masked peace of the assassin and predator at work, but the peace of the sleek landscape over which the war has passed. I have spoken.'

Standing there, on that day of scorching heat and dazzling whiteness, listening to the sound, far off on the distant horizon, of the skins of the atmosphere descending again upon the insatiable city.

I am listening to what you say, Monsieur X, and I think perhaps you are right. I listen to what you say as though it were myself speaking, because it is only when the words being uttered come, not from the others any longer, but from oneself that one really thinks it is the truth: the truth, not just a *story*. You know, before, when you were still there, and I could lift the telephone receiver and speak to you, it was the same thing: I was telephoning myself.

You were in the depths of my being, so much so that I no longer needed to indulge in idle chatter. A few words sufficed. Now, you no longer exist. There is no Monsieur X, any more. Monsieur X died a few days ago. He was felled in his own room, quite senselessly, by a stray bullet. The newspapers never mentioned it. No-one knew about it. A bullet came through the window and struck him in the back. He crumpled dead to the floor, without ever knowing what had happened. Later, they found his body sprawled on the ground, so they retrieved his papers, including his military identification card with a photo on it, and sent them to his mother. It was a ridiculous photo: an unsmiling face staring stolidly ahead, cropped hair, two creases on either side of the mouth. It was nothing at all. Nothing at all had happened.

All the words. There are no more left. The letters one writes on sheets of notepaper, with a ballpoint pen, slipping the sheets inside an airmail envelope, sticking stamps on it, then inserting it in the slot of a letter-box. None of that was of any real importance. It was like the phrases one writes on the pages of a little blue notebook entitled:

the phrases that always say the same thing in different ways.
Today, it goes like this:

> The cold weather has returned. I really like the cold.
> Yesterday the bottle of milk in my room froze
> solid. It seems a long time now since I've had
> a job. Almost run out of money. This morning met
> Danièle, she says it's all fixed with
> Douski, I simply have to phone him. On the whole,
> it wouldn't be too bad working in his
> advertising agency. Slogans are quite fun.
> Maybe I'll phone him later on today.
> It's raining. I really like the rain. No news
> of Monsieur X. Yesterday afternoon, cinema:
> Mizoguchi's Chikamatsu Monogatari.

All this is happening very fast, and I am finding it impossible
to distinguish any longer between the things that have really
happened to me and the things that happened just next to me.
You know, I used to think that one knew what one was doing.
When I was little, I believed you simply built yourself up,
little by little, until one fine day there you were, you had
found yourself. I believed everything had a name. Love,
adventure, faith, art, music. So all you had to do was find out
the name, and you had won. And not so very long ago I used
to believe that some things were profound and others were
not. Now, that's all over.

Monsieur X, I wish you were still there, I would so much
like to speak to you. Sometimes I am surrounded by so much
silence that I can hardly bear it. But that is how you wanted
it. One day, you told me what needed to be done, and then
you left me on my own. No doubt you had a reason for doing
so. All prophets have their reasons. They don't like their

orders to be questioned. They pierce the night for an instant with their searchlight's incandescent beam, and in that flash one sees the thousand years of a landscape. Then they extinguish the light and go away. So I don't know how to manage any longer. I try to remember what I have seen. But it is difficult, very difficult.

You knew all the time what was bound to happen. I imagine that the bullet that hurtled through the window and lodged in your back didn't really catch you unawares. You told me about it yourself, you remember, one day, when I was on the telephone. I can even repeat the exact conversation. I was speaking very low, into the microphone hidden inside the bakelite capsule, and your answering voice was coming through the bakelite capsule at the other end of the receiver, with an odd nasal twang:

Why?

Because it's obvious.

You're too self-confident.

Listen, there's no sense in arguing, diatribes don't amuse me any longer.

What's more, it's all stuff that you've read in books.

There are no more books. Books and all the rest amount to the same thing.

Or you saw it all in the cinema. In *Black God, White Devil*, for example. At some point there is this character who says — Antonio das Mortes, I think, anyhow he says: I have been at war since I was born.

That's true, but I can no longer distinguish between what he says in the film and what I say outside the film.

Do you dream?

Everybody dreams.

But dreaming is something that concerns yourself alone.

That's not true. I dream with everybody else. What do you think a dream is?

A kind of delirium.

Everybody is delirious. Listen, nothing is gratuitous. I

rave, I dream, I analyse, I understand, all those things are done with other people. Never alone.

I am very alone.

No, you are not alone. You are with me, with everybody else.

But I'm frightened.

Your personal adjustment problems are of no interest. It is what belongs to everybody that is interesting.

You're just an unfeeling brute at heart.

No, that's not true. I feel a great deal of compassion for you. But if I took an interest in no-one but yourself, that's to say, if I took an interest in no-one but myself, what would be the good? You see, I know only too well that I don't have very much time left. When I am no longer there I want you to carry on. Don't forget that. Don't slip back, now, into your egocentric little existence.

What should I do?

You must go on looking, as though I were still there. Even if it is difficult, even if your eyes ache with tiredness.

And if, if I see nothing?

You will see everything that is there, you are bound to see it all. Even if you stayed shut up in your room for seventy years, you would see the war in action. Good-bye for now.

Good-bye.

After that, there was a click, and there was nothing more to be heard in the bakelite capsule except the kind of warning siren that goes: wiiii, wiiii, wiiii.

That was the last time you spoke to me on the telephone. After that, I never again lifted the black hand-microphone from its cradle. Everything I know, I owe to you, Monsieur X. You have taught me how not to be alone any longer. Now, I know how to look. In fact that's all I do: look, look. I wander through the city, looking all the time. I have seen many road accidents, many men and women, much crime and love. Before, I didn't know what it was all about. I lived inside the machine, I bought the baited traps, I closed my eyes and opened them again whenever I was told to do so. I walked under the shadow of the huge concrete buildings without knowing what they represented. I read the papers without knowing where their words and photos came from. I lived like a buzzing fly. I was always glued to all the lumps of sugar, with the other flies. It is you who did all that; and I don't even know you. I don't even know your name, Monsieur X. You didn't like being watched. You hid yourself at the back of cafés, or in the rooms of cheap hotels. At night you took out your mighty BMW 500 cc bike. You never spoke to people. When you had something to say you lifted the telephone receiver, and then your voice sounded exactly like all the thousands of other voices; it came from the world of anonymity, reaching me purely by chance. Isn't that extraordinary? You had concealed a microphone in my throat, and when your voice spoke it was I myself who spoke. From time to time you left a message on the floor of the bus, or slipped one between the pages of a magazine in the dentist's waiting room. I would be turning the pages and suddenly I would see what you had written, with a felt-tip pen, in big letters:

HUNGER IS TERRIBLE FOR ALL CREATURES
CAMEL + WHALE = FOR LIFE
HURRAH FOR BASKETBALL

You engraved your messages in the pavement's wet cement. You daubed your letters in red paint across the white façades of public buildings. Or else you drew your little designs of crosses, circles and dots on restaurant tables. I used to pass that way, and when I saw them my heart missed a beat, because then I knew you were still alive somewhere or other.

I have listened to everything you have said, I have read all these messages. Now I know the action to be taken. It is a question of walking into the very heart of the war, without being afraid. I wanted to get away, I wanted to find countries

251

that were at peace. I wanted to get away to some beach fringing the sea, and burrow under the sand-clogged pebbles. I wanted to look at the sea until I was lost in the middle of it. That was a lot of nonsense. There is no escape from this particular war; its little secret signs are to be found everywhere, even deep inside sea-shells. There is no finding that final door that leads into the peaceful little garden. Things once known remain in the memory. The cities are swollen blisters on the earth's surface, full of heat, noise, movement. They call out. I need to go there. I need to be everywhere at once, in the streets, in the armour-plated strongrooms, in the middle of the supermarkets and department stores, at the back of bars, making my way along the lanes of car parks.

Yesterday I too saw a sign. It was strange. I was walking down the centre of the esplanade, between the lines of stationary vehicles. I looked at the parking spaces, marked out in yellow paint along the ground, and all their numbers, 29, 32, 35, 38, 41. Occasionally I switched from one line of cars to another, as I passed by all these tightly sealed metal bodies. There was no-one in any of the cars. The place was completely deserted, immense, solitary, exactly like a windswept cliff at the edge of the sea. The city was far away, enveloping the car parks with its noise. I was confused, because I could see that nothing was happening here, that there was nothing but the silence of the graveyard. I tried reading the licence plates, so as to understand. But they had nothing to say. The engines were cold under their bonnets; the windscreen wipers had not been used for a thousand years and were welded to the glass by dust. It was terrible, you know, to be lost like that in the middle of these great clumps of inert carcases; I could hear my heart thumping in my chest, once more, and the noise of my heels rapping against the asphalt. I walked along faster and faster, between the lines of cars, not looking where I went. And then all of a sudden I saw it: an obscene drawing that spread its white chalk outlines along the asphalt surface between two cars. I just stood there, looking at it. It was a really extraordinary drawing, I assure you, such a beautiful drawing that I shall never forget it. It shone there, on the ground, traced in great strokes that were dazzlingly white. It was so simple and so pure that I didn't at first realize what it represented. There was this series of curved lines that fitted into each other cleanly and unhesitatingly. Like a message in shorthand, with just a few lines to say a whole lot of things. The longer I looked at it, the clearer it became. It was perfect, as beautiful as anything to be seen in the world's museums. It sounds silly, saying it now, but I looked at it without a thought in my mind, just with the strange sort of emotion one would feel when listening to some very beautiful piece of music wafting out of the night. I think that at that moment there was nothing on the whole face of the earth but that drawing; I mean, it shone in the centre of the car park like a star or a fire thorn. It wasn't talkative. It wasn't trying to destroy the world or colonize islands. It wasn't trying to prove anything, it was absolutely without intelligence. The person who had made this hasty sketch there, some schoolboy, perhaps, just out of class, can have had no idea of the masterpiece that he was creating. He had scrawled his sweeping strokes in chalk, furtively, between the great congealed slabs of cars, and then scurried off. The drawing was like the sun, spreading the rays of its rudimentary arms and legs across the ground. At the top, two semicircles with a dot in the centre of each one. Lower down, another dot, barely visible. Then, between the two curves of the wide thighs, a sex like an open eye, and a vertical phallus pressing against it. No face, no soul, no feeling, nothing, only this symbol of action, this diagram that captured the whole of life. The white drawing traced its curves and dots over a surface of several yards, just like a map. It had simply come from the other end of time, something thousands of centuries old, instinctive, quick, absolutely true. Its gesture was depicted on the ground's tarred surface, with a piece of chalk that had led its white trail across the fine grit. And it was the first and last gesture. The drawing was brand-new. It had no age, no setting, no race. Lacking face and hands and feet, it easily carried all the forgotten names. Nothing but a body, not even that, a movement. It was called Venus, Astarte, Gaia. And then, Hel, Sekhet, Uadjit, Bastet, Ta-Ret, Isis, Aphrodite, Kamadeva, Adu-woman, Iyoba, Anahita, Macha, Artemis, Ishtar, Ashtoreth, Atargatis, Belit, Ilat, Ariadne, Anadyo-medë, Shalako-Mana, Ka Atu Ccilla, Muna-Aclla, Chipauac-cihuatl. These were that woman's names, and there were many more besides. That is to say that this obscene drawing contained all manner of things, mysterious simple things that kept fear at bay. You see, as I looked at it I began thinking that that is how writing and picture-making were born. They were not made for analysing, or yearning, but for making a gesture in the middle of this grey expanse, for making a stand against immobility. It was good, discovering a drawing like that, by chance, on the tarred ground. It was like when you see a face you know in the middle of a crowd, a face wearing dark glasses. The obscene drawing stretched its curves and strokes out over the ground, among the tiny bits of gravel embedded in the solid tar. It spread its firm curves apart, it flexed its muscles. At a single stroke it destroyed all the centuries of lies and oblivion. It swept through all the massed hordes of feelings, killing them like flies. Because it was not like glue, because it never clung to you with ideas or phrases. The horizontal structure of fecundity: a different world from that of cinema posters, and photos in erotic magazines. Just a sign that said what had to be said, without flourishes: here I am, I exist, I want something out of life.

Monsieur X, if you are still there, go and take a look at this drawing. You will find it quite easily; it is in the esplanade-cum-car-park, in the fourth lane along, between the one hundred and twelfth and one hundred and thirteenth cars.

Everything that one imagines is true, some time or other. It is you yourself who told me that. I am not the only one to seek for signs of victory. I sometimes find such signs on walls and pavements and plastic tablecloths in restaurants. I am trying to discover the war's mechanism, as are all the others. I do not know any of them. I do not even know when they die. But I know their name. They are called THE INVINCIBLE ARMADA.

They are everywhere. I read the papers, and occasionally I see that they have won a battle. They fight against money, against noise, against enslavement. They fight with everything they have, with words, with photos, with pebbles, with music, or just with silence.

Sometimes I stand in front of the entrance to some great department store that is flooded with light and riches. And I see a little boy peering inside with queer empty eyes. Then I know that he is simply destroying the store gently with his eyes.

Or else I see a North African standing in line at the post office. He is waiting, like all the others. He scarcely even moves. But he is swathed in a sort of whirlwind of silence, and that whirlwind is his weapon of destruction.

Sometimes, too, there is a girl sitting at the terrace of a café in the centre of town. She is wearing a white raincoat and carrying a red nylon travel-bag with TWA written on it. She is drinking a cup of coffee and writing something in a little blue rexine notebook which has stamped on it, in gilt letters, 'EZEJO'T' DIARY. I do not know what she is writing. No-one will ever know what she is writing. She is wearing dark glasses with blueish lenses, and from time to time she raises her head and watches the passers-by. Strange flashes leap from her glasses, shoot straight ahead, and pierce little holes in the bases of the pillars that hold up prisons, museums, banks and new office buildings. Enlist in the Invincible Armada. Stop being blind. It is the eyes that will be the first to be free.

Peace.

Bea X.

From that moment onwards, there has not been much time left for sleeping. How can anyone sleep when so many things are going on everywhere? The girl called Bea B. lies down on the mattress, and rests her head on the foam-rubber pillow. But her eyes remain open. Her eyelids retract, revealing her two eyeballs. A flat grey ceiling hovers in the air, and a dangling cord ends up as a bulb. Everybody's eyes are open. At night, paths of white light stream from neon tubes, head-lamps, lightning flashes, incandescent bulbs, cinema projectors. This indefatigable light furrows the earth and sky with its countless trajectories. Swiftly-moving, untamable light, that seeks to flow through eyes so that it may live within the body. Inside skulls, dreams are starting to run their true-life films. How can anyone feign death when there is so much life and movement around?

Days and nights race past, galloping feverishly along the trails, and through the sombre valleys between the blocks of buildings. There is a terrible amount of movement everywhere. Clouds scurry along the aerial corridors, swim through space, send their shadows gliding over towns.

The girl is living inside the picture that she is in the process of creating: a series of superimposed bars and circles held up by black threads. Distant grey discs, with orange stars, and mauve, pinkish and red cylinders gliding by in front of them. Signs, church steeples. Purplish-blue bottles. The figure 9 standing on its tip, balanced on an ink-coloured streak. It is a picture that she is painting at random, not only with her hands but with her whole body, with her feet, thighs, belly, breasts, shoulders and mouth, a picture that she sweeps with all the hairs of her head and body, that she spits out, vomits, urinates, a picture that is nothing but a rainbow-hued stain slowly spreading out around her.

She does not know what she is doing. She does not know when she started, nor when it will all be over. It is beyond her, and the colours leak out of her, sweat ceaselessly from her body. She studies the picture, trying to understand it. But, each second, she sees a new detail, a magical silhouette of a man running, a shadow lying across the white ground, a snake, a mask, or else a clouded mirror in which the effigy of a chalk-white woman with purple hair floats above the mist.

The picture fades away. The girl has entered by one of the grey openings and so slid through to the other side of the stain. She hears voices now, but she cannot catch sight of anyone. The voices echo, as though inside a grotto or a great amphitheatre. Soft voices springing from all sides at once, voices announcing awful truths with complete indifference. She tries to understand what is being said, but each time that a sentence begins, something breaks in and cuts it off midway.

There are many voices. Hundreds of them, perhaps, emerging from invisible wells. Some speak louder than others, shouting, slurring their words. The girl turns full circle, trying to see the open mouths, or the loudspeakers' black discs. But there is nothing to be seen. Perhaps at that particular

257

moment she is blind, and the voices are amusing themselves by tormenting her; or else it is a torture chamber where all the floodlights have suddenly been switched off, and a confession is being wrenched from her. If only she could succeed in understanding a single phrase, it would all be over with. The lights would come on again, walls would reappear with their windows and doors and all the other holes for getting in and out. But the voices speak faster and faster. Occasionally the girl catches a few words in sequence, but they are mere obscenities, such foul abusive words that a feeling of panic overwhelms her. She too would like to speak. She opens her mouth, opens her throat and nostrils, and breathes air with all her might. The air whistles out of her lungs, but her vocal chords are paralysed, her tongue and lips are dry, and the sounds that come out are not words but the kind of shrill snarl that crocodiles produce.

All of a sudden, without knowing how, the girl discovers an exit. Leaping forward, she escapes as fast as she can. The cries and phrases remain behind. Now she cannot hear them any longer. All she can hear is the sound of her feet slapping the hard ground. She flees barefoot along the asphalt road. It is evening, and the landscape is obscured by the gathering shadows. There are forests, mountains, rivers perhaps. The wind blows, an icy wind that stings the cheeks and takes the breath away. The girl runs frantically along the road. Now her voice is restored, for she can hear it crying harrowing words from deep in her throat: 'Smash! Kill! Smash! Kill!' She is frightened because she knows that it is useless, that no-one will hear her, that they will very soon catch up with her. But she cries out all the same, as she runs. This lasts for days, for years, for an eternity. She never stops running. She is determined not to look back: if she turns her head for even a second, they will be upon her. She glances down at her feet. They are striking the black tarred surface with lightning speed, grazing the soles each time. The gravel lacerates the skin at each stride. She can see her feet being gradually grated away, while the blood flows. She leaves twin trails of blood along the road. She can hear her voice screaming with pain, while her feet continue to pound the ground, murdering themselves, turning into horrible stumps. They no longer make the same sound as they did to start with; now they squelch, like someone running in waterlogged shoes.

There is another noise behind her, now. The sound of footsteps approaching at a gallop, making the ground quake beneath their massive boots. A man running up the road behind her. Or perhaps a car approaching on its four rolling tyres? It is a deep menacing vibration, a noise like very close thunder. It is both: a car with its snarling engine, and a man breathing heavily. Hour after hour the noise creeps slowly closer. The girl is exhausted, breathless. She goes on running, stumbling now over the gravelled roadway. Before her stretch the same distant mountains, massive, black, standing out against the grey sky. She strains her eyes to catch a glimpse of something, anything, a hiding-place, a tree, a tele-graph pole. Her eyes long to see something, but there is nothing new. The tarred road makes a turning in the middle of the plain, then continues in a straight line. What was the reason for that sudden turning? She is scared of traps. She knows that there are traps; someone once told her so. Cun-ning tricks, quicksands, red lights. The girl peers through the shadows, anxious to identify these traps. But she has no time. The galloping noise of the car is right behind her now, and she can make out the distinct sound of each rubber boot as it hits the ground in turn. She sees a city ahead of her. What she had taken for mountains was in fact a city. She enters it. There are vast buildings to her left, to her right, in front of her. She runs along the asphalt esplanades, trying to find a door. But they had forgotten to make doors for these build-ings. All they had made were walls reaching a quarter of a mile into the sky. No-one lives in this city. The girl is quite alone as she runs along the asphalt esplanade, while the giant's dim hulk looms closer. She is so tired by now that she would like to lie down on the ground and go to sleep. She would like to lay her head on the black ground and close her eyes. That is what the man's voice is saying to her, just behind her. She had not been paying attention, but he had been speaking. He had been saying the same thing to her all the time, as they ran: sleep, close your eyes and sleep, lay your head on the ground and sleep. His voice is a peculiar blend of soothing and roaring elements, since he is speaking with his engine. She would never have dreamed that it was possible to talk like that, with an engine. She knows this voice well, this calm and terrifying voice. It belongs to the man who was speaking, just a while ago, in the dark room. He had disguised his voice to give the impression that he was several people; but it was he.

The end is near. One cannot run as far as time itself. The girl collapses onto the hard ground, grazing her hands and her knees. She picks herself up, staggers on for a few yards more. Already the shadow is closing over her like a cloud. Her feet stumble and trip, incapable of running any longer. She can no longer breathe. She is drowning. The buildings are even higher, now, even more vertical. The esplanade is as wide as a prairie. The bits of gravel gleam like little knives. Everything is fierce, cold, everything is shiny, watertight. The man's voice is in her ear. The girl picks herself up once more and starts crawling along the ground. Her half-open mouth gasps for breath. But the man's mouth glues itself to her own, and she starts suffocating. She falls. She begins to fall, and while the man's hands tear at her clothes she sees the sky falling at a dizzy speed. The windowless buildings crumble as their walls topple outwards, crashing against each other. The body embraces her with its steel-hard muscles, the legs grip her so tightly that her bones start snapping. Swarms of bipeds pour out of the shattered buildings and run in all directions, spreading out over the esplanade. The girl would like to call to them for help, but they would certainly never hear her, and besides they have other things to do. The man's hands wander over her whole body, probing deep inside its secret recesses. Teeth sink into her skin, tattooing it with semicircles of blood. All over the undulating splitting ground the bipeds hurl themselves at one another, crushing each other's skulls with bludgeons. The girl watches the mass-slaughter as she lies there, head strained backwards, and now the mob looks just like vermin crawling over a rotting ceiling. She sees a great red glow approaching between the ruined buildings, tongues of flame spewed out by iron dragons. She sees the explosions of dynamite that hollow red holes out of the mass of bipeds, but the holes close up again immediately, and the destructions are soundless. It is all taking place at the bottom of the ocean, in the depths of empty space. It is all taking place far away from reason. The girl continues to struggle against the body that is crushing her and penetrating her, but slowly the struggle turns into a dance, a sinuous crawl. She is helpless. She knows that that is how it is: at the end of every hunt there must be this crushing weight, this pain that becomes ever fiercer, ever more sharply etched, until it turns into enjoyment. She hears the voice speaking very close to her ear, a voice broken by gasps and grunts. It was like a secret that one has known for a long time, a genuine secret. And the voice is splitting her in two, rummaging inside her body. There is nothing hidden there, that is what she would like to say. You will find nothing, no magic stone, no foetus, nothing. Her eyes are rolled back, pressing against the folds of the eyelids, ready to drop out. The swarms of bipeds seethe over the dark ceiling. What are they up to? They cling on, forming moving clusters full of waving feet and feelers, they jump frantically up and down on the endless textured surface, like agglomerating bacillae. They are the image of massacres photographed at high speed, a sequence of snapshots tracing the shapes of their charnel-houses around her. They have constantly changing names, familiar names that she recognizes as they pass by; they are called Pourrières, Babi Yar, Dachau, Cholula, Figueras,

261

Song Mai. But these are no more than parodies, for there are massacres on the way that have not yet found their names. Each time they appear on the topsy-turvy earth, the pain darting through the girl's body will annihilate them. She is gliding horizontally; her skin is sleek with soap, and she is sliding and skidding along. But the man lying on top of her has dug his nails into her, harpooning her. His strange gaze has entered inside her and is examining her. The man fondles each organ, each cell, each gland, each nerve. He surges up inside her like a submarine, and she senses with horror that he is searching for her heart. Like a giant tapeworm, he writhes around in her belly, crawls upwards, explores her entrails inch by inch. He will soon be here, now. It is desperately urgent for her to see what is going on over there, between the ruins, on the dark esplanade, before he reaches her heart. Quick, quick, she has only a few seconds left. Monsieur X advances into her body, hollowing out a cave inside her belly. Only a few seconds left, to understand what is happening over there, what is taking place. An intense glow sets the esplanade ablaze and scorches the eyeballs. What is it? Why is it all happening? Perhaps they are writing words down, over there, words which will resolve all problems. *The solution lies at the far end of time.* The girl can no longer move. She feels heavy inside this body of hers that is lying spread-eagled, naked, on the black esplanade; as though her uterus were filled with concrete. She no longer attempts to rise, realizing that it would be impossible. She is alone, with Monsieur X's face gazing at her from within herself. Then she rolls her eyeballs still farther back in their sockets, trying to see what is happening over there in the future city. She can see the biped population waiting between the ruins. She can see them standing among their dead, and she knows that they have found something. They are far away, they are happy. They are dancing up and down in front of the raging fire. They are at the far end of time, while she is only at the beginning.

At the very moment when, like two pale eyes gazing at the world, she is engaged in reading the beautiful calm words that have been written down, this simple sentence that has cost so much blood, Monsieur X makes a final leap upwards from the depths of her body, impales her, and touches her heart. That is why the earth is in ruins and the girl is lying dead on her mattress, her head resting on the foam-rubber pillow. A little saliva is dribbling gently from the side of her mouth.

From that moment onwards, there has not been much time left for dying. How can anyone die when everything is so alive?

There are deserts. There are plains. There are mountains and rivers. There are unstirring beaches at the edge of the sea. There are places so silent that one might as well be travelling through the depths of space at eighteen thousand light-years per ... There are places so filled with noise that even a train hurtling across an iron bridge would never be heard above the uproar. There are some places that are vast and inaccessible, others that are microscopic. There are searchlights that throw dazzling beams of light, there are blocks of black shadow, unreal colours, fabrics in which each fibre is different, magical books, foolish books, thoughts like termites that think furiously about themselves, explosive thoughts, numbing thoughts. There are women, so many women, beautiful emotionless women, women to love, women to sell, women carrying a child in their belly. There are men who talk and hold beliefs and have a job. Children who play, children who listen to all sorts of things. There is music, dancing. There are religions, systems, armies.

This is war. There are monumental edifices of stone and cement, tall walls, stairways with identical steps trodden by countless feet. Identical steel girders, sheets of corrugated iron, slabs of wood, identical windows. There are voices, millions of voices. Hunched over a transistor radio, in the evenings, one can listen to all these voices talking, until one no longer understands what they are saying. Each voice speaks in its own language, each one shouts and talks in its own way, using the kinds of words and ideas that come naturally to it. There are many pains stabbing out in all directions, each treading its own path along its plantlike nerve. Monsieur X would like very much to experience these pains, but he no longer has the time or the means to do so. There are many dreams that flare up, then die down, behind people's eyes. Dreams that have travelled far, and that have farther yet to go. And aircraft holds are crammed with letters that are travelling, too. Letters going from Helsinki to London, for example, and there is a bit of pasteboard that has LOVE XXX written on it. Letters going from Hamburg to Nevers, including one that runs something like this: dear Alice, just scribbling you a quick line to say hello, no time to write a proper letter at the moment, hope everything's all right with you, I often think about you, when will you be in Oslo, I hope Jean and Daniel are all right, too, and how is Claude, do you like your new job, I'll write you a proper letter in a few days time when I get to Göteborg, looking forward to hearing all your news, love, Nadia.

There are rigid deserts swept by the wind. The light falls on esplanades that are like frozen lakes, the light streams downwards from the sun and touches the black roofs. Open valleys display the endless shimmering of their rivers, peaks flash across a sky filled with birds and flies. There are beaches of tar against which the sea breaks, waves of metal and glass interminably thundering in, retreating, sliding over each other. Sometimes the earth trembles, and a mysterious tide of lava can be sensed flowing somewhere beneath one's feet. Buried deep in the earth, sewers spew their endless tons of excrement and urine, disgorging them somewhere far away, under the sea, or into the bottom of a lime-pit. There are secrets everywhere, extraordinary secrets, terrible secrets, hiding in holes and keeping watch with eyes like spiders'. Jaws, bellies, glands. Blood that bubbles, that pulses jerkily through the pipes. There are noises that go Clunk! or Skoink! though no-one will ever know what causes them. The mute façades are motionless, absolutely motionless. Two years later they have not budged an inch. Machines are digging up the roads, prising up slabs of tar and sending earth cascading into the air: can it really be earth beneath the surface? Along the cold impenetrable stretches of asphalt there are occasionally these openings gouged out by pneumatic drills, and then the flayed skin's window reveals things that should have remained secret, all those cables and pipes and drains, intestines suddenly bared to view, bleeding, alive. Factories belch out columns of black smoke. In brilliantly-lit offices little men in lounge suits are talking, interrogating, breathing into telephones. There is no way of hearing what they are saying, however interesting their words might be. The stores are pyramids: the cohorts climb their steps, then climb down again. There is money. There are deserts of banknotes and cheques; caverns full of gold and platinum; fortified castles full of uranium, in front of which armed men and wolfhounds mount guard night and day. There are waves that travel across the nerves' filaments, running through the invisible networks from one end of space to the other. I'm buying! I'm selling! The warehouse vaults are bulging with mountains of paper, reports dealing with reports, vouchers, documents duplicated in ten, a hundred, five hundred copies, printed on paper that is successively green, pink, yellow, red, grey.

This is war. Nothing is going on, and all sorts of things are going on. Beauty is digging its bottomless wells of power and hatred and hunger and desire. The machines for passing judgment close their valves, slice, erode, decapitate. Who is dying? Nobody wants to die. There are roads that last for centuries, boulevards that stride straight ahead for miles.

The girl will never die. She will disappear, that's all. How can anyone die when everything is so in evidence? She will go and hide herself deep in a hole, without telling anyone. That is what she had always wanted to do; but it was not so easy, simply to vanish in the middle of the crowd as she walked along. And the crowd never dwindled.

There are vast motionless vistas, infinite steppes to be galloped across on horseback. The wind comes from the sea, blowing its wall of icy air, uprooting trees, flattening everything in its path. The dry ground is furrowed by great fissures that time has hollowed out. These are the ravines through which streams of gold wind their way, the gorges through which a roaring of swollen tides echoes at intervals. All is dazzling: the windows, the sheets of mica, the sheets of iron, the tightly-sealed shells, the lenses of sunglasses. The girl can make out all the patterns and camouflages, and guess at all the networks of electric cables. She simply advances among the signs, turning round from time to time to send her own signs of life flashing from her little flat mirror, messages about what she sees. The mirror glitters in her hand, as it reflects the sun's swift sparkle. She is not alone. No-one is alone when he sees these luminous signals.

Occasionally she takes the little blue notebook out of her airline bag and, raising the cover that is inscribed with the title 'EZEJOT' DIARY in gold letters, she writes down what she has just learned: 'It's not easy to renounce God, all gods, but I've finally managed it. Now I feel free and full of strength. It's a very interesting state to be in. I think it may be permanent.'

There are rivers flowing between green banks, and tree-trunks riding down the rivers. There are muddy seas full of dead leaves and rotting oranges. Along the pavement the rain leaves puddles that take hours to evaporate. There are turquoise-blue pools, with chairs around them, and suntanned girls diving in head first and swimming rapidly, shaking out their long, drowned tresses.

There are surfaces as smooth and pleasant as a wool carpet, or lino, or marble paving, or parquet flooring. It is possible to enter all these abodes, for a brief moment, by gliding lightly across these dance-floors. Then one's feet whisk one away to other places, through all kinds of different houses.

Even with the eyes closed one can recognize all these surfaces and chasms. One gropes forward, feeling along the walls: they are granulous and clammy, and rasp the fingers, or else smooth as ivory, solid, resonant, raising their calm barriers. The paintwork is sometimes lukewarm to the touch, sometimes burning hot, sometimes fresh and tacky. One knows many things. One knows the meaning of all the curves and chromium fittings and sharp projections and tufts of hair; one knows all this with far more than one's intelligence, one knows it from within, senses it with the brain that is within the brain.

No need to make up adventures. No need to tell stories. The sun rises, then sets again over the same stretch of territory. The ants and whales each have their own frontier, dotted lines that zigzag across forests of grass and currents of plankton. The girl has set up her frontiers, has built towns and roads between the walls that surround her. Now she has gone to war.

The girl walks through the city, without stopping. She is no longer able to stop. Night and day she plods onwards on her journey. She knows it now, in her heart of hearts: war has been declared. When there is a war going on somewhere, what is to be done? One can:

a) Commit hara-kiri.
b) Knit a green pullover with furious energy.
c) Hide at the back of some cellar.
d) Take photos.
e) Go out into the street.

Or else one can do all that at the same time, and it will still not affect the war one jot. The war is more important than oneself, than one's feelings or one's little phenomenological analyses. The girl has lost some of her fear by now. What had to happen has happened. She walks across all the deserts, along all the tracks and courses, between all the blocks of cement. She sees the accidents, the explosions, the words written on the walls, the signs on the roadway. She counts them as she passes, knowing that they all have a meaning. Clad in her white raincoat, she advances in the light. Her eyes are smarting from lack of sleep, her feet are bleeding inside her shoes. From time to time she crosses paths with Monsieur X, but he does not recognize her. She does not feel like speaking to him. What would be the point? She could stop, and then a few trivial words would follow, while a blazing fire raged just behind his eyes. She would say:

Hullo how are you?

All right ...

What's new?

Oh, nothing ...

Well, then ... Good-bye.

Good-bye.

Good-bye.

And that would mean: I love, I loathe, I would like to kill, make love, spit on people's feet, grind my cigarette stub into someone's eye, vomit, place three bombs behind the store's three pillars. The girl no longer has time to stop. She no longer has time to contemplate the same tree or the same man for two hundred years, to find out how they live.

She runs up the steps. She passes a lapping fountain. She crosses a few public squares. She avoids the cars travelling at sixty-five miles an hour. She listens to a jazz record, something by Coltrane or Art Blakey or Shelly Manne. She goes into a cinema, a café, a library. There are thousands of things: quick, quick. There are gestures, sighs, exclamations. There are !s and ?s and &s and $+ \times i = \S\, 1\; \$\, \text{Fr}\, 367\, [] \;\%\,*/°$s.

269

Everything is dancing, tottering, plunging, gliding, disintegrating. The movements are terrifying, endless. All the glands are sweating, the glands that govern digestion, growth, love, thought. The flesh is bathed with blood, the air closes its cocoon around the plains, the mountains, the oceans.

The girl is walking very early in the morning. She sees cement-lined corridors through which a sort of grey mist drifts. Darkness is still clinging to the doors. The sealed windows are blurred with vapour. There are vehicles moving silently along the pavement. The girl catches sight of one, a big grey lorry being driven slowly over the paving stones. At intervals, men in blue jump down from the lorry and make a rush for the dustbins. They empty these into the back of the giant scoop, banging them down hard, then throw them back onto the pavement. The lorry rolls on, gently, and the girl follows it. She listens to the sound of the engine, and to the kind of groan emitted by the scoop when it opens and closes its jaws.

She follows the grey lorry through the streets for a long time, then she climbs into a bus and travels to the other end of town, as far as a great stretch of wasteland permeated by an odd sense of absence, an odd black smoke. This is the place they call the Refuse Dump. She looks through the linked-wire fencing at the site where the lorries come, one after the other, to tip their loads of rubbish and garbage. In the centre of the wasteland there is a cement building, a sort of factory, with twin chimneys sending up thick columns of smoke. The acrid odour floats down to the ground again, spreading its noxious cloud. In front of the factory there is a mountainous heap of refuse waiting to be burned. The conical mountain seems to be soaring into the middle of the grey sky. It does not glitter, it is not beautiful. The cold air swirls around the congealed mass, while the lorries come and go, adding their fresh accretions to the base. The girl stands there, pressed against the wire-mesh, looking hard at this dark mountain. She stares with all her might. She is determined never to forget this.

270

Her eyes take in each detail, each drab fold, each wedge of rinds, each slab of papers, each package of offal. She feels the dull stale odour enter her, as she listens to the sounds of the decomposition that is smouldering at the heart of the mountain. To one side of it, the factory is hard at work belching out its blackish clouds. Far behind her, at the end of the bare roadway, the city moves and vibrates. But there is no doubt that, here, it is the mountain that reigns supreme, the great drab pyramid made of thousands of dustbin loads. The girl looks at the heaped mass of refuse, her eyes and thoughts equally concentrated. And she knows that this must be where mountaineers come to make their dizzy climbs. Armed with ice-axes and ropes and spiked boots, they come here to make the ascent of the great mountain of excrements. Their boots will search for a foothold in the soft mass, their hands will sink into foul sludge. They will inch their way up, surrounded by the factory's black exhalation, they will crawl up the glutinous slopes, on and on, to victory!

The cities open and close the sluice-gates of their cemeteries, their innumerable cemeteries. Cemeteries of garbage, of dogs, of rats, cemeteries of cars.

Another morning, somewhere else, the girl sees a field of battle. She suddenly sees it stretching out there, below the level of the road, for about a quarter of a mile. It is littered with the carcases of vehicles stacked on top of each other, mountains of rusting hulks waiting in silence. There is not a soul in sight. Upside down, the cars display what should never be revealed, the mysterious underneath, the axles, the sump, the exhaust. Their four wheels lift skywards, tattered remnants of tyres clinging to the rims. Their engines have been torn out. Everything is agape. The bonnets, the boots, the doors, the roofs are yawning black holes. All the fearful signs of mutilation. Here too, the girl thinks; here too. People ought to come here some time, no matter when, tomorrow, the day after tomorrow, a year from now, to collect their thoughts awhile. Those who say that there is no war, that the

271

world has never been so peaceful, should be the first to come. The girl makes her way down the sloping verge, walks towards the linked-wire fence, and looks at the stacks of carcases mounting to the grey sky. She looks at each wheel, each chassis, each disembowelled radiator grille; studies the shattered headlamps, the ripped seats, the dented hubcaps, the smashed windows, the flayed tyres, and all the bumpers, speedometers, steering wheels, crank-cases. Seeing all this, she knows that war, the unknown war, is rumbling on all sides.

In the marvellous cities fringing the sea, the office blocks and public buildings are all asparkle. There is so much whiteness and light that it is wisest to put on dark glasses before entering the shops or bars. But from time to time the walls divide, and through the gap the girl can glimpse the gloomy terrain over which the fighting has just raged, and the hidden piles of corpses. There are those who would have liked very much to make her forget that sight, those who would have liked to prevent her seeing it at all. The brightly illuminated shops were wearing seductive placards, big signs that purred gently: 'Buy! Buy me! Stay young & beautiful for ever! It's *extra* good! Buy me!' Everywhere there were flashes of infra-red or ultra-violet light that struck you full in the face just as you thought you might take a look. To muffle the sounds of war, they had invented thunderous music played on gongs and tomtoms, soft music, nerve-shattering music, rhythms that gripped you in their spell at the very moment when you thought you might hear the voice of Monsieur X yelling: help! Everything was smooth and soft. There were such delectable perfumes, such velvety carpets, such suave liqueurs, such mouth-watering delicacies, such limpid water flowing from the taps, that it was difficult to believe in hunger, and thirst, and cold, and ground knee-deep in mud or muck.

But the girl looks, and this is what she sees: the curtains draw back, the buildings' immaculate façades split open, the phosphorescent windows suddenly peel off their filmy golden skins, the dark glasses become transparent, and slowly there

272

appear great grey slabs that stand silent and rigid, charnel-houses, knackers' yards, rotting slums, swamps, cemeteries. They are all well hidden. They all existed on the other side of life. They were rather like a dream that can be erased on waking, simply by rubbing the eyes. People everywhere were frantically burying their excrements, but the sewage rose again immediately, bubbling up to the face of the earth; and then they could no longer ignore the war.

The girl has gone right up to the grille. She has put her hands against the knitted wires. On the other side of the grille lies a concentration camp; that is what she is staring at with all her might. The huts, put together from planks and sheets of corrugated iron, are lined up, row upon row, along the sunken terrain. The dust rising from the alleyways covers the camp with its cloud. There is not a soul to be seen here, either. There are only distant ghostlike shapes walking down the alleyways, entering or leaving the huts. Ragged urchins are playing among the rubbish-heaps, yelping with their shrill voices. Grossly fat women with childish faces wander through the camp and disappear inside the huts. Time is hourless, here. It is very early in the day, or close to nightfall. The odour of sweat and urine rises from the camp, and the girl breathes it in. She is devoid of feeling. She does not want to know the taste of feeling, does not want to have it in her mouth like an acid-drop. She simply wants to see the war, the one that kills slowly and has no heroes. Occasionally an aeroplane takes off ponderously and flies over the concentration camp. But it drops no bombs, fires no rockets. It just flies very low in the sky, its silver fuselage gleaming, its two broad outstretched wings making shadows on the ground. To the right and to the left, cars are pounding along the motorway, making a noise like the ocean. So the girl goes away. She travels on in search of similar beaches waiting to be discovered behind the white cubes of the brand-new buildings, behind the hills, under the cement bridges, in the depths of ancient dried-up valleys.

These great hells are quadrangular and have a door at each cardinal point; the base is made from slabs of red-hot iron; and the walls close upon these slabs of red-hot iron; and these hells are as broad as they are lofty, they are square, and each face measures a thousand yot, a yot being a thousand wa; the thickness of each of the sides and of the base and of the upper surface is nine yot, and in these hells there is not a single empty place. All the beings in these hells must perforce be packed against each other in great masses, and the fire of these hells never abates for a single instant, but burns everlastingly throughout time's course until the end of ages ...

Trai P'hum (attributed to P'hia Lit'hai, King of Siam).

The girl who was called Bea B. has vanished. She simply disappeared from view, one fine day, without anybody noticing. She melted into the crowd, and nobody knows what has become of her. She has gone off with her red bag containing a small blue notebook filled with writing, a lipstick, a mirror, a packet of cigarettes and a box of matches. She has gone off with her tales and troubles, her adventures with Monsieur X, Danièle, the Invincible Armada, the mighty BMW 500 cc motorbike, the black American sedan, the preserved food in its metal container, Anna Belle, the electric light bulb and the transistor radio.

She has got lost in the middle of the city. It is very easy to get lost there, and the chances are that she will never turn up again. At a pinch one might put a classified advertisement in the newspaper, for example:

Lost, young girl 20–25 years, av. height,
av. build, brown hair, green eyes,
wearing white raincoat, black shoes.
Red airline bag marked TWA, blue notebook
marked 'EZEJOT' DIARY. Special
peculiarity: bites nails. Urgent.

One might also hire a private detective, or launch appeals on the radio. But she would never be found, because she has gone into hiding. She has learned to distrust people who look at her; she has many disguises to throw her pursuers off the scent. She disguises herself as a nurse, or a shorthand-typist, or a fashion journalist, or a bit player in films, or a nude model for stag magazines, or a social worker. She has a whole string of names that will vanish with her: Bea B., Lea D. Lions, Nadia, Florence, Claude G., Tranquilina, Carol, S. D. B., Alexandra Tchkonia, Evelyne…

This is how it all happened. It was evening, in the centre of the city, at the moment when the valves seem to open, and the crowd's torrents gush out. Bea B. walked between the high walls. She had been walking continuously for several days. She had explored cafés, car parks, empty sites, factories, churches, stores, airports. She wound her way through the throng of people on the pavement. She forged ahead through thousands of shadows and reflections. The sky was black, the lights from the lamp-posts and advertising hoardings leapt in all directions. Bea B. used the pedestrian crossings when she wanted to cross the street, and carefully skirted round all obstacles. From time to time she felt a great urge to stop, but on each occasion she immediately encountered the piercing gaze of two eyes fixed upon her, and so she went on a little longer. The buildings opened and closed their glass doors unendingly, and the girl could see yet other unknown beaches, chalky voids, swift combats. She no longer even had the time to distinguish the faces of the combatants. Just sudden flashes, the glassy gleam of a dagger, the rapid phtt-phtt of a pistol fitted with a silencer. Occasionally a shout or a brief cry, 'arrgh!', 'rrhaa!', things like that. Flashing images began to appear, now, all over the place, needles of pain that stabbed through the murky partitions in less than a second, and then faded away. Occasionally, the truncated bellow of a hooter from deep within the mass of snarling cars.

Eyelids raised and lowered a single time: the diamantine star of the eyes' gaze had come and gone like a spark. It was strange, and at the same time perfectly plain. There was, after all, no continuity behind this spectacle in which one had pretended to believe; in the end, there was nothing but these tremors, these false starts, these explosions; gestures swarming everywhere, agitating all the machines; hidden engines shuddering of their own accord. And the girl moved onwards through these impulsive forces.

Then she started drifting with the crowd, letting herself be swept along by it. At one point there was a sort of open mouth in the pavement, and Bea B. saw people being swallowed up by the gaping cavity. She went quickly down the black steps that sparkled with gold particles, and began to walk through the subterranean vaults.

It was a frightening place. Four hundred feet underground, the intestines spread their tubes in all directions: Northern, Southern, Eastern, Western. The human floodtide gushed along these tubes in waves of heads, shoulders, arms, legs. The vague shapes, jammed tightly together, hurried along as fast as they could, then vanished. Other pallid shapes clambered back towards the surface, in a headlong rush for the black staircase that led outside. Already, one was no longer oneself. Already, one had difficulty in distinguishing the features of any girl at all in the dense crowd. One could still see the bright splash of her hair when she passed under an

276

overhead lamp. She queued in front of a plexiglass window that had an opening at the bottom, and bought a little piece of cardboard covered with signs. Then she crossed the foggy grotto and went up to a machine. Standing in front of it, she pressed some of the buttons and watched the itineraries light up on a map. The electric wires were ready and waiting; they outlined the war plans, and showed the movements of the brutish troops in each other's direction. The Western front carried out its encircling operation, while the tanks and armoured cars stormed straight through to the final objective. The girl was probably breathing hard, inhaling the combined odour of the thousands of breaths that were floating along the tube-like tunnels. Maybe she lit a cigarette, at that point, and started smoking as she made her rapid advance through the intestines. Maybe she heard her own heart beating, if it really was her own: there were so many hearts, all beating, there, under the ground.

She was afraid once more. She betrayed her fear by getting her dark glasses out of her bag and propping them up in front of her eyes. When girls put dark glasses on, underground, like that, it means they are afraid.

She walked quickly along the intestinal tubes. The feet of men and women struck the ground all around her, sending out echoes. The tunnel descended in a spiral, plunging ever deeper beneath the earth. The black ground sparkled with mica particles; electric lamps screwed into the ceiling at ten-yard intervals manufactured their own haloes of pale light. The girl plunged downwards with the crowd. She gave furtive glances at the faces of those walking alongside, but they immediately slipped away, were carried far away. On the tube's walls, rows of large pictures placed edge to edge showed women smiling, women in brassières holding a rose in the right hand, children with their mouths full of cheese, babies, cats, packets of cigarettes, more women still smiling, men with their mouths full of macaroni, women with their mouths full of liqueur chocolate.

Bea B. glided along very fast, by the side of the concave wall, stroking the posters with her hand. Sometimes weird-shaped strips had been torn off the paper pictures, or else words — brutal insulting words — were written in black crayon across the smiling faces; or obscene drawings were scrawled over the bodies of the girls wearing brassières, rapid angular strokes designed to express hatred and derision; or there were traces of blows, holes bored into the pubis and bosom, cigarette ends stubbed out on the navel, chewing gum stuck to the tips of the breasts. The girl saw all this, through her dark glasses, as she walked along, and she was afraid.

The gallery continued to plunge towards the centre of the earth. Already, the sound of panting from all sides showed that it was becoming increasingly difficult to breathe. The air swept through the cramped corridor in hot violent blasts that were heavy with fetid odours. It came from the subterranean swampland, an exhalation from the mouth of a great iguana, perhaps, and it was impossible to make headway without lowering the head and leaning forwards. From time to time, stairways opened up underfoot, flights of steps lined with metal that rang under the steady tramp of feet. Fresh galleries followed, funnelling the crowd into separate routes in its plunge towards the centre of the earth. The descent seemed eternal. The surface, the air, the sun fell farther and farther behind, until one forgot they existed. All the forking galleries were leading their jostling throngs towards the same spot, though no-one realized this yet. Sometimes the network of tubes made a pretence of going upwards; a few steps had to be climbed, and the legs had to be hauled up, one after the other. But this was a trick: just ahead there was always another stairway leading downwards again, and then the ceiling suddenly started tilting, and the walls started to sweat moisture. There were also great halls, something like nebulous crossroads, filled with echoing sounds that could be heard coming from a long way off. The monotonous music of an accordion or a flute wailed nasally along the corridors,

278

growing increasingly loud and shrill. At the crossroads one stepped over the outstretched legs of beggars, one made one's way around the robot-like blind musicians interminably churning out the same three notes on their accordions, the cretins, the paralytics, the disabled ex-servicemen chewing at their mouth-organs, the drunkards bawling songs, the ragged women with swollen bellies, whining out their woes. No-one even saw them. The crowd continued to trudge steadily along the sloping pipe-line, gradually losing their sense of direction. The air grew heavier and heavier as it fought its way back, up along the network of tubes, in its efforts to reach the surface. There were sulphurous vapours, a kind of iron dross blackened the ground and walls, and the electric lights could scarcely pierce the gloom. One was exploring the galleries of a volcano, one was dropping to the bottom of its shaft, very slowly, sluggishly, with all one's arms and legs. Perhaps one would never see daylight again; perhaps that was what was written on the little yellow cardboard ticket with a round hole in it. Or else one might shelter there, in the bowels of the earth, for months on end, listening to the faint murmur, the very distant rumbling, of the war that was raging on the surface. Bombs would open craters in the streets, the glass-walled buildings would come crashing down, the overheated engines would explode. And one would wait there, in the underground domain, sleeping on the ground that sparkled with its myriads of mica particles, and one would go on hoping for months on end, years on end, whole centuries.

The girl was swallowed up by the crowd, as she hurried quickly down the slope. From time to time there were metal barriers, and then the human mass split into three segments that pushed tirelessly at the banging gates as they filed through, then coagulated again as they continued on their way. The grubby posters stuck against the walls were always the same, an endless repetition of the same smile, the same breasts, the same babies, the same cigarettes.

Then, all of a sudden, at the bottom of a flight of steps, one found oneself in a long brightly-lit hall, a great grotto with a high ceiling, and walls plastered with gigantic photographs. The crowd spread out along the cement platform and stood there, waiting. There were steel rails emerging from a gallery at one end of the hall and disappearing into a gallery at the other end. The two human masses stood facing each other along the twin platforms, observing those on the other side, and it was as though there had been a great mirror in the centre of the pit where the rails ran. Identical anonymous forms, the men wearing grey raincoats, the women carrying black plastic handbags.

The silence was oppressive. Warm air gusted through the grotto, raising dust and scooping up old newspapers. The giant posters loomed above the crowd, always showing the same images of their gods and goddesses: monstrous children devouring cheese; gigantic men smoking cigarettes; divinely beautiful women, as big as buses, displaying to the sun their mountain of rosy flesh, their forest of golden hair, their red mouths, their greenish-blue eyes, their teeth like ice-cubes. The people gazed at the images with amazement, with humility, with hatred, too, and went on waiting. For these were the idols of war and noise and murder, revealed at last to the eyes of man. There was not a single place in the world where one could escape them, not a single piece of unoccupied territory; their temples were everywhere, their religion was everywhere, at the summit of lofty peaks, in the sun, as well as in the depths of caverns four hundred feet underground.

The six steel rails glittered in the light, down the centre of the pit. They ran over a bed of black pebbles; sharply-defined, bright, invincible rails. They too were observing the scene, and their gaze was so hard and pitiless that it was difficult to stay on one's feet. Eventually, no doubt, some man or woman, knees buckling, would stagger out of the crowd lined up near the platform's edge, and would pitch forwards without even uttering a cry. In the centre of each track there was a third, even tougher, rail resting on porcelain insulators. No-one dared to stare straight at this rail: it was charged with surging electricity, charged with deadly hypnotic powers. Its force opened up dizzy chasms. It was furiously determined to discharge its energy upon anything that came its way: metal wheels, broken bodies, it made no difference.

After a short time, a distant rumbling can be heard coming from all directions at once, and the ground begins to tremble. A light is approaching from deep inside the tube, coming from the other end of the earth, growing gradually bigger. The rumbling has become more unambiguous, now, more urgent. The illuminated coaches are hurtling towards the opening, spitting sparks. The crowd has drawn back slightly, and the long metal machine has roared into the grotto, brakes screeching. The doors have been sucked back by pistons. All the waiting men and women have pushed their way into the coaches. The doors have banged shut. The train is on its way again. All this has happened very fast, in the space of a few seconds at most.

Now one is travelling along inside the galleries. The metal-plated train is speeding through the rock, almost brushing against the walls as it lurches from side to side, and there is so much energy in the air that one might almost be travelling inside a flash of lightning. And one can hear the sound of thunder, too, a steady rumbling that sends its metallic echoes reverberating along the underground network.

That is the way one vanishes. Far beneath the earth's surface, buried under tons of rock and mud, lost in the uncharted labyrinth, one no longer has a name, a thinking mind, a soul, anything at all. One sways in rhythm with the jolts. The train stops briefly in other grottoes, on its onward journey. The faces inside the iron coaches are strange deeply-creased white masks. Their bulging eyes are like fat cock-chafers with glaucous wing-sheaths, as they seek out girls' eyes and settle on them. Just below, their mouths breathe in and out, anus-mouths of anemones. There are women whose red

281

hair is ablaze, women with arched black eyebrows, and nostrils that are black cavities from which snakes come writhing. Masks, masks on all sides, massive casings for the brain's jelly, armour to hide the whole body, its sex, its tufts of hair. At close intervals the doors slide apart and more masks push their way in. They glance warily at each other, press tightly together, quiver like the surface of a mosquito-infested pond. The rapid train streaks along the corridors with their bouncing lines of electric cables at one side. It bursts into the stations like a high-explosive shell. It is bearing its rows of yellow windows ever deeper inside the earth as it twists and turns, makes great circles, burrows its way underground, plunges foot by foot towards the planet's core. It is looking for an exit, an exit that it will never find.

The girl is somewhere down there, now, in a sealed compartment. Her travelling companions are white-masked mercenaries, ruffians carrying the war into the far corners of the globe, devouring each other in the process. She is travelling through all the galleries of the reinforced-concrete shelter, she and the dark glasses of fear, because at that moment, on the surface, a kind of great white bomb is bursting, consuming everything, even the water, with the fierceness of its sudden light. War is the destruction of thought.

The world has begun. Nobody knows where, or how, but the fact remains that it has just come into being. Those who said that its end was near were entirely mistaken, and those who spoke of dotage, decadence, death and so on were speaking for themselves. They were so afraid of youth that they dared not look around.

Today is barely the beginning of the primary era. Great movements ripple over the surface of the earth: great motions of birth, contractions, spasms. Why is it that nobody wants to see these things? Life is striving ceaselessly to emerge from all its enfolding lips, as it burrows its way towards the air.

The war is everywhere. A general state of war means that something is in the process of happening. Volcanoes sprout in the middle of city squares, roads split open, and deep crevasses spurt out a stream of lava and heat and energy. Rock masses shatter into fragments. The sea rages and boils at the foot of the cliffs, scours the echoing caves. There is steam, and electricity, there are clouds, and lightning flashes.

The earth began yesterday. One can still remember with an effort, if one casts one's mind back. Nothing has changed. The unreal landscape is studded with lumpish, barbaric blocks of cement. The iron pipes of the scaffoldings rise in networks above the ground. Waves run busily through the air. There is bracken higher than a sequoia, there are carnivorous plants, carnivorous animals, carnivorous machines. The machaerodus, the dinotherium, the tyrannosaurus were nothing in comparison. Now there are bigger and heavier monsters whose jaws are armed with sabre-teeth, monsters

283

with claws, and talons, and heels for grinding to dust. There are machines as big as mountains, machines that nothing can kill. They lurch blindly forward, gouging with their caterpillar-tracks, uprooting with their hundreds of arms, breathing flames or deadly gases; they own, not just a single heart or head, but thousands of them. When night falls, the sky turns red and trembles above the wilderness of cement. Powerful lights throw bright beams, tall furnaces burn more enduringly than any volcano. This war is alive. It takes empty buildings, fossilized shells, decaying teeth, and gnaws away at them until they are reduced to powder. There are great gestures that sweep space, there are rending winds. When the sun rises in the east for the six thousandth time, it looks just the same as before, like the dilated pupil of a six-day-old baby. Everything within, everything enclosed, is rising inexorably to the surface. Carapaces break apart, and one can glimpse another skin. Everything is full of substance. What place is this? Where does one live? All one can do is to follow the movements of the underground currents. Language can no longer contain itself, it is longer than any speech, it simply writes what it writes, without any prompting.

Youth and newness are unceasing. Eternal buildings. Eternal roads. Eternal airports. Flames that burn for thousands of years on end. Swift birds that make a noise like thunder as they dart across the white sky. There are so many shapes and forms. Beauty is at balance upon the earth, raising its transparent peaks. The circular motorways are loud with noise, quivering rings that gradually unfurl. The trees of the jungle are growing everywhere, digging their roots into the asphalt crust. Tropical creepers, threads, palm-fronds, glass thorns, celluloid fruit, millions of tiny steel filings, they are all alike. There are so many displays of the aurora borealis in shop windows. There are so many meteors flashing around the crystal domes, surging up from the image-machines. There is so much thunder and lightning. There are so many suns, stars, moons, all moving, crossing each others' paths, overtaking each other, according to their mechanical courses. But it is not in the sky that they are to be seen: it is here, on the ceilings and walls. There are so many eclipses, spiralling galaxies, opaque nebulae. Clouds trail smoothly across the rooms. Chiffons return the light's rays: either very hard, and then they are white, or very gently, and, see, they are black.

The world has just begun, as all the cataclysms plainly show. The catastrophe was permanent; that was clear to anyone who knew how to keep his eyes and ears open. When a world is coming into being, there are bound to be these seethings at the core of matter, these blisters disfiguring the skin, these strains and stresses. There are these reddish glows of burning embers, like those of cigarettes, for example; these acrid odours of petrol and oil; these noises of valves and push-rods; these incessant comings and goings. When the world is in the process of appearing, many people encounter death. On the fields of battle, belly pierced by bayonet thrusts, or else kneeling in the mud of the ricefields, face scorched by flame-throwers. Many people have died defending a field, a hut, a bridge. The antediluvian animals kill, and go on killing, and when at last they fall they crush whole towns, whole peoples, beneath them.

All these things are happening all the time. They material-ize beneath the feet as one walks down the street, they materialize before the eyes. There are some things that flash and vanish again within a fraction of a second, glowing sparks inside engines and electric light bulbs, microscopic bombard-ments of slabs of lead. There are things which appear so slowly that no-one knows they are there until generations have come and gone. The war has need of every cell in every brain. Words throng and jostle, covering the sky like bats, multiply-ing like larvae, spreading their haze of plankton, voyaging far into space. There are stars so distant that they might almost not exist. There are specks of dust so near that they penetrate the body and travel in the bloodstream.

The towns and cities have just come into being. They are still trembling with effort, unsure of themselves, their concrete columns teetering on the edge of cliffs. How low the horizon seems! The deep blue of the sky presses down with all its weight upon the fragile bone structures. There is a great deserted square that has started to sprout white stone cubes with narrow windows, and here a little girl is sometimes to be seen. Her feet planted solidly on the ground, she stands in the centre of this square, her hair glowing in the sun. She looks straight ahead, and her eyes register the flimsy ramparts quivering in the wind, the balloons swollen with air. She looks on, uncomprehendingly, but there are many things that she already knows. There is something written at her feet, in black letters. It says, simply:

DACRYL CLOTHES THE BRAVE NEW WORLD

It has all just begun ... The seventy-storey buildings sending their tortuous towers soaring into the sky. The buildings with 8,400 windows, rising higher than the surrounding haze. The 433-foot-high buildings floating above Jacksonville. The 840-million-dollar buildings hollowing out their Aeolian rocks. The high plateaux of cement spreading out their deserts in the air. The pyramids in the sand, the white tombs pointing towards the sun, the temples of Thebes, the Acropoles, the Teocalli, the torch-lit fortresses. Streams of lava, waves of steel, wind, light, all flow between their walls. Crumbling stones dribble the dust of decay. Rocks split in the fierce frost, or shatter under the blows of hammers. Whirlpools slowly advance and retreat; the docks at ports are full of black water one moment, and empty the next. Suspension bridges span the gulfs, tunnels thrust into mountain sides. In a single day the building sites destroy whole years of memories. There are innumerable things striving to appear, seeking to overthrow all barriers in their way. All the mouths are straining together to suck in air, thrusting their gasping holes upwards towards the sphere of space, imbibing greedily with a whistling noise. The world is so vast, so animated. Everywhere there are eyes, lungs, sexes, bellies, nerves. It would be an endless task to witness all the movements, read all the thoughts, count all the microbes. One voyages without ever halting, through the cities and across the newly fashioned spaces, one travels up and down all the world's escalators. One flies through the air, above the stationary clouds. One travels over the countless thousands of roads and avenues and outer boulevards. Here ... there ... what does it all mean? Over there, elsewhere, and equally, above, below, within. It would be an endless task to tell the story of the earth's creation. There are not sufficient words in existence, yet, to keep pace with war. They are not strong enough to use for building brick walls behind which one might feel truly safe. Danger lurks everywhere. Fear is dazzling, fear streaks through the mind at the speed of light. Joy and woe, pain and passion break into foam, waves wafting from the far end of time, and in the same instant they have thrown their bridge across to the opposite shore: and she who wants to understand is exactly like a gnat walking on a window-pane. But meanwhile a woman squats down, ejects her child from the depths of her belly, then buries the plasma and the cord in front of the door of her home. Thought emerges tirelessly from the countless thousands of brains, rises in smoke, sparkles on car bonnets and the windows of skyscrapers. War is thought.

That is how things happened, then, at the beginning of the primary era. Trees and shrubs grew on the tops of buildings. Tables were littered with strange albums of coloured photos showing women's faces and bodies. These books would have loved to be mirrors. They would have loved to speak of beauty, of the future, using simple phrases and very pure illustrations. But they remained mere objects among other objects, mere weapons.

The city closes its series of doors and shutters and blinds and grilles and iron curtains. The dark glasses glitter once again. The golden eyelid that confers invisibility closes over the plexiglass helmets.

Someone has made an attempt to understand. One day, someone began thinking about war, wanted to find out what war was all about, and how it would end. Someone has wanted to break windows in order to breathe, has wanted to launch words in quest of this kind of peace. Then, has vanished.

Those who will see peace are not yet there, have not even been conceived.

I myself am not really sure that I am born.